"I would have thought you'd be a gigolo."

"Why?" he demanded, insulted.

"Well, I don't know..." Jane floundered helplessly. "It's just that you're so good-looking, and I wouldn't think you'd have much chance to use your good looks when you're torching buildings."

He tried to reach for her, but she'd moved out of reach. Later, he promised himself. "You forget," he said evenly, "I'm a con man on the side. Looking like I do, I manage to convince people I'm Princeton and Harvard Law School, and they'll buy anything I sell them."

She nodded. "I can believe it. What are you going to try to sell me?" The question was lightly spoken, but Sandy wasn't fooled. She didn't trust him, on a very basic level. He shouldn't expect her to; he'd done everything to foster her belief in him as a sleazy crook.

"Nothing you don't want to buy," he said.

God, he wanted to tell her the truth....

ABOUT THE AUTHOR

Anne Stuart had her very first work published in *Jack and Jill* magazine at the age of seven, and she has been writing professionally ever since. Recently she built a new house in the mountains of Vermont, where she resides with her husband, daughter, baby son, one dog and four cats.

Books by Anne Stuart

HARLEQUIN AMERICAN ROMANCE

30–CHAIN OF LOVE
39–HEART'S EASE
52–MUSEUM PIECE
93–HOUSEBOUND
126–ROCKY ROAD
177–BEWITCHING HOUR
213–BLUE SAGE

HARLEQUIN INTRIGUE

5–TANGLED LIES
9–CATSPAW
59–HAND IN GLOVE

Don't miss any of our special offers. Write to us at the following address for information on our newest releases.

Harlequin Reader Service
901 Fuhrmann Blvd., P.O. Box 1397, Buffalo, NY 14240
Canadian address: P.O. Box 603,
Fort Erie, Ont. L2A 5X3

Partners
in Crime
Anne Stuart

Harlequin Books

TORONTO • NEW YORK • LONDON
AMSTERDAM • PARIS • SYDNEY • HAMBURG
STOCKHOLM • ATHENS • TOKYO • MILAN

Published May 1988

First printing March 1988

ISBN 0-373-16246-4

Chapter One

Alexander Caldicott yanked off his tie and sent it sailing across the room. It was supposed to land on the lumpy double bed but it fell short, ending up on the stained wall-to-wall carpeting. An ignominious fate for Brooks Brothers' best silk knit tie, and Alexander didn't give a damn. He rolled up the sleeves on his Egyptian cotton dress shirt and sank down in the one chair the sleazy hotel room had to offer. The chair wobbled beneath him, threatening to collapse under Alexander's well-muscled one hundred and seventy-five pounds, but then held still.

Alexander, better known as Sandy, cursed out loud, a solemn, profane curse that was more at home in the Princeton Pike Sleep-a-While Motel than silk ties and Egyptian cotton shirts and a burnt-out lawyer named Alexander Caldicott. It was the worst day in a long line of miserable, depressing days, and even the thought of the Canary Islands wasn't enough to cheer him. It would be more of the same. More forced camaraderie from his fellow man at play, more casual, careful sex from the determinedly attractive female of the species. His travel agent knew just the sort of thing he liked, and had dutifully provided it year after year, with only the settings changing.

But Sandy was sick of it. Sick of hearty friendships from people he'd never see or hear from again, sick of instant relationships that never lasted. He was bored with his apartment in New York, wary of his family in New Jersey, dreading autumn, tired of his MGB, frustrated with his law firm, and sick unto death of everything in his life, up to and including the latest professional triumph that had culminated just that afternoon.

If he hadn't been so burned-out, Sandy thought, he would have known Jimmy was lying. Anyone known both personally and professionally as Jimmy the Stoolie should have been approached with a little circumspection. But Sandy hadn't been paying close enough attention. He'd been too busy trying to get Jimmy off the charges of arson and conspiracy to notice whether Jimmy was being straight with him. He'd been too involved with trying to get through the trial and head for the expensive vacation he now found he was dreading. He'd been too damned self-absorbed to do more than pull off a full acquittal of the charges, only to have Jimmy take him out for a celebratory drink and then inform him he'd been lying all the time.

If you lie down with pigs, Sandy told himself, you were bound to get pig droppings all over you. Maybe he should leave criminal law, head for the nice, clean world of corporate shenanigans. What was the lawyer's line from *The Big Chill*?—"All my clients rape is the land."

Even that sounded deadly right about now. Maybe he'd leave his partnership at MacDougal and Sullivan and never come back. There was nothing keeping him there. No wife any longer, and his family would scarcely miss him. The only people who would mourn his departure would be the mechanic he supported with his temperamental old MGB. Him and maybe a bartender or two.

If only things weren't so damned predictable. If only his life hadn't turned out to be just what was expected of him. Prep school, Princeton, Yale Law School, a partnership in a firm that boasted a social conscience. He'd even had his perfect blond wife, and if Margery hadn't lasted, well that was to be expected too, given today's statistics.

He slid back in the uncomfortable chair, stretching his long legs out in front of him. Maybe he should have asked Beverly to come along. She was always good for a laugh, and maybe she would have kept him from his self-absorbed brooding.

But even Beverly had gotten predictable and tiresome. No doubt she found him just as boring. What he needed, Sandy thought, was something to shake him up. To knock him out of his depression and malaise, something to care about. Anything.

The traffic from Route One almost drowned out the sound of the knock on his door. He sat there for a long moment, unmoving. Not many people knew he was there. He'd deliberately chosen a small, run-down motel instead of one of the big ones that were rapidly dotting the area just outside of Princeton. He wanted to keep a low profile during the three-week trial, and he was sick to death of anonymous hotels. At least the Princeton Pike Sleep-a-While Motel had character. All of it bad.

The knocking came again. Someone was definitely at his door, and the only person who knew where he was staying was Jimmy the Stoolie. The last thing Sandy felt like doing was having another heart-to-heart chat with the little sleaze. Besides, Jimmy should be on his way back to the city by now, an undeservedly free man.

The damnable thing about all this, Sandy thought absently, was that he wasn't upset about a professional criminal cheating the system and getting out when he so richly deserved a few years locked away. As a lawyer it was Sandy's duty to provide the best defense to anyone, guilty or innocent. No, it was the fact that Jimmy had lied, and had pulled Sandy into aiding and abetting those lies, that rankled so badly. It had taken all his willpower not to smash his fist into Jimmy's smiling mouth. If it was Jimmy at the door right now he might very well let his willpower go out the window.

He pulled himself out of the chair. Whoever was outside the peeling door of the motel room wasn't about to go away. The knock was brisk, authoritative, demanding a response. Hell, it sounded just like his mother.

Bright autumn sunlight flooded the dingy room when he threw open the door. For a moment his eyes narrowed against the glare, and then he realized the woman standing there was about as unlike anyone he could have imagined.

She was short, and he liked tall women. She had mousy brown hair, and he was partial to blondes. Her eyes were brown, too, and partially obscured by wire-rimmed glasses that gave her a faintly startled look. Her mouth was too generous, and so was her nose, and her clothes were drab, boring, the sort of things worn by a Midwestern librarian. She couldn't have been much older than thirty, or much younger, either. He stood in the doorway, looking down at her, trying to summon up at least an ounce of polite interest.

"I suppose you'll think this pretty rude of me," she said abruptly, and there was a rasp of nervousness in an otherwise melodious voice, "but I'd like you to help me commit arson."

For a long moment Sandy didn't move. And then he slowly stepped back, gesturing her into the room, and shut the door behind her.

HE WASN'T AT ALL what Jane Dexter expected, but then, a confidence man would have to be attractive, wouldn't he? It would certainly help him in his schemes. And she'd seen the photograph, the elegant, austere blond man with his sleazy-looking lawyer. The evening paper had given the details of the three-week trial, and Jane, too depressed and fractious to concentrate on anything more intellectually strenuous than *"Different Strokes"* reruns on the motel's black-and-white TV, had resorted to reading every single word in the article, drawn by a face she'd recognized.

She'd been staying at the Princeton Pike Sleep-a-While Motel for almost ten days, and she could hardly have missed the beautiful man three doors down. When she hadn't been so involved in her own problems she'd wondered about him, why someone who was clearly so prosperous would hole up in such a down-and-out motel. The royal-blue MGB parked outside his room could either be considered a wreck or a classic, depending on your attitude, but there was no question that the man was used to better things.

Jane had found herself making up stories about him to help distract her when things got to be too much. He could fit any number of roles she fashioned for him. He was tall, a bit over six feet, and beautifully coordinated. His shoulders were just broad enough, his legs long, his hands, from what she could see from a distance, were well shaped. His hair was blond, probably lightened from hours on the deck of a yacht or racing around a tennis court, and his remaining tan set off features that were just this side of perfection. She hadn't gotten close enough to see his eyes, but she knew they had to be perfect Aryan blue. His mouth was thin but sexy, his teeth very white, his cheekbones and jaw chiseled. He even had a perfect nose, damn him.

Jane's favorite fantasy was that he was a deposed Balkan prince, trying to reclaim his family's estates. Failing that, he was the long-lost heir to one of the big industrial families around. He could be a famous football player, but that didn't really fit his regal grace. Or he could be a soap opera star hiding out from voracious fans. The last thing she expected he'd be was a professional criminal, with an arrest record longer than the Brooklyn Bridge. Arson, extortion, and a host of lesser crimes had been thrown against him, and nothing had stuck. He'd gotten off this time, thanks, according to the reporter, to the brilliance of his attorney rather than his own innocence. Jane had looked at Alexander Caldicott's weasely little face in the paper and searched for signs of brilliance in the shifty-looking eyes. It would have been much easier to believe he was the hardened criminal, not Golden Boy.

But the picture's caption identified them quite clearly. Besides, what would a hot-shot lawyer be doing at the Princeton Pike Sleep-a-While Motel? No one in their right mind would stay there if they had any other option, she thought, ignoring the fact that she was doing just that. There was an empty apartment less than ten minutes away just waiting for her, and she'd chosen this decrepit motel, rather than surround herself with depressing memories.

But the man three doors down wouldn't have her reasons. There was no question about it, the astonishingly handsome man she'd been covertly studying for days was nothing more than a professional criminal, ready to sell out to the highest bidder. And he was exactly what she needed.

He was looking at her with an odd, slightly bemused expression in his eyes. On closer inspection they weren't blue at all, they were a deep, unfathomable, smoky gray. And that thin mouth of his was even sexier close up, though he clearly couldn't have thought she was much of a temptation. Jane had no illusions about her charms. If she'd had any, they'd been wiped out two years ago in her ruthlessly amicable divorce. Squaring her shoulders, she looked up into Jimmy (the Stoolie) Calvin's enigmatic eyes, and repeated her opening gambit.

"I'd like you to help me commit arson."

"Would you really?" His voice was deep, unaccented. "Let me fix you a drink and you can tell me why you chose me for such a proposition. Scotch all right?"

"Do you have any coffee?" She looked around the room uneasily. It looked just as bare, just as tattered as her own room. At least she'd managed to brighten her own cubicle with fresh flowers, but Jimmy the Stoolie had added nothing more than a bottle of Scotch to the depressing confines.

"Just Scotch. Besides, this sounds like a Scotch-and-water discussion, not a coffee discussion. Take a seat. I wouldn't trust the chair if I were you. Better sit on the bed."

"Uh . . . where are you going to sit?"

It wasn't an unpleasant laugh, but Jane flushed anyway. "I'll risk the chair. Don't worry, I'm not about to jump on you."

"I didn't think you were," Jane lied, sitting gingerly on the sagging bed.

He had his back to her, and a very nice back it was. He was wearing a white cotton dress shirt that clung to his shoulders and back. The linen trousers fit quite nicely too, and Jane had to control an absent, completely irrational sigh of regret.

"Not that you should walk into strange motel rooms," he added, handing her a glass of whiskey that was far too dark.

"It's not a strange motel room," she said. "I've been sitting in one exactly like it for the last ten days."

"You're staying here, too? I hadn't noticed you."

"No." Jane took a sip of whiskey and shivered delicately. "I'm not exactly noticeable."

He didn't make the usual protests, and for that Jane was grateful. He lowered his body into the chair opposite her, and she watched it creak ominously. His own glass of whiskey was even darker than hers, and she wondered, not for the first time, if she'd made a very grave mistake in coming here. She hadn't allowed herself time to think. She'd been so mad, so desperate at the events of the last few days, that she'd thrown down the newspaper, slipped on her shoes, and marched down the walkway before she could have second thoughts. She was having far too many of them right now.

"So tell me," the man said, "who are you, and why have you chosen me to commit arson for you?"

"I'd ... I'd rather not give you my name right now." She took another sip of the whiskey, wishing it were coffee. "Not until we see if we can come to an agreement."

He really smiled then, not the small wry upturning of his mobile mouth but a full-fledged grin. "We'll call you Madame X then," he said solemnly. "Shouldn't you be dressed in black, maybe with a veil covering your face? You look more like a Midwestern librarian."

"I *am* a Midwestern librarian," Jane said, coming close to hating him for a moment.

"Sorry," he said. "I'm a smart aleck sometimes. Why me?"

"I read the newspaper tonight. About your trial."

"Did you? I didn't bother."

"It was very interesting."

"It must have been, if it sent you to me."

Jane took a deep breath. "It made it clear you were really guilty."

"I beg your pardon?"

"The article made it clear that you were a professional crook, and that only your lawyer's brilliance got you off."

A strange, half-pleased, half-disturbed expression crossed his face. "My lawyer?"

"His name is Calderwood?"

"Caldicott," he corrected absently. "Alexander Caldicott."

"Anyway, he managed to get you off. Though I must say he didn't look that brilliant in the picture."

"Looks can be deceiving."

"Yes," she said, looking at his handsome, patrician face, "they can. So anyway, I have need of an arsonist. That is, if you're looking for work. I would think you'd be at loose ends. After all, you didn't know till this afternoon whether you'd be going to jail or not, so you probably haven't made too many long-range plans."

"No, I hadn't. Caldicott is a very great lawyer," he said with a small grin, "but even he isn't infallible. I thought he'd probably get me off but I couldn't count on it. There's one thing you haven't taken into account, though."

"What's that?"

"Suppose I've decided to mend my ways? Go straight, live a life beyond reproach."

She tried to keep the stricken expression from her face. "That would be wonderful," she managed.

"Liar," his voice was teasing, soft, dangerously beguiling. "Don't worry, Madame X. I have the suspicion that my criminal career is just beginning."

When Ms Jane Dexter left his room forty-five minutes later she was weaving slightly. Sandy had plied her with Scotch, watching with fascination as she began to relax and expand under the influence of Cutty Sark. She'd given him her name within ten minutes, though he had to admit he preferred Madame X. Not that Jane didn't suit her. Plain Jane, the librarian from Baraboo, Wisconsin, back in her hometown of Princeton, New Jersey, looking for an arsonist.

Sandy shook his head in disbelief and poured his half-filled glass down the stained bathroom sink. He'd have to get a copy of that paper. The caption must have gotten their names reversed. It was the first time in his life he'd ever been mistaken for someone of Jimmy the Stoolie's ilk, and the experience was novel enough to be entertaining.

He should have told her, of course. He'd meant to, but she'd looked at him with such wonderful awe and distrust that he couldn't resist stringing her along. For the first time in months the deadly lassitude had left him. That odd little encounter might be enough to make his trip to the Canary Islands entertaining after all. Anytime he got bored he could think back to little Ms Jane Dexter and laugh.

She would wonder about him when he didn't show up for dinner tonight. They were supposed to meet at the steak house in the mall, the most anonymous place he could think of, and there she'd outline her plan. He almost wished he could make it. His flight was at ten o'clock tonight—if he missed it he'd have to go back to New York and that was the last thing he wanted. If they'd picked a decent restaurant he could have sent her flowers and a graceful note of regret. He couldn't see managing that in the cafeteria-style steak house he'd assiduously avoided in the past.

No, she was going to have to wonder about Jimmy the Stoolie. She'd probably figure he went back to his life of crime in the bowels of New York. He wondered if the paper would correct its error. He wasn't about to bring it to their attention, and he doubted Jimmy would. So Ms Jane Dexter would have to make other arrangements, always wondering what happened to her first-choice felon.

Sandy stripped off his clothes and headed for the rusty shower stall. He should be delighted to get away from his self-imposed exile, to immerse himself in the luxurious surroundings that would be provided for him. The memory of Jane Dexter's offer of employment would keep him going. Who knows, when he got back he'd probably find she needed a lawyer. Maybe he could offer his services.

Now if he had even an ounce of decency left in him, he would fight his way through the hordes of teenagers that crowded into the mall and meet Madame X long enough to tell her the truth. If he had any conscience at all he'd warn her against committing the felony of arson, or even conspiring to. They'd laugh over her misunderstanding, admit to the error of her ways, and he'd head off to Newark Airport in plenty of time to get his flight, secure in his own nobility.

He cursed as the hot water turned abruptly icy, and jumped out of the shower, banging his elbow and knee as he went. That's what he'd do. He'd make the time to stop there and meet her, out of pure decency and love for his fellow man. And he'd do it because if he didn't, he'd go absolutely crazy wondering why a conventional-looking creature like Ms Jane Dexter wanted to commit arson. So much for noble motives.

The phone rang as he let himself out the door. He paused for a moment. Apart from Jimmy the Stoolie, only the chief legal clerk of MacDougal and Sullivan knew where he was. Right now he wasn't interested in last-minute details, in the law, in anything at all but getting out of this motel. He'd check in with them once he got to the Canary Islands. In the meantime he was going to settle up his account and head for Quaker Bridge Mall and a woman of mystery. And he found himself whistling as he shut the door behind him.

Chapter Two

Sandy had to park half a mile away from the entrance to the sprawling structure of Quaker Bridge Mall. It was a Wednesday night, hardly peak time for shoppers and browsers, but it might as well have been the height of Christmas shopping instead of a balmy evening in mid-October. He cursed under his breath as he crossed the wide expanse of the parking lot. He'd have to remember to take this hike into account when he left Madame X. He didn't want to miss his plane.

It took him even longer to thread his way through the crowds wandering aimlessly around the enclosed mall. He'd miscalculated where the steak house was, and had chosen the parking lot and entrance farthest away. Once he found the coy, Old English facade he had to wait again, shuffling through the cafeteria line like a bag lady, eyeing his purported strip sirloin with deep misgivings. He knew just what his librarian would be doing: munching politely on a salad, eating barely enough to keep a bird alive. While he, for the first time in months, was famished. It didn't matter if it was strip loin of urban rat, he'd eat it, and the microwaved potato, and the limp salad, and the grease-soaked roll. It took him a while to find Jane in the crowded dining room, and he wondered for a moment whether she'd turned the tables and stood him up. Finally he spotted her over in a dark corner, hunched over her tray, and made his way across the room, only to stop in amazement and stare at her dinner.

He'd never seen so much food in his life. She had the Lumberjack Special, the largest steak the place offered, and it was covered with mushrooms, onions, and green peppers. She had a mound of limp french fries, a half-eaten roll, two desserts, and what looked like a small bathtub of some sort of soft drink. He sank down in the chair opposite her, placing his own more discreet tray on the table, and he wished he'd succumbed to the violently pink strawberry shortcake the place served. Maybe Jane would offer him some of hers.

"Are you pregnant?" he asked abruptly.

It was the second time he'd seen her blush. The first had been when he told her to sit on his bed. He didn't realize women still blushed, particularly women over thirty.

"No, I'm not. Why do you ask?"

"Pregnant women eat a lot."

"So do I," she said defiantly.

"You don't look like you do."

She blushed again, and there was just the tiniest bit of a smile behind the wire-rimmed glasses. Not so plain Jane after all, he thought, biting into his greasy roll. "I thought maybe you wanted to torch the father," he added lazily. "Seduced and abandoned and all that."

The smile left her eyes. "He's not the one I want you to torch."

They ate in silence for a few moments. "You want to tell me who he is?" Sandy said finally.

"Who? The man who seduced and abandoned me or the man I want you to torch?" She managed to sound flippant through the strawberry shortcake that she showed no inclination to share.

"I hope you aren't actually suggesting I set a person on fire," he said plaintively. "I do buildings, not people, and

I have an excellent safety record. No one's ever been hurt in one of my fires, not even a fire fighter.'' Now why was he repeating Jimmy's words to her when he should be telling her the truth, making her see the error of her ways? But if he told her, she might very well get up and walk out, and he'd never know who she wanted to sabotage.

"It's a building. A corporation, as a matter of fact." She'd managed to eat everything on her tray and drain the gallon of soda besides, and Sandy looked at her with new respect.

"I'm listening."

"Ever heard of Technocracies Limited?"

He had, but Jimmy the Stoolie wouldn't. "Can't say that I have."

"It's a research and development firm here in Princeton, run by a man named Stephen Tremaine. It's run along simple enough lines—he provides the space and the funding for research scientists, and they come up with all sorts of things and split the patents. New kinds of baby formulas, new kinds of rocket boosters, new kinds of nail polish."

"And?" he prompted as her recitation came to an abrupt halt.

"My brother worked for Tremaine. He developed a revolutionary process for coating tools and metal machine parts with titanium. It's usually very expensive, but it makes the tools last practically forever. Richard figured out a way to do it cheaply."

"Sounds innocuous enough."

"It should have been. Richard, my brother, has always been intensely idealistic. If there's been a cause he's followed it. He's spent more time in jail than you have, protesting the war in Vietnam, nuclear power, the exploitation of migrant farm workers, environmental polluters, everything. He had very strong principles."

"Had?" Sandy prodded gently.

"He died a little over a month ago," she said bleakly, pain still shadowing her eyes. "He was in a freak car crash in upstate New York. And now Tremaine's planning to take his titanium coating process and sell it to the highest bidder. Do you know who the highest bidders are?"

"I can imagine."

"It'll either be the Defense Department of this country or one even worse. And that would betray everything Richard ever believed in. I can't let Tremaine do it, I just can't!"

"What did Tremaine say?"

"The same old garbage he's always said." Her voice was bitter. "That he understands my feelings in the matter but there's nothing he can do about it. He insists Richard never signed a contract restricting the use of his inventions to peaceful applications. And he says as soon as things get settled he'll take the best offer he can get."

"Hold on a minute," Sandy protested. "What things does he have to settle? I'd think it would be a fairly straightforward transaction."

"I would have thought so, too. But something's holding it up. He wanted access to Richard's apartment, but of course I refused. Not that there's anything useful in there, but I wasn't about to give him anything."

"Who's Richard's heir?"

"I am. Our parents are dead."

"Then anything in his apartment should legally belong to you."

She gave him an irritated look. "You've been hanging around your lawyer too long. I thought of that. Don't you think I've checked into every possible legal alternative? Richard's possessions belong to me, Richard's work belongs to Technocracies. I have no legal claim on the formula."

"If Richard did sign a contract stipulating his work was only to be used for peaceful purposes, wouldn't there be a copy of it among his private papers?"

"I've searched through everything a dozen times. Richard wasn't the most practical of men. He probably wrapped the garbage in it or something. Not that he was practical enough to even wrap his garbage."

Sandy had long ago forgotten to look at his watch. "So what is it you want to torch?"

Jane took a deep breath. "Richard's lab at Technocracies. I'd rather have no one use the formula than to have it get in the wrong hands, and I know Richard would agree with me. You're good at that sort of thing, aren't you? Minimizing the damage, making sure no one gets hurt."

"It would be a waste of time. For one thing, the lab is on Tremaine's home turf. Anything useful in the place would have been gotten out long ago. You'd just be destroying useless information."

"You have any alternatives?"

"Of course," he said, leaning back in the uncomfortable little chair. "We can find out what's holding up the sale of the formula. It must be a damned good reason. There are rumors that Technocracies Limited is in financial trouble. Tremaine would want a fresh infusion of money as soon as he can get it. We might also be able to find a copy of your brother's contract with the stipulation that his inventions be used for peaceful purposes."

"I thought you'd never heard of Technocracies?"

Sandy didn't even blink. "The name didn't ring a bell until you started describing it. Er... my lawyer mentioned something about their troubles. If we can find out what's holding up the sale we can turn it to our advantage."

"You aren't, by any chance, talking about blackmail?" She was carefully folding the crumpled paper napkin on her tray, refusing to meet his eyes, and he watched her hands, the short, well-shaped nails, long, graceful fingers, narrow palms. There was no sign of a wedding band, but he suspected that hadn't always been the case.

"You think blackmail's worse than arson?" Sandy countered. "We'd just use it to keep Tremaine from doing what he shouldn't be doing. Of course we could always see if we could get something for our trouble on the side."

"No!" She looked up then, her eyes intent. "I don't want anything from Stephen Tremaine. I just want to keep the formula from falling into the wrong hands."

"All right. There are legal ways of doing it, if you're prepared to take a chance."

"I'm not," she said flatly. "Besides, what do you know about the law?"

Sandy grinned. "I've picked up some useful knowledge over the years. In my line of work you spend a fair amount of time with lawyers and judges."

"I'll bet."

"No snotty cracks, Madame X," Sandy warned. "Or I just may refuse to help you."

"You're going to help me? What's in it for you?"

"Presumably whatever was in it for me to torch Technocracies Limited. You were planning on paying me, weren't you? In my profession I don't need to get too involved in pro bono work."

She looked startled at his use of the technical, Latin term, and he cursed his slip of the tongue. If he wasn't going to tell her the truth he'd better make sure she didn't guess on her own. And to his surprise it didn't seem as if he had any intention of telling her the truth.

"No," she said slowly. "I suppose you don't. Only lawyers and doctors have to worry about dedicating part of their working hours for the betterment of mankind without payment. I suppose it's lawyers and doctors who have to worry about the tax breaks. Do you even pay taxes?"

"Not if I can help it. What've you got against lawyers? Apart from the fact that no one could help you with this problem."

"What makes you think I've got anything against lawyers?"

"The way your nose wrinkles when you say the word, not to mention that subtly delightful curl of your upper lip," Sandy said.

"I was married to one," she said flatly.

"Not the one who seduced and abandoned you?"

"The same."

"Well, at least he made an honest woman of you in the meantime."

She just stared at him, her dark expression making it clear that the subject was closed. "How do you suggest we go about finding what's going on at Technocracies?"

"My naturally devious turn of mind," Sandy said. "I have all sorts of ideas."

"Such as?" she prompted.

He glanced down at his watch. His plane was leaving Newark for the Canary Islands in twelve minutes. Considering that the airport was forty minutes away, he wasn't going to make it. He looked across the Formica-topped table at his dinner partner. If he had any sense of decency at all he'd tell her who he was. She said she'd checked with lawyers, but clearly she hadn't found one with any brains. There were all sorts of ways to deal with the likes of Stephen Tremaine, and Sandy or any one of his partners could probably put an abrupt halt to Tremaine's machinations. A restraining order at the very least could keep any sale of technology tied up for years.

He should tell her who he really was, what he did for a living, and pass her on to one of his partners to deal with the matter while he arranged for a later flight. They could handle it all in an efficient, businesslike way, just as he could, and there'd be no need for subterfuge, deviousness, or excitement.

He opened his mouth, prepared to confess. "Such as," he said, "infiltrating their ranks. A little industrial spying can go a long way if you have the knack of it."

She was looking at him with a combination of awe and apprehension. "And you have the knack of it?"

"Hum a few bars and I can fake it," he said cheerfully. "How are your secretarial skills? Do you think you could get a typing job?"

"Maybe. As long as I don't run into Uncle Stephen."

"Uncle Stephen? Have I missed something along the way?"

"Stephen Tremaine is my godfather," she said gloomily. "Richard's, too."

"Nice guy," Sandy said. "Scratch that idea. I never really liked it in the first place. I guess we'll have to go directly to plan number two. That is, if you're willing to put yourself in my hands."

She looked daunted, and he wanted to reach over and pull those wire-rimmed glasses away from her doubting eyes. He kept his hands in his pockets, tipping back in the chair and watching the silent struggle that shadowed her face. "Of course, we could always try a more honest approach," he added. "I could find you a lawyer, a better one than you've had before, and he might be able to put a spoke in Tremaine's wheels. What it lacks in verve and imagination it makes up for in respectability."

That word tipped the scales. "I'm sick and tired of being respectable," Jane Dexter said. "I'm tired of being reasonable and seeing other people's points of view and always doing the *proper* thing and not the *right* thing. My brother believed in certain things, and he suffered for those beliefs. I'm not going to allow Stephen Tremaine to destroy his legacy, and I don't give a damn if I end up in jail. I'm going to do anything and everything I can to stop him, and if you won't help me I'll torch the building myself.''

Her words tumbled to a stop. She was breathing heavily, and Sandy noticed absently that there were breasts beneath that drab jacket. Nice ones, rising and falling rapidly in her agitation. Her eyes were sparkling with determination and anger, her mouth was soft and tremulous with emotion, and her hands were clenched around the napkin. And suddenly Sandy forgot about Beverly, forgot about leggy blondes and the Canary Islands.

''We won't start with arson,'' he said mildly enough, re-sisting the impulses that were sweeping through him, most of them indecent. ''We'll begin with breaking and enter-ing.''

Jane Dexter looked panicked. Startled, frightened, wary. And then she smiled, a wide, beautiful smile that reached her eyes and lit her face with a warm glow that was effec-tively destroying any defenses Alexander Caldicott had left. ''I'm in your hands,'' she said simply. And he hoped to God she meant it.

SHE WAS A FOOL, Jane thought as she headed through the crowded walkway, dodging teenagers and senior citizens and infants in strollers. What in heaven's name had possessed her to follow a noted criminal into his motel room, set up an assignation, and then agree to commit a felony with him? She hadn't agreed, she'd encouraged him. Practically de-manded that he break the law. She had only herself to blame when she realized she was to be part and parcel of that criminal act.

She shouldn't look at it that way, but a lifetime, almost thirty-one years, of careful consideration prevented her from doing otherwise. She'd always been cursed with the ability to see the other person's point of view. She could sympathize with the migrant workers, but understand the boss's problems. She could hate the war in Vietnam, but worry about the threat of communism. She could detest American involvement in Central America, but wonder about the freedom in the so-called democracies. She could dislike nuclear power but wonder about the alternatives.

She could even see her husband's point of view when he left her. She couldn't even be angry with him. Eminently reasonable as always, she simply gave him his divorce and let him walk out of her life.

But that fairness, that willingness to see the other side of a question, was degenerating into a wishy-washy inability to make a commitment. Just once in her life she had to change. She had to make a stand—it was all she could do for a brother she'd never really understood or been comfortable around. Idealists were hard to live with, and brilliant idealists were even worse. So while she'd loved Richard, as she'd loved their parents, she hadn't liked him very much. All she could do now was respect his memory, and do this one last thing for him.

Even if this one last thing meant meeting someone most inappropriately named Jimmy the Stoolie at a sleazy motel and heading out for a night of crime. It was the least she could do, it was all she could do. And if the thought of her sober, intellectual parents spinning in their grave was an added fillip, then every cloud had a silver lining. And with a sudden grin, she headed on out into the warm New Jersey night.

SANDY WAS FOLLOWING HER at a discreet distance, careful to keep out of her way. Part of him still couldn't quite believe this small, conservative-looking woman was really eager to embark on a life of crime. Part of him couldn't quite believe he was going to aid and abet her. He'd worked long years for his law degree, passed his bar exam with flying colors, practiced for six years with quite remarkable success. If he was caught breaking into Technocracies Ltd. he could very well be disbarred.

But that wasn't going to happen. For one thing, he wasn't planning to get caught. For another, if worse came to worst Jane had told him enough to put pressure on Tremaine to drop any possible charges.

If he didn't help her he had no doubt at all that sooner or later she'd be storming the slate gray building out on Route 206 with a bucket of kerosene and a book of matches. And while it was none of his business, it hadn't taken him long to realize that he didn't want Jane Dexter locked away, out of his reach. He still wasn't quite sure why. Keeping her safe for now would do until he figured it out.

He hated answering machines, hated the high-tech one MacDougal and Sullivan had bullied him into buying, but now and then they had their uses. Heading toward a bank of public phones, he punched in a few numbers, punched in a few more, and began to record a new outgoing message.

"This is Alexander Caldicott. I'll be out of touch for the next two weeks, soaking up sun in the Canary Islands. If you need to get in touch with me please leave a message with my secretary at MacDougal and Sullivan and someone will help you."

He hung up the phone, grinning. He'd made the break. Now he just had to make sure he survived the next two weeks while he kept Madame X out of jail. Somehow he had the feeling his restless boredom was just about to disappear. Had disappeared, in fact, the moment Jane Dexter had walked into his motel room and asked him to commit arson.

Some days you eat the bear, some days the bear eats you, he thought. Right now he felt as if he'd had a very satisfying dinner of bear meat. And things were only going to get better.

Chapter Three

It was after eleven that night when Jane heard the peremptory knock on her door. She'd spent the past few hours moving from bed to chair to bathroom to bed, unable to settle anywhere. She'd searched through the meager belongings she'd brought east with her, looking for something suitable for a breaking and entering. The best she could come up with was an old pair of jeans and a heavy cotton sweater. The sweater was a dark beige, the jeans so faded they were almost baby blue, but it was all she could manage on such short notice.

She practically flew to the door, expecting a cat burglar. Jimmy the Stoolie had changed from his elegant suit, but the smoke-gray running suit wasn't what she'd imagined an experienced crook would wear. He was looking her up and down with an amused light in his eyes that was becoming all too familiar. Why he should find her so amusing was beyond her imagining, but she didn't like it.

Jane took the offensive. "Is that your idea of the sort of thing to wear when we're breaking into a building?"

He strolled in, closing the door behind him with a quiet little snap. "I was tempted to ask you the same thing," he said, "but I decided to be polite."

Jane flushed, determined not to back down. She didn't like Jimmy the Stoolie, she didn't like his patrician good looks or his East Coast aristocratic manners. It didn't matter that the manners were phony, they still reminded her of all the golden men who'd never really had time for her. "I don't have to be polite," she said sweetly. "I'm the boss."

"Actually I meant to talk to you about that." Sandy dropped down onto her bed, making himself completely at home. "If you're going with me tonight you're going to have to do as I say."

"I'm going with you," she said determinedly. "And I haven't the slightest intention of doing what you tell me."

"Then you aren't going," he said flatly, stretching out on the bed. "You seem to forget, I'm the one who's experienced in these matters. I wouldn't think a librarian would have much experience with 'B and E.'"

"I read a lot." Her voice was ridiculous, defensive, and the man's eyes crinkled in a wry smile.

"Reading isn't good enough. You're going to have to trust me, trust me enough to know what's best. When I say duck you'll have to duck, when I say run, you run. No questions asked, no arguments, no democratic decisions. If you can't accept that then the deal is off."

Jane stood there watching him, chewing her lip in frustration. What he said made absolute sense, but the last thing in the world she wanted to do was give him any sort of power over her. Her self-esteem, her peace of mind were too precarious to entrust to this charming con man.

On the other hand, if she didn't do as he said she had no doubt at all he'd walk out and refuse to help her. When it came right down to it he probably did know best about such things, much as it galled her to admit it.

She was asking him for help, she'd have to learn to accept it. "All right," she said finally, "we'll do it your way. This time."

He moved swiftly then, coming off the bed in one fluid, graceful movement and reaching her side. She backed away quickly, coming up against the door, and he reached a hand out to steady her, the laughter fading from his eyes. "Don't be so nervous, Jane," he said softly. "I'm not going to hurt you."

She drew herself upright. "You startled me. And I think it's understandable that I'd be edgy. I've never broken into a building before."

He nodded, sober for once. "The first time is always the hardest."

She looked at him curiously. "What was your first time like?"

He shook his head, a smile once more curling the corners of his mobile mouth. "You wouldn't want to know," he said softly. "You'll do as I tell you?"

"Yes."

"Don't sound so sulky, Jane. I may very well save your life."

She had to stop the sudden clenching of her heart. "It's not going to be that dangerous, is it?" she demanded.

"I made a few calls. Tremaine favors armed guards and patrol dogs."

"What?"

He shrugged, grinning that disarming grin. "This wouldn't be any fun if it was too easy. Trust me, Jane. Do as I say and we'll be just fine."

"And if we're not?" she said, resisting that charm stonily.

"Then I know a heckuva lawyer."

And Jane, remembering the weasely little face in the grainy newspaper photo, snorted derisively before following him out into the brightly lit New Jersey night.

THEY DROVE through the sparse nighttime traffic in the blue MGB. It ran a little rough, and Jane gave it a doubtful look as her companion sped down the wide roads. "Are you sure this is the car to take? I'd think we'd want something reliable for a quick getaway."

"This car's reliable," he said, clearly stung. "It's in classic shape—you don't see many like these nowadays."

"Amen," muttered Jane. "It needs a tune-up."

"It had one three days ago."

"Doesn't hold it long, does it?"

He glared at her. "Suddenly you know about cars, too, Madame X?"

"I read a lot."

He managed to hold the glare for perhaps fifteen seconds longer. And then he laughed, a short bark of humor that lessened the tension filling the car. "Now is not the time to pick a fight with me. We've got a challenging night ahead of us—we don't need to be at each other's throats."

"It keeps me from being nervous." She slid down in the leather seat, stretching her legs out in a useless effort to relax.

"Well, it makes me edgier. Cut it out." Without warning he cut the wheel to the left, pulling into a narrow, vacant lot and stopping the car behind a billboard advertising Tanqueray Gin. Jane had a sudden, intense longing for a tall glass of the stuff, forget the tonic, as Jimmy the Stoolie bumped to a halt, flicking off the key with one well-shaped hand.

"Am I allowed to ask questions?"

"Feel free. I need blind obedience, not silence," he replied, pulling on a pair of leather driving gloves that he hadn't bothered to wear before. "Look in the glove box. There should be another pair in there."

"Why don't I just promise not to touch anything?" Jane suggested brightly.

"Put them on." There was no room for argument in his tone of voice. "Your pal Tremaine's building is just beyond that vacant warehouse. We're going to walk from here."

Jane opened her mouth to protest, then shut it again. All she could do was trust this stranger and do as he ordered. Six hours ago she'd never spoken a word to the man, now she was in the midst of committing a felony. The Baraboo Board of Libraries wasn't going to tolerate a felon in their employ, nor were most libraries in her experience. They tended to be a conservative bunch, quick to condemn and slow to understand. No, if they were caught her career was down the tubes.

She could tell Jimmy the Stoolie she'd wait in the car. She could tell him forget it, she'd changed her mind. After all, Uncle Stephen doubtless thought he was doing the right thing. He must have good reasons for believing he had the right to sell the process to whomever he chose.

But he was wrong. And she couldn't let Richard's life mean nothing. She pulled herself out of the car, taking a deep breath of the night air. It tasted of damp earth and autumn and the tang of exhaust. "I'm ready," she said, meeting her companion's curious gaze.

If only he didn't have such beautiful gray eyes, she thought. If only his smile wasn't completely bewitching. He smiled at her then, and it took every ounce of effort to keep from melting. "Good girl," he said. "Keep your head down and follow me." And Jane followed.

Technocracies Ltd. was a sprawling complex of buildings on Route 206 just north of Princeton. In the daylight it was beautifully proportioned, perfectly landscaped, a spacious, elegant place to work. At night, that moonless night in particular, it was a dark, ominous huddle of buildings. The decorative shrubs hugged the building, menacing shapes to add to Jane's already terrified state of mind. The parking lot was empty, but somehow she failed to be reassured.

The guards, and she truly believed her accomplice when he told her there were guards, must have parked somewhere.

Jane did as she was told, following her companion's tall, well-built figure as he approached the building, hiding in his shadow as he in turn hid in the shadow of the building. He moved with unerring instincts, directly to a bank of doors, and stopped in front of one of them.

"Are you going to use a credit card?" she whispered. "I've never seen anyone jimmy a lock."

"Shhh." He pulled something out of his pocket, and she leaned forward, curious to watch a lock pick at work.

Her companion held up a key, inserted it in the lock, and opened the door, gesturing her inside. She went, stopping dead still inside and turning an accusing glare on him.

"Where'd you get that key?" she demanded in a fierce whisper. "And don't tell me it's a skeleton key—I know better."

"I wouldn't think of telling you any such thing. Where do you think I got it?" He stood there looking down at her, patient, amused, and she was sorely tempted to kick him in the shins.

"From my godfather? Maybe you figured you could get more money from him if you strung me along and reported to him."

"You do have a devious mind." He was clearly admiring rather than offended. "I never even thought of that. The idea has merit, but it's full of holes. Tremaine doesn't sound like the sort who'd appreciate my offer of assistance. He'd probably just turn me in to the police and double the security. Guess again."

Her nerves were at a screaming pitch, her palms damp and slippery inside the over-large pair of driving gloves he'd forced her to wear. "Now isn't the time to play games."

"Why not? It eases the tension."

"For you, maybe. Not for me."

He took pity on her, his gloved hand cuffing her chin lightly. "Cheer up, Madame X. If you're going to embark on a life of crime you'll have to be cool, calm and collected. I got the key off your key ring."

"Mine?" He surprised her into a little shriek, and the hand that had cuffed her chin immediately covered her mouth, pushing her against the wall.

"Not that cool," he muttered in her ear. "We aren't supposed to be here, remember?" He removed his hand. "You had a set of keys lying on your dresser. Presumably your brother's? Everything was nicely marked—apartment, beach house, Vermont house, L-1, L-2, Techno. It didn't take a great criminal mind to figure the last key would get us in here without having to resort to credit cards and jimmies and the like."

"I should have thought of it myself," she said, self-recrimination warring with another, less acceptable emotion. He was standing close enough for her to feel the body heat emanating through the expensive gray sweat suit. The feelings he aroused in her were disturbing, unacceptable, and inescapable. She was reacting to him as a woman reacts to a man she wants, and she was a hundred times a fool to do so.

"That's all right," he said, still not moving, too close, too damned close. "All part of the service."

"Service?" The word was breathless. She could lean a little closer in the darkened hallway and be touching him again. It was tempting, very tempting.

"Jimmy the Stoolie's Rent-a-Crook."

It was enough to break the hypnotic spell. "Are we going to search this place or not?" she snapped, remembering to keep her voice to a whisper.

"I suppose we'd better. It's now—" he checked the ultrathin gold watch on his strong wrist "—eleven fifty-three. Tremaine uses Foxfire Security Systems, which means two men, two Dobermans, and probably two guns, will be here sometime after one o'clock. They have three stops before this one, and it depends whether any of my colleagues have chosen tonight to break into one of Foxfire's other clients' offices. I don't expect we'll be so lucky, so we'd better be out of here no later than quarter of one. Okay?"

She stared up at him. "How do you know all that?"

"Professional secret. Quarter of one okay with you?"

"Fine," she said, fighting back the distrust.

"Then let's go."

It was damned lucky she was gullible, Sandy thought. He couldn't very well tell her he'd called a colleague who'd called a client who'd called a friend to find out how Technocracies Ltd. handled security. She probably didn't want to know the sordid details, anyway. She'd rather believe he had some sort of criminal osmosis.

The keys had been a stroke of good luck. They'd get through the night with similar luck, if his sources had been correct. As they moved through the empty hallways he wondered what the real Jimmy would have done if Madame X had shown up at his motel room.

Tried to seduce her, for one thing. And while that reaction hadn't been Sandy's first, it was becoming more and more appealing.

Except that prim and proper Jane Dexter wasn't the sort to fall into bed with a professional criminal. He'd have to overcome all her misgivings, all her doubts, all her very strong defenses.

The thought was challenging. Could he make someone want him so much she'd be willing to turn her back on years of security and ethics? The question had never come up before. The women he met knew he was a well-paid, unmarried lawyer of healthy habits and well-mannered disposition. They were running no danger at all getting involved with him.

With Jane it was a different matter. If she ever went to bed with him she'd be taking untold risks. If she went to bed with him it would be an act of faith and trust such as he'd never experienced. The more he thought about it, the more he wanted it.

"This is it," Jane said abruptly.

For a moment he didn't know what she was talking about. And then he looked at the heavy walnut door in front of them, the raised bronze lettering announcing the executive offices. "In there?"

"Where else? You told me there wouldn't be anything in Richard's lab, and I expect you're right. Uncle Stephen's office is the best place to start."

Uncle Stephen's office, he thought glumly. He'd been hoping to back her into a corner in some empty little lab. "All right," he said easily, reaching for the doorknob. The heavy brass handle didn't budge.

Jane was watching him, her eyes steady and curious behind her wire-rimmed glasses. "I don't suppose you brought a key for this one?"

"No sarcasm," he uttered. "We'll have to be inventive." The idea of breaking into an office with his gold American Express card would have appealed to his sense of humor if he had any kind of assurance he'd be successful. He pulled the thin sliver of plastic from his wallet, squatted down, and tried to look as if he knew what the hell he was doing.

It didn't help having Jane breathing down his neck. He could catch a slight trace of the perfume she was wearing, something faintly flowery that was nevertheless more sensuous than innocent. He spared himself a brief glance over his shoulder at her intent face. Plain Jane indeed. He wanted to push her over onto the too-expensive carpeting that lined the hallway and forget about her damned brother.

He turned his attention back to the task at hand. He heard the little click, and ignored it, refusing to believe it would be that easy.

"You did it," Jane whispered, reaching past him and turning the handle. The weighted door swung open.

"Of course I did." He rose to his full length, towering over her, hoping it was too dark for her to notice his astonishment. "Of course it took me a little longer than usual."

"I'll start with the receptionist's desk," she cut in. "Why don't you check out Uncle Stephen's office?"

The moment he saw the bank of teak filing cabinets he knew why she'd given him the good part. He had no hope whatsoever that the files were unlocked, and one desultory little yank proved him correct. Jane Dexter probably expected him to use his much-abused American Express card on each one of those file cabinets, something he wasn't about to do. It had been dumb luck the first time. He had no faith at all in his ability to repeat that particular miracle.

He didn't have to. Tremaine hadn't locked his desk, and sitting in the top drawer was a small gold key ring. The man was either innocent of wrongdoing, or supremely self-confident. From what little Sandy had heard of Stephen Tremaine, he had a very good notion it was the latter.

He was halfway through the files when Jane joined him. She sat cross-legged on the floor, leafing through the folder he'd handed her, her head bent like a studious little girl. She must have felt his eyes on her, for she looked up, directly into his face.

"You're awfully good at this sort of thing," she said. "The files were locked, weren't they?"

"Yes." He felt no need to enlighten her further. Better to have her think he was almost omnipotent. "It all comes with practice," he added modestly.

"You know, you just don't look the type." She closed the folder and reached for another one.

"What type?"

"Oh, you know. Hardened criminal and all that."

He considered making a crude joke, but resisted the impulse. While he might consider the past few hours in the nature of an adventure, Jane Dexter took it much more seriously. "We've already agreed," he said solemnly, "looks can be deceiving. You, for instance, look like a very conventional middle American. Instead, beneath that mild exterior hides the heart of an adventuress."

"Beneath my mild exterior hides a panic-stricken woman," she said tartly. "We're getting nowhere. There isn't even any mention of Richard's name in the personnel files. No contracts, no insurance packages, nothing."

Sandy nodded. "You're right. Which in itself is a sign we're on the right track. There should be some trace of your brother, some mention. How long did he work here?"

"Seven and a half years."

"Someone has carefully expunged all trace of him from the records. The only way to get his files will be through the computer." He eyed the silent screened monolith in the outer room with deep misgivings. "I don't suppose it would hurt to check. We don't have much time left. I'll clean up in here and you can see what the computer has to offer."

"See what the computer has to offer?" she echoed. "I don't know a thing about computers."

"Why not? I thought you read a lot."

"Not about computers, if I can possibly help it. I'll clean up and you try the computer."

Sandy sighed. "It would be a waste of time. I don't know anything about computers, either."

She just looked at him for a long moment. And then to his surprise she laughed, a deep, throaty chuckle at complete odds with her prim exterior. "We make pretty inept spies."

"But I'm hell on wheels at breaking and entering."

"You're hell on wheels at finding keys," she corrected. "Better put Uncle Stephen's back in his drawer."

She didn't miss much, he had to grant her that. For a moment he wondered how long it would take her to realize the newspaper made a mistake, that she wasn't consorting with a dangerous felon but a mild-mannered lawyer. And what would her reaction be when she did find out? He thought he might prefer the Dobermans.

"We'd better get out of here," he said suddenly, remembering. "It's ten of one, and those guys might be early."

Together they slammed the teak file drawers shut. Sandy almost forgot to relock the outer office, but Jane reminded him, and then they were racing down the hallway, their sneakered feet silent on the heavy carpeting. He didn't know whether the sound of traffic from 206 had gotten louder, or whether it was his own overstimulated heart roaring like that. The heavy glass door clicked shut behind them, and they were outside in the damp night air.

Headlights split the darkness as someone pulled into the parking lot, and he grabbed Jane's hand, pulling her along, panic and adrenaline rushing through him. She went with him, her gloved hand tight in his, and moments later they were off the property, heading toward the highway. The streetlights were bright, too bright, illuminating their figures, and Sandy could hear the slam of car doors, the muffled growl of ferocious canines as the two of them slid down the embankment, landing in a tangle of limbs.

They'd been seen. A flashlight shone in their direction, more like a spotlight, and a rough voice called out. "Hey, what are you two doing down there?"

Sandy didn't have much choice in the matter. The dogs were coming closer, the strong beams from the spotlight circling over their heads. He ripped off his gloves and stuffed them in his pocket, noting with approval that Jane had done the same thing without having to be told.

A dog snarled. A tightly leashed dog, Sandy devoutly hoped. A few more feet and they'd be seen. He looked at Jane's panicked expression and did the only thing he could think of. Yanking her onto his lap, he shoved one hand down her sweater and set his mouth on hers.

Chapter Four

It was the last thing Jane expected. Her heart was pounding wildly, her breath coming in tortured gasps, terror and a twisted sort of excitement were racing through her body. The feel of his hand on her breast, even through the lacy bra, shocked and aroused her. His mouth was on hers, wet, hot, seeking, his tongue and lips taking complete, unquestioning control of her and overwhelming any ounce of restraint she might have had. Too many emotions were batting at her, too much adrenaline, too much stimulation. She snaked her arms around his neck, pressed her breast against his hand and kissed him back, wanting nothing more than his mouth on hers, that desperate, erotic claiming that was shaking her to the very marrow of her bones.

Dimly she heard the dogs barking. Lights were flashing over her head, and for a moment she thought it was the force of his kiss making her see stars. Then she thought it was lack of oxygen causing the lights to go on in her brain. He tore his mouth away, gasping for breath, and she realized those celestial lights were flashlight beams.

"Helluva place to bring a lady, buddy," a voice called from above them. Her companion was looking at her, eyes glittering in the artificial light, and his breath was coming as rapidly as hers. Then he turned his head toward the intrusive beam of light.

"What can I say? We were out jogging when we decided to...er...take a little break. You wanna turn those lights off?" His voice was disgruntled, a man interrupted in the throes of passion.

"Better pick someplace else, pal," another voice said, less amused. "This is private property, and you're trespassing."

Slowly the man beside her uncoiled his body and rose, shielding her from the light. "We'll do that. Sorry to bother you."

"No trouble. Just be glad I didn't unleash the dogs." An exuberant snarl punctuated that flat statement, and Jane shivered.

Jimmy the Stoolie was playing his part to the hilt. He put an arm around her shoulders, pulling her trembling body against his, and started down toward the road. She could feel the inquisitive, unsympathetic eyes following them, and she shivered in the warm night air.

"Do you think we fooled them?" she whispered under the noise of the traffic.

"Probably." They were back at the car by then, and he released her, too quickly, the action reminding Jane it had all been part of a very efficient charade. "You're quick," he said, his voice approving. "For a moment I thought you were going to hit me."

"The thought crossed my mind," she lied. Hitting him had been the last thing she'd contemplated. "All in a day's work."

THEY DROVE BACK OUT to Route One in silence. It was well past one in the morning, and traffic had thinned to a muffled roar. Jane's heart had slowed to a dull, steady throb, her hands were dry, her stomach in knots. She glanced over at her companion. Jimmy the Stoolie seemed lost in thought, his gray eyes intent on the driving, his strong hands gripping the leather-covered steering wheel loosely. One of those hands had cupped her breast. That practiced deftness must have been pure instinct on his part. He couldn't have consciously caught the tiny bud of her nipple and teased it into swollen arousal with attack dogs and armed guards looming overhead. An accident of nature, Jane decided, sinking gloomily in the seat.

"What next?" he asked as he pulled in front of her peeling motel-room door.

Tension shot through her body. "What do you mean?" She couldn't deny the pseudo embrace in the ditch beside 206 had aroused her, but she certainly wasn't about to jump into bed with a professional arsonist and con man. Particularly when she'd known him for less than twelve hours.

Again that slow smile, as if he read her mind. "What do we do tomorrow? Unless you're ready to call it quits."

"I'm not. Even if tonight was a total washout that doesn't mean there aren't other possibilities."

"I wouldn't say tonight was a complete failure. The fact that your brother's personnel file was missing suggests there's something going on . . ."

"I *told* you something's going on."

"So you did. But one has to consider all the possibilities. And you might have been racked with paranoid delusions due to unresolved grief over your brother's untimely death."

"Do you hang out with a lot of pop psychologists along with lawyers?" she questioned sweetly.

To her surprise he flushed. "Just worth considering," he said. "You're still determined to go through with this?"

"Still determined. With you or without you. Are we going to torch the place?"

"No, we're not going to torch the place," he said wearily. "Violent little creature, aren't you? I've got a few tricks up my sleeve."

"Such as?"

"Leave it to me," he said mysteriously. "I'll give you a call tomorrow morning and we'll make our plans."

She was being dismissed. She breathed a sigh of relief, but felt disappointed that she wouldn't have to fight him off. She hadn't really expected to, but after the tangle in the ditch she couldn't help her mind from considering such things.

It was a waste of time. People who looked like her companion were never interested in plain Janes, and people who lived as she did weren't interested in compromising themselves with professional criminals. They were nothing more than partners in crime, and unless they ran across more Dobermans and armed guards he wouldn't have to touch her again.

He reached over and caught her willful chin, his long fingers cool against her heated flesh. "Earth to Jane, come in please," he murmured.

"Sorry, I was distracted." She was still distracted, by the look, the scent, the heat, the touch of the man beside her. She pulled back, and his hand dropped too readily. "Tomorrow," she said, climbing out of the car and locking it behind her.

He was coming with her. She couldn't read his expression in the artificial light, wasn't sure she even wanted to. "There's no need to see me to the door," she said hastily.

"I'm not. I've got the room next door."

The darkness covered her embarrassment quite nicely. "Since when?"

"Since this evening. I'd already checked out when you came up with your charming proposition. When I reregistered I had them move my room. I thought it might come in handy."

I'll just bet you did, Jane thought, then wiped out the fantasy. Why in the world was she so paranoid about the man's intentions? He'd said and done nothing to suggest he had any physical interest in her. For all she knew he might even be gay. No, scratch that. The man standing tall and straight in the lamplight was definitely, distressingly heterosexual. And even if her instincts told her he wanted her, her intellect assured her that fantasy was nothing more than wishful thinking on her part.

"Tomorrow, then." Her voice was steady, showing none of the tangled thoughts racing around in her weary brain.

"Tomorrow," he agreed, standing by his door as she fumbled for her key in her back pocket.

He waited until her door closed behind her, waited until he heard the distinctive sound of bolts being shot into place. "Damn," he muttered to himself, opening the peeling green door that was a twin to Jane's. "How do I get myself into these things?"

Of course the answer to that, he thought, pouring himself a generous shot of Scotch and dropping down on the bed, was that he didn't. This was the first time he'd ever gotten involved in a situation rife with such lies and complexity that it simply boggled his mind.

He'd had more than a few bad moments that night, starting with the locked file cabinets and ending with her crack about pop psychologists. That was exactly what Beverly did for a living, and her conversation was dotted with phrases like "meaningful relationships" and "getting in touch with yourself." He'd always been revolted by her psycho-babble, and then to find he was doing it himself . . .

He drained the whiskey, stretching out on the lumpy mattress that was even worse than the one in his previous room. He considered turning on the TV—Princeton was in range of both New York and Philadelphia and even without cable there was always something on. The Princeton Pike Sleep-a-While Motel's only cable channel was an x-rated one. Clearly the place was misnamed—here people didn't usually rent rooms just to sleep.

Dirty movies were the last thing Sandy needed. He could still feel Jane's light, strong body beneath his, taste the surprising enthusiasm of her soft mouth. He was beginning to think he'd been mistaken in chasing after Amazons for all these years. He was rapidly growing partial to small brunettes, a Jane who wasn't very plain after all.

He cursed out loud, a nice, rounded obscenity he'd picked up from a teenage nephew, and was about to say it again when he heard a rapping on his wall.

"Is something wrong?" Jane's voice was muffled but unmistakable. He wondered what she was wearing, and he groaned.

"It's nothing." He sounded admirably calm. "I just stubbed my toe."

"Oh. Good night, then. Pleasant dreams."

Pleasant dreams, he thought cynically. Who would be innocent enough to wish a stranger pleasant dreams? Only a Midwestern librarian who was totally ignorant of how she affected him. He was going to have dreams, all right. He was going to dream about that slender, warm body of hers wrapped around his, he was going to dream about that soft, lovely mouth and those surprisingly generous breasts of hers. And he was going to have nightmares about what she was going to say when she found out who he really was.

He turned over on his stomach, shoved his face into the foam pillow that smelled of stale cigarette smoke and moaned. It was going to be a long night.

IT WAS TEN THIRTY-FIVE in the morning when Jane finally surfaced. She blinked sleepily at her watch, then sat bolt upright, jumped from the bed and raced to the window. Pushing the sickly green curtains out of the way, she saw in relief that the MGB was still in place. He hadn't taken off in the middle of night, never to be heard from again.

Not that it wouldn't have been a good thing, she thought as she rushed through her shower. If Jimmy the Stoolie were gone she'd be on her own, and sooner or later she'd have to give up in defeat. With a professional by her side the possibilities were endless, and so were the risks.

She had her morning ablutions down to a science, one that usually lasted seven and a half minutes. Today, in a hurry, it took her twelve, making sure the minimal mascara and liner were just right, even bothering with a slash of tinted lip gloss and a pinch of color on her pale cheeks. She braided her wet hair, tossing it over her shoulder, and grimaced at her reflection. She wasn't doing it for him, she reminded herself. The opinion of her partner in crime meant absolutely nothing to her. No, she did it for her own flagging sense of self-esteem.

By five of eleven there was still no sound from next door, no knock on her door, no jangling telephone. She considered her options. She could bang on the wall, but that seemed a little intimate. She wouldn't have done it last night, but that curse floating through the thin walls had a desperate edge to it, and she'd been afraid he'd hurt himself.

She could walk out into the bright sunlight and knock on his door. But what if he were still asleep? She didn't fancy having him stagger to the door in rumpled pajamas, or even less.

She picked up the phone and dialed the desk. For a moment her mind went blank, forgetting his last name. She could hardly ask the bored-sounding clerk for the room of Jimmy the Stoolie, could she?

Calvin, that was it. Jimmy Calvin.

"No one by that name," the gum-popping voice replied, and the phone slammed down.

Jane counted to ten, dialed 0 once more, and said in her sweetest voice, "I know he's registered. He's in the room next to me."

"Then why don't you go and knock on his door?" Slam.

Jane counted to fifteen, dialed 0 and said, "Because I don't want to disturb him. Could you please ring his room for me?"

There was a long-suffering sigh on the other end of the line, accompanied by a loud snapping of gum. "There's no one in 4-A, and the man in 6-A isn't James Calvin. He's registered as Alexander Caldicott."

SOMEONE WAS CHASING after him, someone with a huge mallet, twice the size of an average man, and that person was slamming the mallet down on the ground, causing a major earthquake. It was Yosemite Sam, his red handlebar mustache bristling, shouting and cursing as he slammed the mallet down and the entire landscape hopped. It didn't hop as fast as he did, and he realized without much enthusiasm that he was Bugs Bunny.

The pounding continued, the dream faded, and Sandy sat bolt upright in bed, realizing he wasn't Bugs Bunny racing through a Southwestern desert, he was Alexander Caldicott in a motel in New Jersey.

The flimsy door was trembling with the force of someone's fist. "Wake up," Jane Dexter said fiercely from the other side and Sandy had one more realization. He was neither Bugs Bunny nor Alexander Caldicott, he was Jimmy the Stoolie. And he sank back into the pillow with a groan.

"Go away," he said weakly. It was too early and he was too hung over to face her and the truth he knew would have to come out. He'd have to tell her—sometime during the sleepless night he'd come to that conclusion. He'd take her out somewhere, not a cafeteria like that godawful steak house but someplace restrained and elegant, where she wouldn't dare throw a scene. She'd be embarrassed at her mistake, but he'd be charming, and they'd both end up laughing about it.

She didn't sound like she was laughing right now. "Wake up, Jimmy!" she said, still pounding. He could see the cheap panel vibrate, and he knew she wouldn't give up.

"I'm coming," he groaned. He'd resorted to finishing the bottle of Scotch around four-fifteen, when sleep had still eluded him. He didn't know whether he'd finally drifted off or blacked out, but the end result was the worst headache he'd had in his entire life.

He stumbled to the door, yanked it open, and stood glaring into the sunlight. Jane was glaring just as fiercely. "It's about time." She bit off the words, stepping into the room. He reached beyond her and shut the door, shut out the blinding sunlight that was threatening to split his skull. "I have something to ask you." And then her voice trailed off as she noticed what he was wearing.

Sandy ignored her, collapsing back on the bed. The weakened frame shook beneath the force of his body, but he didn't care, just lay face down in the tangled covers as he waited for Jane to pull herself together.

It wasn't as if he was stark naked. He'd slept in his briefs and T-shirt—both were a sedate navy blue, and if she'd been married she'd been bound to see someone in a lot less. Hell, there was more to his underwear than he usually wore swimming. God damn all librarians and people who pounded on his door demanding answers when he had the world's worst headache . . .

"Why are you registered under the name Alexander Caldicott?"

All self-pity vanished, and he stared down into the creased white sheets, his beleaguered brain working overtime. He'd always had the ability to think fast, particularly in crucial situations, and now wasn't the time to come up with the truth. She'd probably break a chair over his head.

He rolled onto his back and eyed her calmly. Her normally pale face was still slightly pink, and she kept her eyes fastened above his neck. For a moment he had the sadistic wish that he had slept in the nude. If she was going to react like a Victorian virgin she might as well have something real to panic about.

"I'm registered under Caldicott's name because he's responsible for my bills," he said blithely, obscurely pleased that he wasn't actually lying.

"Why?"

"Part of a deal we worked out. He'll be reimbursed. It just helps with record keeping and all that."

She looked doubtful, then guilty. "Actually, I suppose I should be paying for your room."

"I draw the line at being a kept man," he said in his most solemn voice, and her cheeks flushed pink again. He wondered if he could get her to come a little closer. If he could just manage to trip her, get her onto this too soft bed with him, she might very well respond as she had last night.

Speaking of response, he thought with a silent groan, rolling onto his stomach once more. She might not have noticed if she kept her gaze on his face, but he had the suspicion it was taking every ounce of concentration she possessed to keep from letting her eyes drift lower.

"I didn't mean to offend you...you're teasing me, aren't you?"

"Yes."

She sighed, sinking down into the powder-pink vinyl chair that was the one improvement this room had to offer. "I'm too gullible."

He grinned at that. "Very true. And no, you don't need to pay for my room. We'll work out the finances later."

"But I don't even know if I can afford..."

"You can afford me. And if you can't, I may be into doing a little pro bono work after all."

"I couldn't accept that," she said stiffly.

"We'll work something out." He still didn't dare roll over again. She was having the most amazing effect on his senses, and she wasn't even a blonde. "Listen, let me grab a shower and then we'll head on out."

"Head on out where?"

He grinned. "Back to Technocracies, of course. Breaking and entering netted us very little, so it's back to plan one. It's time for a little industrial espionage."

Chapter Five

"This is an incredibly stupid idea," Jane hissed as she trailed Sandy down the same carpeted corridor they'd traversed less than twelve hours ago. It looked different in the daylight, bland and professional and distinctly unthreatening.

Neither of them bore much resemblance to the two burglars of the night before. She could scarcely recognize Jimmy the Stoolie. His wheat-colored hair was slicked back and parted in the center, his aristocratic nose was marred by a pair of glasses, he walked with a stoop-shouldered slouch, and his tie was knotted badly. For such minor changes the results were considerable, turning the golden prince into an attractive nerd.

She didn't know if her own transformation was as effective, though her companion had assured her it was. She'd gone in the other direction, fighting him all the way in the confines of his sleazy hotel room.

"Haven't you got anything livelier to wear?" he'd demanded, eyeing her sensible khaki suit and white blouse with disgust.

"No."

"Didn't that lump of a jacket come with shoulder pads?"

"I threw them out."

He snorted derisively. "I believe it. We'll have to wad up some tissues. We need to give your clothes some shape."

"It has quite enough shape, thank you."

"Stop arguing." Before she'd realized what he was doing he'd reached out and unfastened the top two buttons of her white oxford shirt. She batted at his hands, but he ignored her, yanking at the material until his critical eye found something to approve. "One would never know you had breasts under those clothes," he muttered.

Outrage and amusement warred within her, and for once amusement won. "I think people are supposed to take it on faith." She jerked away from him, taking the wadded up tissues from his hand. "I can manage from here, thank you." She turned to the mirror, tucking the tissues under her bra straps to form makeshift shoulder pads. "They'll probably slip and I'll end up looking like the hunchback of Notre Dame."

He came up behind her, and his fingers were deft in her tightly braided hair. "They'll be too busy looking at your cleavage." He spread her damp hair around her shoulders, fluffing it slightly, gazing at her with an expression she couldn't quite fathom.

"Satisfied?" she demanded, turning to face him and instantly regretting it. As usual he was standing too close, and he'd touched her too much already for her peace of mind.

He wasn't through touching. "Almost. Change the sensible shoes to something a little spikier, put on more lipstick, and these—" he reached out, unwound the curved stem of her wire-rimmed glasses from her ears and pulled them off "—have got to go."

"Mr. Calvin," she began fiercely.

"Who?"

"Calvin. It's your last name, isn't it?"

He had the grace to look slightly flustered. "It's an alias."

"I'm not surprised."

"So is Jimmy." He peered through her glasses, shaking his head and blinking. "Call me Sandy."

"Sandy?" she echoed.

"Short for Sandor Voshninsky," he said blithely. "That was my favorite alias and I haven't used it for a while. You don't need these glasses."

"I get a headache without them."

"Join the club. I already have one." He reached up and settled her glasses on his own classic nose, peering through them. The transformation was instantaneous. He looked nearsighted, slightly wimpy and suddenly approachable. Jane found she didn't like that approachability one bit.

"I don't think we're going to fool anyone." She reached down to button her shirt, but he caught her hand, stopping her, holding it far too long. "If Uncle Stephen hadn't left for Europe I wouldn't even consider it. It's a lucky thing we met at his house and not at the office. I know his executive assistant never forgets a face, and once she sees me . . ."

"We don't have to fool them for very long. Listen, this is a simple scam. I know they'll hire me—I can talk anybody into anything."

"I believe it," she muttered.

"And you only had to look at the cluttered desks around there to know they're behind on their clerical work. You show up with the proper credentials and they'll jump on you like fleas on a dog."

"Charming figure of speech."

"Good help is hard to find nowadays. Everyone wants to be a chief, no one wants to be an Indian."

"How come I got elected to be the squaw? Why don't I tell them I'm a research scientist and you're the typist?"

"Because you don't have the experience to carry it off," he said bluntly. "I do. All you have to do is smile and lean over."

"Sexist pig," she said mildly. "How do you know the person hiring me is a man?"

"I don't. You'll have to adapt. If it's a man, you flirt very, very discreetly. Show him those terrific legs you try so hard to hide. If it's a woman, pull your skirts down and come on strong and subdued. Play on the sisterhood angle, but don't let her feel threatened."

She stared at him for a long moment, trying to ignore the flush of pleasure that had swept over her when he mentioned her terrific legs. She did have good legs, but she hadn't expected him to notice. "You have the most devious, manipulative mind," she said.

He leaned closer, and for a brief, startled moment she thought he was going to kiss her. Instead he reached under her jacket and adjusted the wad of tissue. "Thanks," he said cheerfully. "But you're showing great promise yourself."

Right now she didn't feel the slightest bit promising. Jimmy, no, Sandy had called Technocracies Ltd. And apparently the company was in dire need of temporary secretarial help. She didn't even understand half of what Sandy said about himself. All that mattered was the end result. Sandy had an appointment with the chief of personnel, Jane was to be interviewed by the other end of the corporate ladder.

"Cheer up, Madame X," he murmured at the door of the personnel office. "You'll do fine."

To her amazement she did, though she had a few schizophrenic moments. Charlie Pilbin, a harassed-looking middle-aged man, interviewed her, and she dutifully hiked her skirt up, leaned forward, and spoke very seriously of her interest in word processing. She hadn't a snowball's chance in hell of being hired if she admitted she knew nothing about computers, and she'd managed to pick up enough information in her job at the Baraboo City Library to sound knowledgeable. She could only pray Sandy rescued her before she actually had to confront one of the electronic beasts.

There she was, being as subtly seductive as she could possibly imagine, when the door opened and a woman walked in. Jane didn't need an introduction to know who the newcomer was. Richard had been loud and hostile about Elinor Peabody, and the vivid word pictures still lingered.

Stephen Tremaine's executive vice-president was a stunningly attractive woman in her late thirties. From the tips of her leather-shod feet to the top of her silvery-blond hair, a distance that encompassed almost six feet, the woman emanated poise, intelligence, and the kind of ruthless determination that had always given Jane a headache. Some people were so sure of things in this life, and nothing ever swayed their intense certainty.

Whereas Jane was far too likely to view all the possibilities and have a wretchedly hard time choosing which one was the least of all evils. She rose politely, looking up at Elinor Peabody, and knew one thing without any doubt. The woman was trouble.

"Is this the new temp?" Ms Peabody inquired abruptly. Jane was too nearsighted to be sure, but it seemed as if the woman's icy gaze took in Jane's appearance, not missing a detail, and found her wanting.

"It is." Charlie Pilbin clearly didn't like being interrupted, and he didn't like Elinor Peabody. Jane didn't need glasses to ascertain that—his tone of voice made it very clear. "Judy Duncan, meet Elinor Peabody, Stephen Tremaine's executive assistant."

"Executive vice-president," Ms Peabody corrected him. "The promotion went through last month, remember?" She nodded at Jane, a curt greeting. "You're familiar with IBM computers and software?"

"Yes," Jane lied.

"Elinor, I haven't finished interviewing her yet..." Charlie complained, but Ms Peabody sailed right over his objections.

"You don't need a life history for a temporary employee, Charlie." She was using a "be charming to the subordinates" voice that Jane found fascinating. She could hear Charlie Pilbin's teeth grinding. "I'm sure Judy will be able to catch on quickly enough, and you can finish up the paperwork later."

"But..."

"Thanks, Charlie." She put a hand on Jane's arm and swept her from the room with a backward glance. "It doesn't do any good to be wishy-washy about these things," she announced. "If you find a home at Technocracies Limited, you'll soon learn that Stephen Tremaine's creed is fast decisions and deal with the consequences. You seem *reasonably* well-equipped. I have no doubt you'll do just fine."

Jane began to grind her own teeth, but Elinor Peabody was too caught up in her own master plan to notice. Five minutes later she found herself plunked in front of a computer screen, staring at blinking amber blips and trying to wish away the cold sweat that had broken out on her forehead.

At least Ms Peabody had turned it on for her. Jane leaned forward, peering desperately at the letter *A* flashing back and forth and praying for guidance.

"Are you nearsighted, Ms Duncan?" Peabody demanded abruptly.

Jane kept staring at the screen, then belatedly realized the woman was talking to her. How could Jimmy...no, Sandy keep his aliases straight?

"I have new contact lenses." The lie came so easily Jane was secretly horrified. She'd always prided herself on being scrupulously honest and completely straightforward. She'd slipped into the shadowy life of half truths so easily she wondered if she'd ever make it back out again.

"You shouldn't let vanity get in the way of efficiency," Elinor Peabody intoned, and Jane swallowed a retort. Elinor Peabody was born with the kind of beauty that very little could tarnish. Perfect bone structure combined with an indomitable will left nothing to chance. If she ever needed glasses she'd probably order her eyes to improve. Doubtless those china blue eyes of hers would comply.

"I won't, ma'am," Jane muttered, reaching out and pushing a key. The damned machine beeped at her, and once more Elinor Peabody raised her head.

She rose and circled the wide teak table that served as a desk, coming to loom over Jane's unevenly padded shoulders. "Sorry, I forgot to let you into the file. You need two passwords, and I'm not about to give either one of them out." She leaned past Jane and began tapping on the keys, and Jane got a full dose of her perfume. Poison, by Christian Dior. Wouldn't you know it, Jane thought with a sigh, cursing her partner in crime for getting her into this mess.

"There you go." Ms Peabody moved back. "It's certainly a simple enough task. Just enter the new tax information for each employee, then go on to the next one."

"Simple enough," Jane muttered, peering at the screen. Personnel files at her fingertips, if she could just manage to move from one name to the next.

God bless them, the creators of the software provided a help file at the top of the screen. Holding her breath, Jane pushed a key. To her amazement, a personnel file appeared in bright amber. Adamson, George Social Security #156-42-5917.

She pushed another button. Allman, Gregory. Astor, Jacob. Her face was flushed with triumph, and she pushed her irritating mop of hair away from her eyes, hunching closer. Computers were easier than she'd ever imagined. What a fool she'd been to be terrified of them. Bachman, Joyce. Ballard, Alice. Butler, Charles. Cashill, Patricia. Davis, Alexander. Debrett, Piers. Dunbar, Glenn. Eddison, Larry. . . .

She stopped, perplexed. The personnel files held records for all employees, past and present. Larry Eddison had retired four years ago, Alice Ballard had worked as a consultant for three months in 1978. Where was Richard Dexter's file?

She looked up at the Help file, but this time the programmers let her down. They refused to tell her how to go back, only how to move forward. All she could do was forge on ahead and hope the damned files would start all over again when she got to Z.

Fairbanks, Robert. Kellogg, Roger. Peabody, Elinor. Sullivan, Nancy. Tremaine, Stephen.

That answered one question. The files covered everyone, from corporate head to mail clerk. Richard's file must have been deliberately deleted.

Xanatos, Grigor. Zallman, Yeshua. And then a blank screen, with nothing more than a blinking, taunting letter *A*.

She allowed herself a brief glance over at Ms Peabody, but her golden head was bent over her spotless desk, the bright sunlight gilding it. Jane managed a silent snarl and went back to the screen. It had been fairly simple so far. All she had to do was punch a few buttons and the program would reappear. It had been remarkably easy when Ms Peabody did it, and despite Jane's deep-rooted feelings of inferiority she told herself that anything Ms Peabody did, she could do.

The computer disagreed. For long minutes it sat there sullenly, flashing that bright *A* at her while she pushed keys and combinations of keys. And then suddenly it went wild, letters and numbers and figures that looked like they were part of the Greek alphabet began hurling themselves onto the screen. The damned thing began buzzing, a rude, grating noise, mocking her, and then, just as Ms Peabody rushed to her side, the entire screen shuddered and went blank.

Dead silence reigned in the office. "Move out of the way," said Ms Peabody. The words were bitten off, and Jane moved.

The older woman sank gracefully into the chair Jane had vacated, bowed her head in what appeared to Jane as silent prayer, and set her fingers on the keyboard. Jane held her breath.

But even the indomitable Ms Peabody couldn't coax life from the recalcitrant computer. After long, fruitless moments she moved away, icy rage vibrating through every cell of her elegant body. "Twenty-three years of personnel records lost, Ms Duncan," she said in a deceptively mild voice. "I think, I'm afraid, that you won't do for Technocracies Limited."

Her very calm was terrifying. Jane managed a weak smile, wondering whether she ought to plead, ought to protest. She decided she'd be lucky if she escaped with her life. "I'm terribly sorry..."

"Just leave," said Ms Peabody, sweeping past her and heading for the phone. "Marcus," she said into the receiver, "bring me that new computer genius you hired. It's an emergency."

Jane was still hovering by the door. Ms Peabody fixed her with an icy stare. "You can leave anytime," she said, then looked over her shoulder at the opening door. "There you are, Marcus. Let's hope your new wonder boy is all he's cracked up to be."

Marcus turned out to be a middle-aged man complete with nerd pack and pot belly. In his wake came Sandy, a Band-Aid wrapped around one corner of *her* glasses. He was stooping just slightly, his coat flapping around him, and as he passed Jane he reached out and pinched her backside, well out of view of the other two people in the room.

"What seems to be the trouble, ma'am?" His voice was nasal, just this side of an adolescent whine, and it took all Jane's willpower not to giggle.

Ms Peabody opened her mouth to speak, then spied Jane still lingering at the door. "Go!" she thundered. Jane turned and ran.

THEY'D TAKEN BOTH CARS, and Jane couldn't rid herself of the suspicion that Sandy hadn't had much faith in her chance of success. It was understandable—she didn't have much faith either. She drove home through the early-afternoon traffic, muttering under her breath, replaying the scene in her mind and coming up with alternatives that cast a more flattering light on her efforts.

She slammed into the room, yanked the tissues from underneath her bra straps and squinted into the mirror. Her cheeks were flushed, her thick brown hair tangled, and she couldn't see without her glasses. It had been dangerous enough driving home, peering through the windshield of her Escort. It would be foolish indeed to go out again.

She flopped down on the bed. She was starving, she was edgy, she was tired, and her head ached. Surely Richard wouldn't demand this kind of sacrifice on her part. He was dead, surely he was past caring.

He might be, but she wasn't. As tempting as the thought might be, she couldn't turn her back on her responsibility. Today had taught her a lesson, however. Subtlety wasn't her strong suit. When Sandy came back she'd ask him about pipe bombs.

The spiky high heels he'd made her wear hurt her arches. She kicked them off, reaching up to fasten her blouse, then dropped her hand. *The hell with it,* she thought tiredly, rolling onto her side and curling in on herself. There'd be time enough to change later.

She always hated sleeping in the middle of the day—her worst nightmares came then. She dreamed she was in a car, rolling over and over down an embankment and then bursting into flames. But the fire smelled of pepperoni and onion, not of gasoline, and the brightness wasn't the bright glow of fire, it was the meager bedside light. And that wasn't Death leaning over her, it was Sandy, squinting through her glasses, holding a square white box that could only contain pizza in front of her nose.

Jane looked up at him. "I'm not going to ask how you got in here without a key," she said in her calmest voice. "I simply want to know whether there are anchovies on that pizza."

"What if there are?"

"I'll scream for help."

He grinned at her, flipping open the lid. "No anchovies. I guess our unholy alliance continues for a bit."

Slowly, wearily Jane pulled herself into a sitting position. Sandy had plopped himself down on the bed beside her, helping himself to a generous slice of pizza. Reaching out, she pulled her glasses off his nose and settled them on her own. The metal frame was warm from his body heat, and she wished she'd let him hand them to her.

She touched the white Band-Aid that was wrapped conspicuously around the frame. "Did you have to break them?"

"Don't worry—the Band-Aid is for effect, nothing more. You certainly screwed up their computer." He finished his slice of pizza, crust and all, and reached for another.

Jane decided she'd better move fast or she'd starve to death. "I told you I didn't know anything about computers. Neither do you. What happened when they found you couldn't fix it?"

"They still don't know. The PC in Ms Peabody's office is completely out of whack. They think I'll be there first thing tomorrow morning to pull the personnel files from its bowels."

"Oh, God," Jane murmured.

"Is that 'Oh, God' in response to the splendor of the pizza or the destruction of the computer?" Sandy had put his long legs up on the bed, his tie was off, and he'd rumpled his blond hair into a spiky punk look.

"Both," she said, reaching for another slice. "So neither of us gets to go back."

"Just as well. Your boss of five minutes found out who you are. By tomorrow they'll tumble to the fact that we were hired together."

The pizza began to feel like lead in her empty stomach. "How'd she find out?"

"Who else but your beloved godfather?" Sandy said, kicking off his shoes and making himself comfortable. "Eat that last piece and you die."

She eyed it wistfully. "It might be worth it. How did Uncle Stephen know?"

"He had an anonymous tip that you broke into the place last night."

"How in heaven's name did he know that?" she demanded, horrified.

"Very simple," said Sandy. "I told him."

Chapter Six

Plain Jane looked absolutely adorable sitting there with her blouse gaping open, the Band-Aided glasses perched on her nose, her lips red from the pizza. "You did what?" she demanded.

He smiled sweetly, ripping apart the last piece of pizza, and handed her the smaller portion. "I gave Uncle Stephen an anonymous tip. I thought it would be useful to see how he reacted—whether he called the police or went to ground."

"And...?"

"No sign of cops anywhere around the place. Ergo, he's trying to cover up something. Unless he has a soft spot for you and doesn't want to get you in trouble." He frowned suddenly. He hadn't thought of that possibility until now, but if it had been up to him he wouldn't have turned Jane in.

"Uncle Stephen doesn't have a soft spot for anything without a bottom line. Don't you think you were taking a big risk? They may have connected us sooner than you hoped. If he had called the police you would have been back in jail so fast your head would swim."

"Back in jail? I wasn't in jail before."

"What about the arson and conspiracy charges? Didn't they arrest you?"

Thank heavens for his ability to think fast. "You forget, Alexander Caldicott is one of the world's great lawyers. He got me out on bail before they even locked me up." Not strictly true, Sandy thought. The real Jimmy the Stoolie had spent an uncomfortable night in custody before he'd managed to spring him on his own recognizance.

"I still think you were taking too great a risk." Jane sat up and tucked her feet underneath her. "I didn't find anything I didn't already know. Richard's personnel records have been deleted from the files."

"Everybody's personnel records have been deleted, thanks to you."

"Don't be pedantic. Before my little mishap I went through all the employees. They had everyone listed who'd ever worked there, from Stephen Tremaine on down, and no mention of Dick whatsoever."

"Dick?" Sandy echoed, momentarily diverted. "As in Dick and Jane?"

"Our parents weren't very imaginative." Her narrow shoulders were hunched defensively.

"I don't suppose you have a younger sister named Sally?" He knew he shouldn't push it but he couldn't resist.

"Living in Dubuque with her second husband and three children," she said gloomily. "Could we get back to the subject?"

"Not yet. Where is sister Sally during the grand quest for your brother's legacy?"

"They never got along. Dick wasn't that easy a person to be around. People with such high principles seldom are. He didn't have much patience for compromise, or for people he considered his intellectual inferiors. Which included just about everybody."

"Did it include you?"

"Oh, me most of all," she said with unfeigned cheerfulness. "I was anathema to him. The little peacemaker, with no more conviction than a willow tree, swaying with each strong breeze. He was right, I'm afraid."

Sandy had a sudden swift desire to punch Dick Dexter in the teeth. "Your brother sounds like an intolerant, pompous idiot."

If he expected an argument he wasn't about to get one. "I'm afraid he was," she admitted. "But I loved him anyway. And I mourn his death, though not as much as I should. I suppose that's why I feel so guilty. I just . . . can't really comprehend that he's gone. I don't believe it." She sighed. "I suppose that's a fairly common reaction to untimely death. Sooner or later it'll sink in. In the meantime, I have to do what I can to preserve his memory."

"Urrmpphh." Sandy knew the sound from his throat was uncompromising, and he didn't care. He wasn't motivated by any great liking for Richard Dexter. His motivations were pure and simple—keep Jane out of trouble. And have the undisputed pleasure of moonlighting as a con artist while he was doing it.

"We're not making much progress," she added. "I've been thinking—Uncle Stephen has to sell the process because Technocracies is in such big trouble. If we burn the place it would render the situation obsolete. Either he'd be out of business entirely and we won't have to bother, or he'll get so much from insurance it'll solve his cash flow problems. You can do that, can't you? Torch an entire building?"

"Don't look so eager," he growled. "Yes, I can, and no, I won't. You're not thinking clearly again. If the place is destroyed and Tremaine is out of business he'll cut his losses and sell anything negotiable to the highest bidder. We've already ascertained that we don't know where the process is."

"Oh," said Jane, disappointed.

"And I beg to differ with you. We're making more progress than you realize. I spent an inordinate amount of time in the executive washroom trying to clean computer grease from my hands. Ceramic tile is excellent for carrying sound. Your godfather put off his trip to Europe, and for a very good reason.''

"Which is?"

"He can't sell the process if he doesn't have the process," Sandy said triumphantly.

"He doesn't have it?" Jane shrieked. "Who does?"

"No one. At least, no one has all of it. Your brother didn't work exclusively at Technocracies Limited. He had at least one private lab, and maybe more, and your buddy Tremaine hasn't the faintest idea where they were. All he knows is that when Richard died there was an important piece of information missing from his work at Technocracies. Without it the process is useless.''

He was unprepared for her response. Unprepared for the blazing smile that lit her face, turning her from passably attractive to a raving beauty. He was unprepared for the whoop of joy, unprepared for her to launch herself at him, flinging her arms around his neck and kissing him soundly on the cheek. And he was unprepared for her immediate withdrawal. He reached out, trying to capture her arms and keep her tight against him, but she'd already slipped away.

"Our troubles are over," she said, her eyes alight.

"No," he said, "they're not." He hated to disillusion her, but she'd figure it out sooner or later, and he didn't trust her without his restraining presence. She was too damned bloodthirsty. "Tremaine isn't going to give up. They're hiring private investigators to find Richard's laboratories. Sooner or later the information is going to turn up, unless you think he would have destroyed it.''

She shook her head. Her hair was still loose from her earlier transformation, and it tangled appealingly around her narrow face. "He wouldn't do that. He was too egocentric to destroy anything he'd invented.''

"And of course he'd have no reason to do so, would he?" he prodded. "It was only a coincidence that a vital part of the process is missing. Wasn't it?"

Jane was lousy at dissembling. "Not exactly."

"Not exactly," he echoed. "What have you neglected to tell me? If we're going to be partners in crime we can't keep things back from each other." He didn't suffer more than a slight twinge at the thought of all he was keeping from her.

"I didn't think it was that important. Dick was always paranoid—I just thought it was part of his persecution complex."

"What was?"

She made a face. "He called me a couple of days before he died. He must have had some sort of premonition. He said if anything happened to him I had to make sure Uncle Stephen didn't misuse the titanium coating process."

"Was that a premonition?" Sandy asked. "Or did he know he was in danger?"

Jane sat very still. "You think it wasn't an accident?"

"I don't know what to think. There's a lot of money at stake, and Stephen Tremaine is not known for his ethical restraint. You know the man better than I do. Do you think he'd balk at murder?"

"Absolutely," Jane said. And then a moment later, "At least, I think so."

"Thinking's not good enough. I think we're going to have to be extra careful. If he's killed once there's nothing to stop him from killing again."

"This is ridiculous. No one's killed anybody. You sound like some sort of murder mystery. People don't go around killing other people."

"Yes," he said gently, "they do."

The dingy motel room was silent, with only the sound of the traffic from Route One filtering through the thin walls. In the distance Sandy could hear the sound of a television set turned up too loud, the noise of a shower two rooms over. And the sound of Jane's steady, troubled breathing.

"Have you ever killed anyone?" she asked finally.

"No." He could say that both for himself and for the real Jimmy the Stoolie. Though of course he shouldn't have taken Jimmy's word for it—the man was a pathological liar. But in his years of practicing law he'd learned to tell, not necessarily who had and who hadn't committed murder, but who could and who couldn't. Jimmy definitely fit in the hadn't and couldn't category.

But Jane Dexter was a question mark. Common sense told him a civilized Midwestern librarian wasn't about to go around wreaking havoc, but her frustration level was high. And if it turned out that Stephen Tremaine really had murdered her brother, he had no idea what her reaction might be.

"We have several options open to us," Sandy continued. "We can drop everything, hope that Tremaine never finds the missing part of the formula, and go our merry way. Or we can try to outfox him and find the rest of the formula before he does. After that it's up to us. We could always sell it to the highest bidder ourselves . . ."

"No."

"Just a thought. Or we can destroy it. Or just salt it away someplace until we make up our minds."

"Or we can torch the place."

Sandy shook his head. "Jane, Jane, you must curb these violent impulses. It wouldn't do any good at all. Tremaine's no fool—he'll have copies of the formula."

"Then I guess we really have no option at all. We'll have to find the rest of the formula before he does. That way we can blackmail him into selling it to someone we approve of, and Richard will be satisfied."

Richard won't care, Sandy wanted to point out, but he tactfully controlled himself. "Personally I approve of the highest bidder, but I bow to your wishes.'' He shifted on the bed, moving imperceptibly closer. Jane was so caught up in her plans that she didn't even notice.

"How much does Uncle Stephen know? Does he have any idea where Dick's labs might be?"

"I'm not sure. He and Peabody got a bit . . . distracted, and gentlemanly restraint forced me to stop eavesdropping."

Jane snorted. "I hadn't noticed you plagued by gentlemanly restraint. Are you telling me Uncle Stephen is sleeping with Ms Peabody?"

"I don't think they were sleeping."

Jane shook her head. "The swine."

Sandy shifted closer, so that his thigh pressed against hers. "Some men are," he said innocently.

"They are indeed. We'll go back to Dick's apartment," she said decisively.

"Now?" While the bed they were sitting on wasn't terribly comfortable, it had the undisputed merit of being readily available.

"Tomorrow. I went through that place with a fine-tooth comb but I might have overlooked something."

Sandy nodded. She smelled like flowers and pizza and soap—an undeniably erotic combination. "It would help to have a fresh look at the place."

"And you're exceedingly fresh. Move your leg."

He didn't. He looked at her for a long, thoughtful moment. She didn't blink, though he could tell she wanted to, she didn't fiddle with her blouse, though he knew she wished to hell she'd rebuttoned it. She just looked into his eyes with an I-dare-you kind of glare, and Sandy Caldicott couldn't resist a dare.

He shifted, smoothly, gracefully, so quickly that she didn't have time to squirm away. In seconds she was sprawled on the bed, beneath him.

"I didn't know you numbered rape and assault among your crimes," she said through gritted teeth. His face was inches away from hers, and behind the wire-rimmed glasses her dark brown eyes were blazingly angry and not the slightest bit frightened.

"I'm not going to rape or assault you," he said in his most reasonable voice. "I'm just going to kiss you."

"I don't want to be kissed."

He was holding her hands down, his hips were pinning hers, and her breasts were pushing against him. "Tough. I deserve something for combat pay. Not to mention the pizza." And he dropped his mouth down on hers.

She tried to jerk away, but he let go of her hands and caught her jaw, holding it in place for a long, leisurely kiss. He could feel her hard little fists pounding at him, but he ignored them, lost in the sweetness of her lips. She bounced her hips, trying to throw him off, but it only aroused him more. And for all her fight, for all the anger in her hands, her mouth was soft, pliant, and opening to him.

She was no longer beating at him. Her arms had slid around his neck, her tongue had reached out to touch his, and her body was softening beneath him as his was getting harder and harder. She made a little noise in the back of her throat, half a moan, half a whimper, and he wanted to hear more. He wanted to hear her crying against him, wanted to feel that surprisingly lush body wrapped around his, he wanted to turn off the lights and shut out the depressing little motel and lose himself in Jane Dexter's wonderful body.

He paused for breath, lifting his head to look down at her through passion-glazed eyes. She lay there, panting, her lips slightly swollen from his kisses, her eyes closed behind the glasses. Beneath the closed lids, hot tears were pouring down her face.

Sandy jumped away as if he were burned, cursing loudly and profanely as guilt swamped him. "For God's sake, Jane, it was only a kiss!"

She opened her eyes and to his disgust and amazement she grinned at him. "Neat trick, eh?" She pulled herself to a sitting position, rebuttoned her blouse almost to her neck, and stood up, keeping well out of his reach. "It's my one accomplishment. I can cry any time I want to."

He just stared at her. No longer did he have any desire to push her back on the bed. There was nothing he hated more than tears—like most people he couldn't deal with them, could do nothing but feel guilty. He felt tricked on the most fundamental level, and his temper was fraying around the edges.

"I'd be more than happy to give you something to cry about," he snarled.

"You would."

"I beg your pardon."

"You would give me something to cry about," she said calmly, moving over to the wavery mirror and wiping the tears off her cheeks. "You'd give me nothing but trouble and misery, and I'm not about to let myself in for it. I've had enough misery in the past couple of years to last me for a long time, and I'm not going to make any more mistakes when it comes to men."

"And I'd be a mistake?"

She met his eyes in the mirror. "The biggest," she said, sighing. "So we'll keep this as a business partnership, all right? I'm sure you can find someone who's more your style. Some leggy blonde who's not into commitment."

"They're all into commitment," he said gloomily, ignoring the little shock he'd felt at her words. How did she know he liked leggy blondes? Hell, who wouldn't? Except right now he had no interest in leggy blondes whatsoever. He was only interested in petite, bespectacled ladies with rumpled brown hair and tears still glistening in their eyes.

Crocodile tears, he reminded himself. "I think," he said, "I've had enough for one day. I'm going to bed."

"Good night." She was cool and unmoved, watching him as he headed for the door.

Sandy considered sulking. He considered slamming the door, he considered telling her what he thought of her phony tears. And then his sense of humor surfaced. "It's not going to work," he said, opening the door and standing there in the cool night air.

"What isn't?"

"You're not going to be able to keep from making mistakes."

"I can try."

"Yes, you can. But it won't do you any good. And next time I kiss you I won't mind if you're awash in tears."

She glared at him. "There won't be a next time."

"Oh, yes, there will." He shut the door behind him, stepping out into the night. And through the thin walls he heard her voice.

"Yes, there will," she said out loud. And Sandy, his good humor totally restored, headed back to his own room.

RICHARD'S APARTMENT didn't look any different from the last time Jane had been there, three days ago. The boxes she'd packed were still neatly stacked in the hallway, the curtains were drawn, everything exactly where she'd left it. She stepped into the musty smelling apartment, waited until Sandy closed the door behind them, and announced, "Someone's been here."

"How do you know?" He wandered past her into the boring, box-shaped apartment. "Is anything missing?"

They'd gotten along fine, eating breakfast together and being very careful not to touch each other. Now, alone in the closed-up apartment, Jane was remembering the night before, the brief, overwhelming moments on that concave mattress, the feel of his body on hers, the lean muscle and sinew and bone that had felt unbearably delectable covering hers.

Quickly she wiped out that thought. If Sandy remembered she'd seen no sign of it—his temper had been cheerfully unimpaired that morning. Maybe he'd gone out and found a leggy blonde. No, she would have heard it. The walls were paper thin between their rooms.

But those few moments on her bed were probably more commonplace to someone like...like whatever name he chose to use at the moment. While for her they were a shattering revelation.

"Jane?" Sandy prodded.

"I can't tell. I just get this feeling that someone's been snooping around."

Sandy shrugged. "Either you're as paranoid as your brother was or Tremaine's detectives have been both efficient and unscrupulous. Your guess is as good as mine." He crossed the dull beige wall-to-wall carpeting and peered behind the curtain into the parking lot below. "When were you last here?"

"Three days ago. Plenty of time for someone to come in and search the place." She stared at the neatly piled boxes with a sense of oppression. She'd spent days packing everything away. She could only hope Sandy wasn't about to suggest they unpack everything.

Apparently Sandy had something else in mind. "Well, if someone broke in while you were gone they didn't find what they were looking for."

"What makes you say that?"

He let the curtain drop and turned to face her. "Because Stephen Tremaine and two suspicious-looking characters just drove up. And unless I miss my guess, they're heading up here to give the place one more look."

"We've got to hide."

"No, we don't. You have every right and reason to be here. I, on the other hand, ought to make myself scarce. I'll be in the bedroom while you get rid of them."

"But what do you expect me to do? Sit here and twiddle my thumbs while they break in?" she demanded, both frightened and furious.

"If they have any experience at all they'll ring the doorbell," he said calmly. "That's the first rule of 'B and E.' Make sure the place is deserted. All you have to do is answer the door and send them on their way."

"And if they won't go?"

He grinned, that disarming, golden-boy grin that didn't belong to someone known as Jimmy the Stoolie. "We'll deal with that when we get to it." Right on cue, the doorbell rang, and Jane jumped.

"Get the door, Madame X," he prompted, disappearing into the bedroom. "Time for Act Two."

Chapter Seven

Jane stood in front of the door, wiping her damp palms on her khaki trousers and taking a deep, calming breath. The doorbell rang again, and the doorknob twitched, suddenly, suspiciously. For half a moment she was tempted to let them break in, just to see their reaction when they came face to face with her. And then she thought better of it. She had no desire to initiate a confrontation—the past thirty-six hours had been far from blameless on her side as well as theirs.

"Coming," she called, and heard the thud as someone jumped back from the door as if burned. "Just let me fiddle with these locks," she said cheerfully, making a great deal of noise before swinging open the door. She looked directly into her godfather's flinty eyes and flashed him her widest, most guileless smile.

"What the hell are you doing here?" Stephen Tremaine demanded gruffly, striding into the room with his two goons at his side. He was a short, barrel-chested man in his late fifties, with a shock of carefully tended white hair, a perpetual tan, and small, unsentimental slate-blue eyes that he used to stare down competition. He didn't believe in wasting time on social amenities, and he stood there in his beautiful suit, staring at Jane, tapping one perfectly shod foot in a blatant demonstration of just how impatient he was.

"How nice to see you, Uncle Stephen," she almost cooed.

"You just saw me last week," he snapped. "What are you doing here?"

"Packing Dick's stuff away."

"You already did that."

There was no way Stephen Tremaine would know that, if he hadn't already been in the apartment. Jane felt a sudden surge of satisfaction at having trapped him, whether he knew it or not. Maybe she was developing a talent for intrigue. "I had a few more things to take care of," she said calmly. "Speaking of which, why are you here? And who are your friends?"

"They don't matter," Tremaine said, walking past her and peering at the stack of boxes. "I hope you realize that anything pertaining to Dick's work legally belongs to Technocracies?"

"Of course." Her tone was dulcet. She wouldn't ask him again, she'd wait.

He poked one stubby, well-manicured finger at one of the boxes, snorting audibly. And then he moved on, prowling around the apartment like a caged beast, his two goons standing silently by the door. As long as he didn't head for the bedroom she would let him poke and pry all he wanted to. If he found anything interesting, all the better for her.

He stopped at the window, whirling suddenly. "Where were you yesterday?"

She didn't bat an eye. "Here, packing. Where were you?"

"At work. We had trouble with some temporary workers. Some fool woman messed up our computer system, and a so-called hotshot destroyed one of our terminals." His eyes were accusing.

"It's so hard to find good help nowadays," Jane said with a sympathetic sigh.

Tremaine just looked at her. She knew what he was thinking, as clearly as if he'd spoken his thought out loud. He was trying to decide whether or not to accuse her of infiltrating Technocracies. She knew by his tiny nod that he'd chosen not to. "Yes," he said, "it is."

"We all have our problems," she said vaguely, wishing he'd leave.

He was suddenly solicitous, moving back toward her and taking her damp, cold hands in his hot, hard ones. "But it's you I'm worried about, Janey. This has all been too much for you, losing Richard and then having to come east and pack up everything. I know Princeton doesn't hold very many happy memories for you. Why don't you let me finish things up for you? I have a staff who can handle these matters. They'll finish packing, ship the stuff back to you, and close up things. You've been through too much already. Go back to Wisconsin and let me do this for you."

Damn, he was good, Jane thought, letting him squeeze her hands and look earnestly into her eyes. He was about as earnest as a tarantula. "You're sweet to offer, Uncle Stephen," she said. "But I've got some time off, and it helps me to be here."

His tough little hands tightened painfully on hers. "I think you're making a mistake. I think you should go back and leave things to me."

"No." The word was only slightly ragged, and she met his eyes fearlessly, not quailing before the sudden flare of rage in them. "No."

He dropped her hands, stepping back a pace or two, and then he smiled once more, displaying small, sharp teeth. "All right, Janey," he said. No one ever called her Janey. "Suit yourself. I only wanted to save you needless grief."

"I appreciate the thought."

He nodded. "Then we'll leave you to it. I'll just use the little boy's room before I go..." He was heading toward the bedroom, and Jane felt her heart leap in panic.

She opened her mouth to stop him, to protest, then shut it again. There was nothing she could say that could possibly sound reasonable. She shut her eyes, listening to the sound of the bathroom door closing, waiting for Tremaine's exclamation of surprise.

There was no sound at all but the noise of running water. Jane opened her eyes, to look into the blank, emotionless faces of Tremaine's prepossessing escort. She managed a shaky smile. "I left the bathroom sort of messy," she said in explanation. Neither of the goons said a word.

Minutes later Tremaine was back, anger in his eyes, a smile on his mouth. "We'll be going now, Janey. That is, if you're sure I can't help?"

"I'm sure, Uncle Stephen. You've done more than your share already."

The smile vanished. "Don't count on it." And he was gone, the two henchmen following closely behind him.

She stood there, sagging against the wall, as she listened to the sound of their footsteps receding into the distance. Her hands were still shaking, her forehead was covered with a cold sweat, and she wished to God she could go back to Baraboo and forget about any lingering familial debts.

She crossed the room to the window, watching as Uncle Stephen got back in his Mercedes. "Sandy?" she called out, not moving from her vantage point. "Are you still here?"

"Still here," he said from directly behind her, his advent silent on the thick beige carpeting. "Your godfather's a curious man."

"Where were you hiding?"

"In the bathtub with the shower curtain drawn. Fortunately your brother favored navy-blue shower curtains, and Tremaine didn't think to check. I was able to watch him without him seeing me." He leaned forward and stared at the window, and for a moment she watched his profile, that perfect, chiseled line, the strong nose, the beautiful eyes, the rumpled blond hair.

Jane sighed absently. "You watched him? You pervert."

"What was I supposed to do, stare at the grout? Besides, Tremaine didn't do anything one usually does in a bathroom. He checked the medicine cabinet, under the sink and he even lifted the back of the toilet and looked in the tank."

"Why?"

"I imagine he was looking for something. Whatever it was, he didn't find it."

"So where does that leave us?"

He shrugged. "We'll just have to take up the search."

"Even though we're not sure what we're looking for? It might not be the formula."

"Even though we're not sure what we're looking for," he agreed. "Let's start with the boxes."

She looked at him with complete, utter loathing. "I just spent days packing them."

He leaned forward, and to her shock he brushed his lips across hers. "Then we'll just repack them," he said sweetly. He moved away before she could react, before she could hit him, before she could twine her arms around his neck and kiss him back. "Let's get started."

THE PARKING LOT outside Richard Dexter's lakeside condominium was brightly lit. All the Hondas and BMWs and Saabs gleamed in the artificial light, radiating a glow of financial well-being. Some of that glow penetrated the shambles of what had once been a spotlessly organized apartment, illuminating the littered floor. Sandy looked across the room at his partner in crime, just barely suppressing a grin.

Jane was sitting, shell-shocked, in the midst of a mountain of papers, her eyes glazed behind her wire-rimmed glasses. "I cannot," she said faintly, "look at one more piece of paper."

"It's probably a lost cause," Sandy agreed. "Whatever Tremaine is looking for isn't here. It would help if either of us knew the faintest thing about chemical engineering. None of Richard's notes makes sense to me, even the shopping lists.''

''I know,'' Jane said wearily, stretching out on the mounds of paper. She was wearing pants for a change, and the crumpled khaki fit her long legs and delectable rear quite nicely. ''No one could ever read Richard's handwriting. Maybe Uncle Stephen has the missing part of the formula and he just can't decipher it. Maybe we've read a dozen copies of it and not known what it is.''

''Maybe, but I don't think so. Your brother doesn't sound like he was a very subtle man. Would he be likely to hide it among similar stuff so no one would notice?''

''Nope,'' Jane said, taking off her glasses and closing her eyes. ''He'd put it somewhere obvious. He probably thought no one could ever find his secret lab and he's left it locked in a file cabinet. Maybe he didn't even bother to lock it.'' She sat up, pushing her tangled hair out of her eyes. ''We've got to find the lab, Jimmy.''

''Sandy,'' he corrected absently. ''Do you think we'll have any better luck recognizing it there?''

''No. We'll just have to burn the place down.''

''Not again! The trick to a life of crime, dear heart, is only resort to violent action when you've used up all the alternatives,'' Sandy said reprovingly. ''We've still got a lot of options left.''

''Such as?'' There was a delightfully pugnacious tilt to her chin. Even in her overtired, underfed state she still had a bloodthirsty streak that never failed to enchant him.

''I can't give away trade secrets,'' Sandy said, wondering how long he was going to be able to stall her. ''In the meantime, I think I'd better feed you. You get nasty when you haven't eaten.''

''Anything,'' she said longingly. ''Just so long as it's hot and there's a lot of it.''

"Burger King?"

She smiled beatifically. "Heaven," she replied. She scrambled to her feet, slipping on a precarious pile of papers.

He was there to catch her before she could catch herself. He could have just caught her arm, but he couldn't resist sliding his arm around her and pulling her upright. She looked up at him, startled, and he heard her sudden intake of breath, felt the tension and undeniable awareness in her body as it rested lightly against his.

She bit her lips, and he wanted to do the same thing. He didn't. "Why are you looking at me like that?" he asked quietly, not releasing her.

"I just wondered why you do what you do."

He felt his mouth curve up in an involuntary grin. "What would you think I'd do for a living?" he countered.

"I would have thought you'd be a gigolo."

He released her quite abruptly. "Why?" he demanded, insulted.

She was so tired and hungry that she'd lost half her defenses. "Well, I don't know..." she floundered helplessly, "it's just that you're so damned good-looking, and I wouldn't think you'd have much chance to use your looks when you're torching buildings."

He tried to reach for her again, but she'd moved out of reach. *Later,* he promised himself, watching her pick her way across the floor. "You forget," he said evenly. "I'm a con man on the side. Looking like I do, I manage to convince people I'm Princeton and Harvard Law School and a silver spoon, and they'll buy anything I sell them."

She nodded. "I can believe it. What are you going to try to sell me?" The question was lightly spoken, but Sandy wasn't fooled. She didn't trust him, on a very basic level. He shouldn't expect her to, he'd done everything to foster her belief in him as a sleazy crook. It shouldn't bother him in the slightest.

"Nothing you don't want to buy," he said.

Her smile was slightly lopsided. "That's just what a con man would say."

He wanted to tell her the truth, but that would only brand him a bigger liar and far less trustworthy than he'd proven so far. For the time being he had to keep his mouth shut. "Be nice to me," he warned, "or I won't take you to Burger King."

It was the right thing to say. She smiled, the shadows leaving her eyes. "I'll hitchhike if I have to."

"Don't worry, Madame X. I have to keep my partner in good working condition." He'd reached her by then, and he kept himself from touching her.

"What about all this?" She gestured to the mess.

"What would happen if we just left it for a few days?"

Her smile turned into a full-fledged grin. "Sounds good to me. Maybe I'll take Uncle Stephen up on his offer of assistance. Can you picture Elinor Peabody repacking these boxes?"

"It boggles the mind. Come on, partner. It's fast food time, and then maybe we'll see if *The Untouchables* is playing anywhere. We could use a few pointers on how to be real criminals."

"Aren't you a real criminal?"

Damn, he had to watch every word he said. Even exhausted and starving, Jane Dexter was too damned sharp. "There's always room for improvement," he said cheerfully, snapping off the light and plunging the trashed room into darkness.

Within minutes they were crammed into his MGB and heading toward Route One, the engine coughing and jerking and sputtering. Neither of them noticed that Stephen Tremaine's goons were watching them from the front seat of an anonymous sedan. Or that the American car pulled out and followed them into the warm October night.

"WAKE UP, LAZYBONES." The voice was coming from a spot unacceptably close to her ear. Jane reached up and batted at it, pushing her face deeper into the pillow.

But the irritating voice wasn't the sort to be easily routed. "Wake up," it said again, and as Jane slowly struggled up from the mists of sleep she recognized it as Sandy's. Beside her. On the bed.

Her eyes shot open and she flipped over in sudden outrage. She would have taken the sheet with her, but Sandy's body was keeping it in one place. She ended up sitting there, wearing nothing but an oversize T-shirt that had ridden too high on her thighs, glaring into her felonious partner's smoky-gray eyes.

"How did you get in here?" she demanded. "And don't tell me you picked the lock. I've seen you in action—you do much better with a key."

"We have a connecting door," he said, unchastened. "I took the precaution of unlocking it last night."

"Take the precaution of locking it, buster," she snarled. "And get off my sheet."

He moved, reluctantly, and while he kept his expression suitably sober, she could see the light of laughter lingering in the back of his eyes. "You're grumpy when you wake up."

"I'm grumpy when I'm woken up," she corrected. "What time is it, anyway?" She peered out at the sunshine filtering through the threadbare curtains. "We didn't have anything planned, did we? You were just going to get in touch with a few of your underworld contacts and see what you could dig up."

It must have been her nearsightedness that made him look so peculiar for a moment. Almost guilty. She reached for her glasses, settling them on her nose, and his expression was as bland as ever.

"It's after ten. And the situation's changed."

She pulled herself up, wrapping the sheet around her body, suddenly alert. "What's happened?"

"Your godfather took off this morning for parts unknown."

"And just how do you know that?"

"I don't sleep till all hours of the morning," he said in a lofty tone. "I woke up at six, went running, and then decided to kill some time waiting for you to emerge from your beauty sleep. So I staked out Tremaine's house. I got there just in time to follow him and his two henchmen to the Mercer County Airport."

"Where's he going?"

"I couldn't very well walk up and ask him, now could I?"

"You're supposed to be a con man," she grumbled. "Why didn't you con it out of the flight controller or whoever they had working there?"

"I thought I'd con it out of Tremaine's wife."

Jane sat back, running an absent hand through her sleep-tangled hair. "We could certainly try."

"What's this we? You don't run a con on people you know," he said severely.

"Of course you don't. But I've never met Annabel Tremaine."

"Why not?"

"She wasn't home the other day when I met with Uncle Stephen. She's his second wife—the first one dumped him when she got tired of his playing around. I imagine Annabel will do the same when she finds out about Elinor Peabody. Particularly since Annabel was Uncle Stephen's administrative assistant when he was married to Aunt Alice."

"Sounds like *Dynasty*," Sandy drawled.

"Uncle Stephen has the morals of a reptile. So how are we going to con Annabel?"

Sandy looked blank for a moment. "Give me a minute. It'll come to me."

"Door-to-door salesmen?" Jane suggested. "Religious fanatics?"

He shook his head reprovingly. "We wouldn't even get in the door. What about environmental activists? Save the dolphins and that sort of thing."

"Uncle Stephen probably eats dolphins for breakfast. We need something more esoteric."

"Loons?" Sandy suggested.

"Loons," she echoed. "I like it. They have a summer place in Maine on a lake with loons. That should appeal to Annabel enough at least to let us in. Once we do that, it's up to you to get the information out of her."

"Why up to me?"

"You're the professional crook around here," she said. "Aren't you?"

For some reason Jimmy the Stoolie alias Sandy looked abashed. "So I am," he said with the air of one making a discovery. "So I am."

Chapter Eight

It was just after one when Jane's rented Escort pulled up in front of the Tremaine's home on Cleveland Lane in the heart of old Princeton. Jane sat behind the wheel for a long moment, admiring the stately grace of the huge old house, with its ancient boxwoods, its perfect landscaping, its beautiful flagstoned walkway up to the wide front door. When she looked more closely, though, she saw signs of decay that she hadn't noticed in her earlier visit. The box-woods needed trimming, the red paint on the front door was faded and just beginning to peel, the dead leaves of autumn lay scattered on a lawn that hadn't been cut. The signs weren't obvious, just the subtle warning signals that all was not well with the Tremaine finances.

"Nice place," Sandy said in a neutral tone of voice.

Jane shrugged. "I grew up in a house very much like this one. A little smaller, a little more haphazard looking, but the same general idea."

"Was your father a captain of industry like Tremaine?"

"Not exactly. My parents were college professors."

"I didn't think even Princeton paid its professors well enough to afford this kind of life-style."

"Princeton doesn't." Jane stared out the window, trying to fight the old sense of inadequacy that was settling down around her. "They came from an older class of moneyed educators. They inherited enough to enable them to indulge themselves in teaching. My parents were so impractical they couldn't have survived if they had to do anything as simple as follow a budget and live on their salaries.''

"Your brother didn't sound very practical, either."

"He wasn't. But I am," she added with a trace of defiance. "Sensible Jane." The plain was left unspoken, but she knew he had to be thinking it.''

"How'd you get along with your parents?"

"Sandy, they've been dead for more than seven years now. They were killed in a plane crash when they were on their way to a conference. It's not the issue right now."

"Maybe," he said, "maybe not."

Jane allowed herself a weary sigh, answering him anyway. "I got along with them about as well as I got along with Richard. In other words, they basically ignored my existence.''

"Why?"

"Richard was enough of a challenge for them. He was extremely gifted, even from the start. He could read by the time he was three, solve algebraic equations when he was five, balance mother's checkbook when he was eight, which was the most impressive feat of all. In comparison I was just a normal little girl, walking when I should, talking when I should, playing with dolls and reading Nancy Drew books. My parents must have thought I was a changeling.''

Sandy just looked at her. "What about your sister? Was she one of the brilliant ones?"

Jane shook her head. "Sally went the other route. When she saw how things were she decided to be stupid. She was always in the lowest classes in school, got rotten report cards, and simply refused to try. The funny thing about it, though, is that in certain ways she's much smarter than my parents or Richard ever were. She just hides it.''

"So we've got the brilliant Dexters, the slow one, and or-
dinary old plain Jane. Is that it?" His voice was just slightly
taunting, and she turned from her perusal of the old house
to stare at him in outrage.

"How dare you . . . ?" she began.

"Isn't that what you've been calling yourself? All your
life, even now, when you should be years removed from the
slights of childhood, you go around dressing like plain Jane,
thinking like plain Jane, acting like plain Jane. Maybe you
should learn to lighten up."

"Maybe you should learn to—" she stopped the obscene
sentiment before she uttered it, replacing it with something
safer "—should learn to mind your own business. I'll be
whoever I want to be."

"Exactly. And you've chosen to be plain Jane."

Outrage and hurt had vanished long ago, to be replaced
by a simmering, bristling anger. "Well, honey, you're a fine
one to talk. You've decided to be Jimmy the Stoolie, Sandor Whatsisname, among other names. How many aliases
do you have?"

He blinked for a moment, like a lizard facing bright sunlight. "At least I have a little variety in my life."

"I like constancy."

"Do you ever find it?"

"Not in someone like you," she snapped.

"Were you looking for it?"

That silenced her. He was sitting very still in the passenger seat of the stripped-down Ford, his thick blond hair
rumpled over his high forehead, his tanned, beautiful face
composed and no more than slightly curious. He was wearing a suit that was far too conservative and far too expensive for either a conservation fund-raiser or a felon, but she
had to admit he was absolutely gorgeous. And completely
out of reach.

"No," she said. "I wasn't." But even though she knew better, she would have liked to have found constancy of any sort in the man beside her.

"Are you sure?" His voice was soft, beguiling, teasing at her senses. *He's a con man,* she reminded herself. *He knows how to use people.*

"This conversation is going nowhere," she said abruptly. "Are we going to talk to Annabel Tremaine or aren't we?"

He smiled at her, that brilliant, heart-stopping smile that she knew would haunt her. "We are. Actually, I am. You're going to stand by and look serious and concerned while I pitch her. Think you can handle that?"

"I can handle anything you dish out."

The golden smile broadened to a grin. "I'll hold you to it."

It took a while for someone to answer the door. Jane could hear the melodious chimes echo through the house, but there was no sound of life, or scurrying footsteps. "No one's home," she hissed. "Let's get out of here."

"Tremaine went alone, and someone kissed him good-bye," Sandy said, pressing the doorbell again. "And that BMW was in the driveway this morning and it hasn't been moved. She's home."

"You're wasting your time."

"You can always wait in the car, Jane," he said, not bothering to look at her.

"The hell I . . ."

The door swung open, and a slender, willowy figure stood in the darkness of the hallway, peering out into the bright autumn sunlight. Jane watched in utter fascination as Sandy smiled at the shadowy figure. He knew just the right level of wattage to turn on. Not too overwhelming—the shy creature hiding from them would have probably run. Not too subdued, just enough to coax Annabel Tremaine out of hiding.

"Hi," he said, his voice warm and soothing and just faintly tinged with a Southern accent. "I'm Ashley Wilkes and this is my wife Melanie. We're representing the Northeast Conservation Alliance for Saving the Loons. James MacDougal suggested you might be interested in helping us in our quest. We tried to call before showing up like this, but there was no answer."

Jane allowed herself a cautious, curious glance at her companion. She had no idea who James MacDougal was, but apparently Annabel Tremaine did. She also hadn't read *Gone With the Wind* very recently. She opened the faded red door wider, exposing herself to the brutal sunlight, and smiled up into Sandy's beautiful gray eyes, ignoring his putative wife completely.

"This is rather a bad time," she said vaguely, running a slender hand through a carefully styled mane of silver-blond hair. "My husband's away right now, and I'm afraid I'm between maids, but if you want to come in..."

"We'd love to," Sandy said firmly, turning his back on his beloved Melanie and putting one strong hand under Annabel's elbow. Jane followed in their wake, allowing herself the brief, totally satisfying treat of sticking her tongue out at his beautiful back.

Annabel Tremaine must have been between maids for quite a while. The house was very dark—all the curtains were drawn, shadowing the disarray. Their hostess picked her way with exaggerated care over the piles of clothing, magazines, and dishes, dropping down on a damask-covered sofa and pushing a chintz comforter onto the floor.

"Could I offer you a drink?" she cooed, and everything clicked into place for a confused Jane. At eleven o'clock in the morning Annabel Tremaine was well and truly sloshed.

"It's a little early," Jane said, sinking down on a chair, jumping back up again and removing an empty wineglass before reseating herself.

"It's never too early," Annabel said cheerfully, blinking at them. "What about you, Mr. Wilkes?"

"Not right now," he said.

"You wouldn't mind getting me something, now would you?" Annabel purred.

"How about a cup of coffee?" he suggested calmly.

"Mr. Wilkes, I've been drinking since eight o'clock this morning, since my husband walked out the door. Why should I go and spoil such a carefully acquired state of bliss?"

"You don't look very blissful," Sandy said in a gentle voice.

Annabel blinked again, and slow tears ran down her beautiful cheeks. She was perfectly preserved, anywhere from forty to sixty, with wide, slightly dazed eyes, neatly coiffed hair, beautiful clothes, and makeup applied to her perfect features with a master's hand. Her advanced state of inebriation didn't even put a dent in her physical beauty. Clearly she didn't make a habit of drinking all day, or it would have begun to take its toll on her exceptional looks.

"I'm not blissful," she agreed with a trace of petulance. "I don't want you to think I'm a drunk. I only do this when my husband goes out of town. He's just been doing it a little too often, and I know he's seeing her, and I don't care. Not one tiny bit," she added defiantly.

"I'm sure you don't. How about some coffee?"

"How about some vodka?"

"It's all gone."

"Damn." Annabel had slumped sideways a bit, but she pushed herself back into a sitting position, crossing her shapely ankles. "I'll have to send out for more. I only hope we still have credit at the liquor store. Stephen's been closing all my accounts. He's put me on a budget. Would you believe such a thing? I'm sure he hasn't put Miss Goodbody on a budget."

"Miss Goodbody?" Sandy echoed. He hadn't taken a seat, he was hovering in the doorway, and Jane suddenly realized his problem. He didn't want to take advantage of the woman. It would have been a simple matter to mix her another drink from the bottle of vodka that was, in fact, half-full, and then pry any information he wanted out of her. Instead he wanted to sober her up. Jane's partner in crime had a conscience. The notion was startling and yet, not really surprising.

"My husband's mistress," Annabel said tearily. "Oh, he calls her his vice-president or something like that, but I'm not fooled. How do you think I got him in the first place? Back then they didn't have to make their mistresses executives—they could keep them as secretaries until they dropped them."

"He didn't drop you," Jane said.

Annabel looked crafty. "I was too smart for him. I'm too smart for Miss Goodbody, though she doesn't know it."

"I'm sure you are."

Annabel's fine blue eyes squinted at her. "Who are you?" she demanded suddenly. "What are you doing here?"

"We're here to save the Loons," Jane said somewhat desperately, as Sandy still stood silently by.

"It won't do you any good," Annabel said firmly. "My husband shot a loon two years ago. Nearly went to jail for it. He hates the damned things and their awful noise."

Trust Uncle Stephen to shoot an endangered species, Jane thought. "When will your husband return? Maybe he'd like to assuage his conscience by making a donation."

"My husband has no conscience," Annabel snorted. "And I haven't the faintest idea when he'll be back."

"Where's he gone?" Jane demanded bluntly, when Sandy still said nothing.

Annabel focused her rapidly blinking eyes on Jane. "Why do you want to know?" she said belligerently. "And what are you doing here?"

"We're representing the Save the Loons Foundation," Sandy finally spoke, moving into Annabel's wavering line of vision. "Perhaps we should come back when your husband returns."

"I don't know when he'll return," she said fretfully. "He's gone off to upstate New York and I haven't the faintest idea why. But I can guess who went with him. Elinor Goodbody."

"Peabody," a dulcet voice corrected from behind Sandy. She'd entered the house so silently no one had heard her coming. Elinor Peabody looked much as she had two days ago—perfectly groomed, perfectly collected, perfectly angry. Rather like a sober version of Stephen Tremaine's wife.

Annabel had struggled to her feet, weaving slightly. "Elinor," she purred, suddenly all affability. "What brings you here?"

"I promised Stephen I'd check in on you. He was worried you might get too lonely. But I see you have visitors already." Her eyes met Jane's, bright with mockery, and Jane waited for the boom to fall.

"They're from the . . . what did you say you were representing, dears?" Annabel inquired dazedly.

"The Save the Loons Foundation," Sandy said.

Elinor's eyes ran the length of Sandy's cool, elegant body, and Jane followed that gaze with an odd tightening in her stomach. One she called uneasiness, refusing to give another, more elemental name to it. "And I imagine you're their resident computer whiz," she murmured silkily, gliding over to him.

"Actually I'm not very good at computers," Sandy replied in a low, caressing tone of voice that had Jane clenching her fists. "I'm better working with people."

"I'm sure you are."

Enough was enough, Jane thought, rising from her chair. "We'd better be going," she announced abruptly. "We'll come back when Mr. Tremaine returns from his trip."

"That would be nice," Annabel said vaguely.

Ms Peabody turned an amused gaze back to Jane. "In the meantime, the two of you devoted conservationists might pay me a little visit. I have a great interest in saving loons."

Jane just stared at her. Sandy broke in, smooth and unruffled as ever. "We'd be more than happy to accept any help you have to offer, Ms Goodbody." He let his eyes travel her elegant, voluptuous length just as she had surveyed him. Jane growled low in her throat.

"Peabody," she corrected gently. "Why don't you come by my place tonight around eight? I'm sure we can be a great help to each other."

"We'll be there," Sandy said.

Elinor's mouth turned down in a sour little smile of acceptance. "If that's necessary. In the meantime, why don't you leave Mrs. Tremaine to me? She does this every now and then, just to punish Stephen."

Jane looked back at her hostess, startled, and discovered Annabel sound asleep on the sofa, snoring slightly. "Maybe he deserves it," Jane said.

Ms Peabody's smile broadened. "Maybe he does. Tonight at eight. My address is in the phone book—I imagine two resourceful people like you can find it."

"I imagine we can," Sandy said. He moved slowly, easily over to Jane and took her arm in his. He had to feel the clenched muscles, the tension vibrating through her, but he said nothing, just patted her hand gently. "Till tonight."

Neither of them said a word as they walked through the darkened house. Only when Sandy shut the peeling red door behind them did Jane finally speak. "Do you suppose Annabel is safe with that she-wolf?"

Sandy smiled. "Don't you like Ms Goodbody?"

"She's a snake."

"A snake who seems willing to help us. I don't imagine there's much Elinor doesn't know about Stephen Tremaine's affairs."

"Then you don't know Uncle Stephen," Jane said, climbing into the Escort. "He doesn't know the meaning of the word indiscreet. Anything Ms Peabody knows she had to worm out of him."

"First she's a snake and now she's a worm," Sandy said, sliding in beside her. "You didn't mind her all that much before. Why all the sudden hostility?"

She paused in the act of starting the car, turning to look him directly in his guileless gray eyes. Except, she reminded herself, she'd never known anyone so full of guile in her entire life. "I don't like what she's doing to Annabel. I don't like the fact that while she's busy ruining one woman's marriage she seems ripe for a fling with you. I don't trust her willingness to help, and I don't trust..." The words trailed off, and she turned her attention to the dashboard of the car.

"You don't trust me," he finished for her, quite gently.

"Is there any reason why I should?" she muttered.

"Yes." His hand covered hers before she could start the car, pulling it away, and she had no choice but to look at him. "You should trust me because we're partners, Jane."

"Partners in crime."

"Whatever," Sandy dismissed her cavil. "We're in this thing together, and if we can't trust each other, if you can't trust me, then we may as well give it up right now. Is that what you want?"

She looked at him, at his stern, unsmiling mouth, his stormy eyes, his unflinching expression, and she was ashamed of herself. "I trust you, Sandy," she said. "I do trust you. For a crook you're very honest," she added, hoping to coax a smile from him.

There was no answering lightening in his face. "Or for an honest man I'm very crooked," he said. "Let's get out of here. This place depresses me."

Jane looked back at the subtle signs of decay around the beautiful old house, thought back to the beautiful woman passed out on the damask sofa. "Me too," she said. And she put the car in gear.

SANDY SLUMPED DOWN in the uncomfortable bucket seat, pulling his sunglasses out and propping them on his nose. Not for one moment longer could he meet Jane Dexter's trusting gaze, not for one moment longer could he even stand to see his own reflection in the glare of the windscreen.

The names he was calling himself were so obscene he almost blushed. He had no excuse in the world—if he were any sort of decent human being he'd put a stop to this charade right now. He'd tell Jane Dexter who he really was, that he'd never broken any more laws than the average liberal college student growing up in the early seventies had broken, and that he'd do everything legally in his power to help her.

He believed her when she said she trusted him. That made it all the worse. He'd taken her very rational distrust of men, of him, and turned it around so that she was starting to open up to him. Sooner or later she'd find out the truth, whether he had the guts to tell her or not. And worse than her rage, worse than her justifiable fury, was the thought of seeing those trusting brown eyes clouded with hurt and betrayal.

"What was that?" Jane questioned, her eyes trained on the early afternoon traffic clogging Elm Road.

"What?"

"Did you say something? I thought I heard you groan."

Sandy scooted upright in his seat, shoving his sunglasses back up his nose. Now was the time to tell her. Before things got any worse. "Just clearing my throat," he said, flashing her his most charming smile, the one that could melt the heart of the stoniest judge.

And Jane, bless her poor, gullible heart, smiled back at him, and he started calling himself those names all over again as they headed back toward Route One.

Chapter Nine

It was a cool, clear night in October. The smell of burning leaves still lingered in the evening air, the dampness of a late rain mingled with the scent of autumn closing in. Outside the Princeton Pike Sleep-a-While Motel the air was filled with exhaust from the ever-busy Route One. By the time they reached Elinor Peabody's cozy little stucco house in the Riverside section of Princeton the more soothing sights and scents took over, reminding Jane of her childhood, of Halloweens spent trudging the broad, beautiful streets around her parents' house and collecting chocolate bars that she'd never eaten.

Dick had never bothered going out on Halloween, even when he was little. He preferred to stay home, reading, to dressing up in outlandish costumes and racing around the usually staid residential streets. By the time Sally was old enough for trick-or-treating, certain people had taken to putting razor blades in apples, and Halloween in the suburbs came to an abrupt halt. Jane still missed those earlier times, especially on a night like this, when the sights and smells of her childhood came rushing in on her, leaving her absurdly vulnerable as she hadn't been in years.

Elinor Peabody's house was a pale peachy color with aqua trim, carefully landscaped grounds, and an inground swimming pool in the back. Years ago Riverside had been one of the newer sections of town, a place for young couples and tacky houses. Sandy had casually informed Jane that the house was now on the market, and Ms Peabody was asking four hundred and fifty thousand for a place not much larger than her parents' garage. She'd probably get it, too.

The MGB coughed to a halt outside the well-tended walkway. At least with Ms Peabody there was no sign of imminent decay. "You want me to wait in the car?" Jane finally broke the silence that had lasted since Route One.

His face was shadowed in the car. "You might have a long wait," he said, his voice giving nothing away. "Ms Peabody had a lean and hungry look. If I go in without you I might not escape with my virtue intact."

Jane discovered the sheltering darkness could be beneficial as well as frustrating. There was no way he could see the dismay on her face. "Well," she said finally, "if you're willing to make that sacrifice for the cause I shouldn't stand in your way." Her voice was stiff and unhappy.

He leaned across the front seat, his face inches from hers, the warmth of his breath brushing her mouth. "I'm not," he said softly.

She couldn't keep the relieved smile from wreathing her face, and this time he was close enough to see it. His eyes were sober, watching her, and his mouth drew closer until it feathered her lips.

And then he pulled away. "Besides," he said in a more normal voice, "we decided that despite my gorgeous looks I'm not a gigolo. Now wouldn't be the time to start. Unless you feel like supporting me yourself?" He didn't wait for an answer to the astonishing question, merely climbed out of the low-slung car and moved around to open her door.

If Elinor Peabody was disappointed to see Jane accompany Sandy, she was masterful enough to disguise it. She was also masterful enough to maneuver Jane into a hard chair some distance away, and Sandy into the overstuffed sofa beside her. She was dressed for success that night, in a flowing aqua jumpsuit that complemented a cleavage well-hidden in her daytime uniforms. Her silky blond hair was a tawny mane down her back, and Jane was knowledgeable enough to recognize the subtle difference in her makeup. Ms Peabody was on the prowl, and she wasn't going to let someone of Jane's caliber stand in her way.

Jane stiffened her back in the uncomfortable chair, listening with only half an ear to the idiotic pleasantries about the balmy fall weather and Princeton traffic. This time she wasn't going to give in without a fight. She'd caved in too many times, in her childhood, in her career, in her short-lived marriage. She was through with being understanding, with sitting back and letting other people have their way.

She rose from the chair, crossed the room and sank down gracefully in an overstuffed chair to the left of the sofa, stretching her legs out in front of her, inches away from Sandy's. Her legs were better than Ms Peabody's, even if she didn't have a model's figure and tawny hair and perfect eyesight.

"Why didn't you tell Annabel who we were?" she demanded bluntly, breaking through the polite fencing. She was prepared for Sandy's disapproval of her precipitous question, but he said nothing, leaning back against the cushions with the air of a man about to enjoy himself.

"Annabel wasn't in any condition to comprehend anything, Ms Dexter," Elinor replied sweetly. "I didn't want to confuse her any more than necessary."

"You're the reason she was in that state in the first place." Jane went on the attack.

"No, I am not." Elinor leaned forward, forgetting her languid pose, forgetting Sandy. "No one's responsible for Annabel's drinking but Annabel herself. And maybe Stephen helps a bit. But you've got to realize Annabel doesn't do that very often. Just every few months when she's angry with Stephen and feeling sorry for herself. She doesn't have a serious drinking problem.''

"Yet," Jane said.

"I didn't invite you here to discuss Annabel Tremaine's domestic problems." Elinor carefully recovered her composure. "As a matter of fact, Ms Dexter, I didn't invite *you* at all."

Sandy finally stirred himself. "I don't go anywhere without my boss," he said lazily.

"Your boss? I wondered how you two fit together. Somehow I didn't imagine you were lovers."

Jane swallowed the growl that threatened to erupt. Instead she leaned forward, putting a predatory expression on her face that would have done Ms Peabody proud, and placing a possessive hand on Sandy's knee. She felt the slight quiver of surprise beneath her hand, and then he was still, watching all this with great curiosity.

"You haven't impressed me as someone with much imagination," Jane cooed. "Sandy is my...associate. We're in this together. In every sense of the word." Sandy's knee twitched again, and Jane suspected she'd pay for this later.

But Ms Peabody merely nodded, her sultriness turned off, all business despite the flowing loungewear. "I'm prepared to help you."

"Why?"

Ms Peabody's smile was quite frightening. "Let's just say I have a score to even up with Stephen Tremaine. I'm a firm believer in looking after my best interests. But I don't think my motives concern you. I think what matters to you is what happened to your brother."

Jane's languid self-control vanished. "I beg your pardon?"

"Was I wrong? I thought these elaborate charades were connected with your brother's death."

Jane had the eerie sense of things swinging out of her tenuous control. "Uncle Stephen wants to sell Richard's titanium coating process for defense purposes, either to this country or to another, hostile one. I owe it to Richard to keep him from doing that."

"Do you now?" Ms Peabody murmured. "How are you planning to stop Stephen?"

"Part of the process is missing," Jane said. "You know that as well as I do. If I can find it before Uncle Stephen does I'll destroy it."

"And your brother's life work at the same time? You're very severe, Ms Dexter."

"He would have wanted it destroyed, rather than have it used for military purposes," Jane said firmly.

"I imagine you're right. Your brother always was a royal pain." She rose, crossing the pretty pink chintz room and pouring herself a drink. Straight vodka, and she didn't offer them anything. "I'm afraid I can't tell you where the missing part of the process is. I don't know any more than Stephen does. He thinks it's in Richard's private laboratory, and we don't really know where that lab is."

"Neither do we," Sandy drawled, finally entering the conversation. "Where did Tremaine go today?"

"Upstate New York. He's gone to the area where Richard had his accident."

"Does he think he'll find some clue there?" Jane demanded. "Richard was just passing through, heading for Vermont when his car went off the road. I wouldn't think he'd learn anything there."

"Maybe not. All I can tell you is he isn't any farther along in his quest than you are. He hasn't the faintest idea where the lab is, and all his private detectives aren't helping. Is that what you are, Mr...?" She let it trail, eyeing him over the rim of her glass of vodka.

"Just Sandy," he replied modestly. "And no, I'm not a private detective."

"Then just what are you?"

Time to intervene again, Jane thought, rising briskly. "We appreciate your help."

Elinor shrugged. "It wasn't much."

"You could keep in touch. Let us know if Tremaine comes up with anything."

"I could. We'll see how I feel."

Jane headed down the hallway, Sandy strolling casually along beside her, when she turned to look at Elinor's still figure. "I just wish I knew why you were willing to help us."

Elinor's smile was icy. "Let's just say I didn't bargain for getting involved in murder."

"He couldn't have been murdered," Jane insisted for the twenty-seventh time. She was sitting cross-legged on her motel bed, her hair shoved behind her ears, her glasses slipping down her generous nose, her blouse unbuttoned lower than she doubtless realized. Sandy looked at her and controlled a wistful sigh.

"Why not?" They'd repeated this conversation too many times for him to remember. "Do you think Stephen Tremaine is incapable of murder?"

"Not necessarily. But I can't believe he'd risk it. I wouldn't think the stakes would be high enough. Damn that woman! How could she just say something like that and refuse to explain?" Jane fumed, bouncing on the bed in her agitation.

"Ms Peabody knew exactly what she was doing. She wanted to get you riled up and not thinking straight." He was lounging against the wall by their connecting door, trying to decide how he could get beside her on the bed without having her throw a major fit.

"She succeeded. Do you suppose that was why she did it? That this was all part of Uncle Stephen's plan to get us so confused we went off in a thousand directions?" Her eyes were swollen with unshed tears. He knew she'd shed tears in the darkness on the long drive home, but she'd refused to cry in front of him.

"It's always a possibility." He managed a casual stroll over to the front windows on the pretext of looking out into the artificially lit parking lot. That little maneuver got him a few feet closer to the bed and kept her off guard. If only she'd start crying again he'd have an excuse to comfort her. He'd been on fire since she'd made that phony pass at him earlier—he could still feel the imprint of her hand on his knee and hear the very real possessiveness in her voice.

Jane shook her head. Her thick brown hair was coming loose from the braid down her back, and her glasses were slipping down on the end of her nose. "I don't think so. There was real hostility in her voice when she talked about Uncle Stephen. I think she's definitely out to get him. I just don't know whether getting him involves lying or not."

Sandy crossed to the bed, leaning over her and resting his hands on the sagging mattress. "If she was telling the truth, if Richard really was murdered, then this isn't a game anymore. It's a matter for the police."

"Is that what it's been to you? A game?" Her voice was tight and throbbing with tension, and she was so angry she didn't realize how close he was, didn't comprehend the possibilities when he sat down on the bed beside her.

"No," he said, pushing a strand of hair back from her flushed face. "But it wasn't a matter of life and death, either."

"I keep forgetting," she said bitterly, not moving beneath his hand.

"Forgetting what?" His voice held no more than mild curiosity as he reached out and pushed the glasses back up her nose. He would have liked to have taken them off her, but he decided that would be pushing his luck.

"That you're an amoral criminal, selling your expertise to the highest bidder."

He wasn't even affected. He looked down at her, a gentle smile on his face. "But at least my body's for free," he said, and kissed her.

He more than half expected the reaction he got. For a moment her mouth softened beneath his, her whole body radiating warmth and desire. The next moment he was shoved away, the stinging imprint of her hand on his jaw as he toppled off the bed and onto the threadbare carpet.

He looked up at her from his ignominious position, sprawled on the floor. She was kneeling on the bed, holding her hand and staring down at him in shock and dismay. Her hand must hurt her a good deal, he thought, because it sure as hell hurt his face.

"I've never hit anyone in my life," she said, her voice dazed. "Not since I was eight years old."

He kept a straight face for a moment longer, then grinned up at her. "Maybe you should have hit your ex-husband," he said, sitting upright on the hard floor. "Not to mention your self-centered brother."

"Don't. He's dead."

"That doesn't mean he wouldn't have benefited from a good wallop," Sandy said gently.

She stared at him for a long moment. "God, Sandy, what am I going to do?" she said finally.

There were a number of possibilities, most of which she'd find completely unacceptable. He'd already mentioned the police, and clearly she hadn't liked that idea. He'd tried another pass, and while she'd been more amenable, common sense had reared its ugly head. That left only one possibility. The real Jimmy the Stoolie and his impressive underworld connections.

"What we're going to do," he corrected gently, "is get a good night's sleep. I'm going to make a few phone calls, see what I can stir up, and tomorrow we'll head into the city."

"Why?"

"Because if Stephen Tremaine really was responsible for your brother's death, you can bet your cookies he didn't do it himself. He hired someone. And in New York we can find out exactly whom he hired."

"How?"

"I have friends," he said modestly. "Friends in low places. We can even stay in my lawyer's apartment while we're checking out leads."

"Your lawyer pays your bills and lends you his apartment?" Jane said, mystified. "Why?"

Sandy shrugged. "What can I say? He likes me."

"Are you blackmailing him?"

This being a criminal has its drawbacks, Sandy thought, swallowing his outraged protest. Righteous indignation had no place in his scheme of things. "No, I'm not blackmailing him," Sandy said patiently, with only a slight edge. "He owes me a few favors, I owe him a couple. It all works out."

"So the glorious Alexander Calderwood owes favors to a gangster," Jane mused. "Remind me not to hire him if we get caught torching Technocracies."

"Caldicott," Sandy corrected, the edge coming out. "And you couldn't ask for a better lawyer."

"I could ask for a more honest one."

He just managed to keep from growling. "Besides, I'm not a gangster. I'm just a minor talent."

"True enough. You can barely manage to pick a lock."

Enough was enough. Sandy's romantic mood was thoroughly banished by now, his jaw was throbbing, and Jane was looking decidedly cheerful. "We'll go tomorrow."

"Fine," she said, lying back on the bed, seemingly unaware that her skirt had ridden up her thighs, exposing those beautiful legs of hers, that her glasses were sliding down her nose again, and that no matter how mad he was right now he still found her absolutely delicious. "I don't think we'll find anything, but it will help matters to know for sure."

"You've decided Tremaine didn't kill your brother?"

"I don't think so. Call me irrational, but I think I'd know. I trust my intuition about people, and I just don't think Uncle Stephen could have done it. It had to be an accident."

Sandy had made it to the connecting door, but he stopped for a moment. "You trust your intuition about people," he echoed. "What does your intuition tell you about me?"

He would have given ten years off his life to have been able to read her mind right then. Whatever she was thinking, it was powerful. Her eyes widened, her mouth grew soft and tremulous, and for two cents he would have crossed the room and landed back on the bed with her.

And landed back on the floor, no doubt. Within seconds she'd wiped the incriminating look from her face, tightening her mouth and narrowing her eyes. "That you're nothing but trouble," she answered. "Good night."

That was true enough, he thought. But he wished he knew what else she'd been thinking for that brief moment before her defenses shuttered down again. "Pleasant dreams," he said, hoping they'd be lustful ones.

There was no question that his would be.

THE WHIMPERS WOKE HIM. It was sometime in the middle of the night—the Princeton Pike Sleep-a-While Motel didn't supply digital clocks to succor the insomniac, and he could only peer at his thin gold watch and guess that it was after three. The fluorescent lights from the parking lot glared into the room, and he lay in the uncomfortable bed, his ears straining for the sound that had pulled him from a deep sleep.

Maybe the sparsely populated motel had rented the room on the other side, and right now some energetic couple was being slightly vocal in their endeavors. Or maybe some stray alley cat was lurking outside, prowling along the cracked cement walkway, looking for a juicy mouse. Or maybe, he thought, as the sound came again, his partner in crime was crying.

He pulled himself out of bed, and headed for the connecting door, grabbing for his bathrobe as he went. Not that she hadn't already seen him in his underwear, but in her current fragile state he didn't want to do anything to alarm her further.

He wouldn't have put it past her to barricade the connecting door, but it opened easily, silently at his touch. He expected a shriek of outrage when she realized he'd faked locking the door, but all that came from the narrow figure on the bed was another muffled whimper.

The eerie blue-yellow light from the parking lot outside cast gloomy shadows in the shabby room. He could hear the distant roar of trailers barreling down Route One, but Jane slept on, oblivious, lost in her own nightmare world of misery.

He should leave her alone, he knew that. He should go back to his own room, slam the door loud enough to wake her out of her tear-laden sleep, and let her work out her problems by herself. What the hell did he have to offer her but more lies?

The bed sank beneath his weight as he sat down beside her. He touched her shoulder, gently, hoping just to jar her out of the nightmare but let the sleep continue.

Her eyes flew open, staring up at him, dazed, myopic, filled with unshed tears. "What are you doing here?" she demanded in a husky voice.

"You were having a nightmare," he said softly, reluctantly pulling his hand back.

"I was dreaming about Richard and the car crash. I was in the car with him, falling down the embankment, rolling over and over and over." Her voice shuddered to a halt.

"You're safe," he said, knowing how lame it sounded. He wondered how he was going to be able to touch her again. He'd probably end up on the floor.

"I suppose I am." Her eyes narrowed as she looked up at him. "What are you wearing?"

"A bathrobe," he replied, startled.

"A F C." She reached out and traced the telltale monogram. "Don't tell me you stole your lawyer's bathrobe?" There was more weary amusement than indignation in her voice.

"Of course not," Sandy said, glad the darkness hid his expression. "I just borrowed it."

"You're an unregenerate scoundrel, Sandy or Jimmy or whoever you are."

"I'm afraid so," he agreed, feeling suddenly very guilty. Maybe now was the time to tell her, now in the timeless hours between midnight and dawn. The longer he waited the worse it would be. "Jane," he began earnestly, steeling himself.

"Good night, partner," she said, interrupting him gently but firmly.

"But I wanted to . . ."

"Good night."

He had no choice. At least he could comfort himself with the knowledge that he tried. Not hard enough, but he did try. He sat on the bed, looking down at her.

"Good night," he said. And without another word he went back to his room, closing the door silently behind him.

Chapter Ten

"I wouldn't trust Elinor Peabody further than I could throw her," Jane said, huddling deeper into the leather car seat as they sped toward New York.

"Neither would I," Sandy said reasonably enough. "That doesn't mean she can't be useful."

Jane gave her clothing a look of disgust. The artfully streaked and tattered jeans had clearly seen better days, the top resembled something Geronimo might have worn. At least it covered her. Beneath it was a metal studded leather bra that Sandy had presented with a flourish. She wouldn't have worn it at all if the feathered shirt hadn't provided a few desperate gaps, and she would have given anything to be able to wrap her underdressed body in a nice, enveloping raincoat.

Her hair was even more absurd, but by the time she'd attacked it she'd become reckless, getting into the spirit of the thing. It stuck out every which way, aided by mousse, styling gel, and the kind of teasing she hadn't seen since her brother went to the senior high school prom with Rita Di Angelo in a fit of teenage lust never repeated in his noble manhood.

But the hour-long, cramped ride into the city in Sandy's MGB was giving her more than enough time for second thoughts, and every time she glanced at her reflection in the mirror she cringed. The blue, purple and pink streaks radiating above her eyes were visible even without her purloined glasses, and the black lipstick made her look like the bride of Frankenstein. She shivered delicately, looking out over the New Jersey Turnpike, and hoped her left earring wouldn't catch in the feathers. She'd closed her eyes when Sandy had inserted the diaper pin in her right ear, and she still couldn't bring herself to look closely at it.

It was long past dusk, an early autumn chill was in the air, and the smell of New Jersey exhaust penetrated the closed windows of the little car. Jane had drawn the line when Sandy had tried to douse her with some sort of musk that smelled more like pesticide, but maybe that would have been better than the sulphurous fumes rising from the sprawled-out megalopolis surrounding Newark.

"You could have stayed home," Sandy said gently.

"I wouldn't exactly call the Princeton motel home," Jane said, allowing herself another, surreptitious glimpse of Sandy's spiked blond hair and torn T-shirt and swallowing the sigh of part disgust, part lust. While she looked like a cross between Cyndi Lauper and Vampira, Sandy managed to look like a punk Don Johnson. Certain things in life weren't fair.

"What would you call home?"

"The second floor of a run-down Victorian house in Baraboo, Wisconsin. I used to live in a boxy apartment but it drove me crazy."

"Somehow I don't see you as a Victorian."

"Don't you? I've been called prudish in my time." She knew her voice sounded raw, but she hoped he wouldn't notice.

Sandy noticed everything. "Who called you prudish? Your ex-husband?"

"Yes."

"Does he have anything to do with your Victorian lifestyle?"

Jane sighed. "I wish you wouldn't be so damned nosy. Why don't we change the subject?"

"Lovely weather," he said obediently enough.

There was a long silence. "You really want to know about my marriage?"

"Only if you want to tell me."

"If I wanted to tell you I would have brought up the subject myself."

"Yes, I want to know about your marriage," Sandy said, dropping all pretense.

"All right. It doesn't take long to tell. I met Frank at the University of Wisconsin. I was taking a night course in Japanese Socialism and he was rebounding from a messy divorce."

"Japanese Socialism?" he echoed in a voice of horror. "Why in the world would you willingly choose to study something that dry?"

"I thought it was time to try something new. I'd already had enough arts and sciences to keep me going. Do you want to hear about my academic career or my marriage?"

"We're getting near the turnpike exit. Which takes the shorter amount of time?"

"Definitely the marriage. Frank was teaching the course, which was unspeakably boring. He'd just been divorced by his wife of five years—apparently she needed to find herself and he'd been holding her back. So he cried in my arms for a while, then figured there probably wasn't much of me left to find, so he proposed, and I was fool enough to accept."

"Why?"

It was a good question, one she hadn't considered in a long time. She gave the unrepentant Sandy her most severe look. "Because I was in love with him," she said firmly.

Sandy, of course, wasn't cowed. "Really?"

She didn't hesitate. "At this point I don't know any-more. Maybe I married him because he looked like Dustin Hoffman and he was man enough to cry. I should have re-alized one should never marry a man who's crying over an-other woman."

"What happened?"

"His ex-wife found herself, Frank got over his rebound and went back to her. It was all very civilized and decent, everybody was terribly sorry about the whole bloody mess."

"Did you put up any kind of fight?"

"Are you kidding?" Jane tossed her frizzy mane over her feathered shoulder. "I'm much too reasonable a person. I'm cursed with seeing everybody else's point of view. They both made a mistake and they'd suffered too long for it. I bowed out gracefully and flew to Mexico for a fast divorce so they could get remarried on their old wedding anniversary."

"Nice. What did you give them as a wedding present?"

Jane glared at him. "What makes you think I gave them a wedding present?"

"You'd already been such an incredible sucker I'm sure you didn't stop there. I bet you refused alimony."

"Of course."

"What about community property?"

"Stop sounding like a lawyer. We'd only been married seventeen months. We hadn't had time to accumulate much more than a car and a time-share in Bermuda where we spent our honeymoon."

"What happened to them?"

"I gave them up. I don't like Saabs and I never want to go to Bermuda again."

"Did he give you any compensation?"

"Sandy..."

"Didn't you have a lawyer?" He was sounding posi-tively incensed.

"Of course I did. A friend of Frank's took care of the details."

"A friend of Frank's shafted you."

"I didn't want anything," she said, anger and desperation making her voice tight and hard. "I just wanted my freedom."

"You didn't get anything else." Sandy didn't look at her, concentrating instead on the heavy evening traffic as he headed for the Lincoln Tunnel. "Not even your self-respect."

If she hit him they'd probably swerve into another car and die. Still, the thought was tempting. With great difficulty she swallowed her rage. "My self-respect doesn't depend on material possessions."

"That's good. Let's just hope it isn't influenced by being screwed by people who once cared for you." His voice was tight with anger, and that emotion finally stirred Jane out of her own fury.

"What does it matter to you how I'm treated? If *I* don't mind why in the world do *you*?"

"Are you trying to tell me you don't mind?" he countered.

She thought about it, carefully, prodding at the remembered pain like a tongue prodding a sore tooth. "I mind about me," she said finally. "I mind that I made a fool of myself. Apart from that, it's all ancient history."

He didn't have to say anything, his skeptical expression was reaction enough. She tried to shove a deliberately careless hand through her teased and tangled mane, but her fingers stuck in the rough mass. "All I know," she added sweetly, "is that I'll never let a man make a fool out of me again."

His derision vanished. "Good idea," he muttered, turning his attention back to the narrowing road.

YOU'RE GETTING MORE and more foolhardy as time goes on, Sandy berated himself as he maneuvered the car down the crowded, narrow streets of the Lower East Side. He'd had plenty of chances to tell her the truth, plenty of times when he could have set things straight and then sat back and let others take over this incredible mess. Instead here he was, wandering around places he shouldn't be seen, looking for people he shouldn't even know existed.

He wouldn't have done it if Elinor Peabody hadn't called up with a name. A name he knew. Anyone else and he would have left it alone, but the coincidence made it unavoidable.

Years ago, when he was first practicing, his partners had handed him a case too dirty for them to soil their patrician hands with. When Gregory Matteo had shown up in his office all Sandy had known was that he was squeezed into a thousand dollar suit too small for his fat, sweating body. After talking with him Sandy had watched the contradictions mount. The man had an income and a title ill-suited to his meager intellect, combined with a bullying attitude that irritated Sandy enough to look further into the man's background. He'd been accused of assaulting a police officer. He'd actually been beating his girlfriend, but she'd refused to press charges, so only the policeman who'd tried to stop him ended up going to court.

He'd gotten him off on a technicality, a maneuver that required no great brilliance on his part, but Matteo had been almost pathetically grateful. And he'd made a firm promise: if Sandy had ever needed anything, he had only to send word to his notorious father, Jabba Matteo himself, and that wish was granted. And as Sandy had watched the man waddle away he'd wiped away an icy sense of relief that it was over so quickly.

Jabba Matteo was so powerful, so dangerous and so rich that his very existence was almost a secret. The media that didn't hesitate to stake out presidential campaigners and malign anything that moved seldom mentioned his name, and then only in the most circumspect manner. Even Sandy didn't know the extent of the senior Matteo's activities, and he didn't care to. All he knew was that one of his quasi legitimate forms of employment was arms dealing, and that Matteo owed him one. Once Elinor Peabody mentioned his name, the die was cast.

Getting in touch with him had proven the major challenge, one that Sandy had chosen to meet in typically brazen style. Three blocks away, their guide to the underworld was waiting in Ratner's delicatessen, probably stuffing his ratty little face with strawberry cheesecake. The real Jimmy the Stoolie was waiting for them, and it was going to take all of Sandy's quick thinking and mental juggling to keep Jane and Jimmy at arm's length.

"So how come your lawyer hangs out with godfathers?" Jane queried as he pulled up beside a boarded-up building and switched off the car. "I didn't think Alexander Caldicott was a hireling of organized crime."

"He isn't. He knows a friend of a friend. I should have thought of him myself. If anyone in New York knows anything about arms dealing, Jabba's the man. He'd also be likely to know if anything…unpleasant…happened to your brother."

"Something unpleasant happened to him, Sandy. He died."

"I know," he said hastily, trying to keep from staring in total fascination at her streaked and painted face. He could barely see the normal, so-called plain Jane beneath the gold and purple stripes, the spiky, tangled hair and garish mouth. He still wanted to kiss that mouth, black lipstick and all, and he was still far too partial to what lay beneath the metal-studded leather bra, but for the present he struggled to keep his mind on business. He'd explained the situation to

Jimmy, and the little weasel had promised his full cooperation in exchange for a break on his legal fees, but Sandy
wasn't fool enough to trust him. If Jimmy thought he could
get some sort of advantage out of his information he'd try
to, and the next few hours would prove harrowing indeed if
Sandy wasn't extremely careful.

"Isn't that your lawyer?" Jane murmured, reaching for
the door handle.

Jimmy the Stoolie was sauntering toward them, a smarmy
smile on his rodentlike face. Sandy just watched in growing
dismay. He'd told Jimmy to borrow a suit from his ward-
robe—they were close in size and the doorman would let him
in. Needless to say Jimmy had chosen the best one he
owned—a Giorgio Armani he kept for special occasions.
Jimmy had already dripped a faint trail of strawberry on one
lapel, and that was probably the trace of whipped cream just
beside the pocket. Sandy bit his tongue in outrage.

"There you are, Jimmy," the real Jimmy said, displaying his prominent teeth in a condescending smile. "I wondered when I'd see you again. Not in any trouble are you,
my boy?"

"None at all," Sandy said between his teeth. "It was good
of you to meet us."

"Not at all, Jimmy, not at all. After all, you've kept me
busy these past few years. It's no trouble to lend you a
hand." He put his newly manicured hands on the car, leaning down to leer at Jane. "You must be Jimmy's little
friend. Do you realize what sort of man you're hanging out
with, Miss . . . ?"

"No names," Sandy snapped, getting out of the car and
fiddling uselessly with the lock. He hadn't been able to lock
the MGB since 1978, but he always made a pretense of it in
case someone happened to be looking.

And Jimmy was looking very carefully, his attention torn
between the leather bra and the exterior of the MGB. "He's

a pretty unsavory character," Jimmy continued, opening the door for her and watching with undisguised admiration as she slid her luscious legs out. Those tattered jeans did nothing to disguise their long, graceful length, and Sandy was on the edge of shoving Jimmy out of the way if he didn't stop drooling.

"Then why do you do so many favors for him?" Jane asked sweetly.

"Favors?" Jimmy echoed, mystified as well as entranced.

"Pay for his motel, cover his bills, even lend him your monogrammed bathrobe," Jane said innocently. "How do you know he won't run off with all your things?"

"Don't forget the apartment," Sandy piped up helpfully. "It was very decent of you to lend us your Park Avenue apartment since you're going out of town."

"You know," Jimmy mused, leaning forward and peering beneath Jane's feathers, "I may stay in town after all. There's plenty of room for you at my place anyway, but I might as well be a good host."

Sandy came over and slung a friendly arm around Jimmy's shoulders, grinding his bones with just enough pressure to make his accomplice turn pale without actually groaning in pain. "We appreciate the thought, Alexander, but we know how important that Baltimore case is. We'll just have to let you go."

Jimmy smiled weakly. Baltimore held a great many unpleasant secrets, most of which Sandy knew. "You're right, Jimmy," he said. "We'll have to do it some other time."

Sandy released his crushing grip, carefully moving Jimmy out of the way and taking Jane's arm in his. "Where's Jabba? Does he know we're coming?"

"He knows," Jimmy said, and Sandy couldn't miss the uneasiness in his voice. "I'm not sure your friend is going to like the company."

"My name's Jane," she said, and Sandy could feel the tension beneath the feathers. "And I'm used to him. How bad could things get?"

Jimmy laughed, a high-pitched, nasal giggle. "Used to him?" he echoed, looking at Sandy's thinly disguised patrician profile. "Honey, you ain't seen nothing yet."

"Sandy?" He could hear the beseeching note in Jane's husky voice, and he placed his hand on top of her arm, pressing slightly.

"You don't have to come," he said. He wished there was some way short of the truth that could keep her miles away from Jabba Matteo. But Jane Dexter was nothing if not a determined woman, and even the outlandish costume he'd provided hadn't deterred her.

"I'm coming," she said, her momentary hesitation gone.

He looked down into her somber eyes, surrounded by the rainbow streaks. She didn't trust him, and she was wise not to. But the one thing she could trust him with was her safety. Tonight, for possibly the first time in her life, he was deliberately leading someone into a dangerous situation beyond her own control. He had to count on the hope that it wouldn't be beyond his.

He managed a casual shrug. "Suit yourself," he said, ignoring Jimmy's admiring expression. "But remember to keep your eyes down and your mouth shut. We're heading into a patriarchal society, and no one's interested in equal rights around here. Understand?"

"Understood." She tried to pull away from him, but he held fast, his fingers tightening on her arm. The more he held on, the more she tugged, and in another moment they would have been involved in a wrestling match in the middle of the Lower East Side, when Jimmy decided to intervene.

Sandy was so startled he released her, and Jimmy took her arm with more graceful aplomb than he'd shown in his entire misspent life. "I'll take care of her, old boy," he murmured. "You just take care of yourself." And he started off down the littered, crowded sidewalks, Jane walking meekly enough beside him.

Sandy didn't move for a long moment, staring after his best Armani suit on Jimmy's stooped shoulders, watching Jane's magnificent legs and that absurd tangle of hair. Others were watching, the curious, sullen eyes so prevalent in a domain of criminals. Watching Jane and Jimmy's progress, watching Sandy, watching the MGB that couldn't be locked. Sandy gave it one last worried glance. He loved his aging, impossible-to-tune car with a passion he reserved for nothing else, and he couldn't rid himself of the miserable possibility that when he returned it would be gone.

But it was a choice between his car and Jane. And to his surprise there was no question at all which one mattered. Without another glance at the shiny blue finish, he hurried down the sidewalk after his former client. He could always buy another car.

Chapter Eleven

What in the world am I getting myself into, Jane thought as she moved along the broken sidewalks. She was in a part of New York her parents had always warned her about, and she was on the verge of meeting people she scarcely believed existed. The only protection she had was her own somewhat limited abilities, a felon who looked like a prince, and a lawyer who looked like a felon. Between Sandy and his lawyer there wasn't much choice, and if she had any sense at all she would have stayed at the motel in the first place instead of dressing up in such outlandish gear and walking the streets of the Lower East Side.

Her sense of uneasiness had been growing by the day, by the hour, compounded by the sudden intensity of the situation in which she found herself. Something bothered her about Sandy, and she couldn't quite pinpoint what it was. Something that didn't ring true, and every time she felt she was coming close to understanding it he'd do something distracting like kiss her. It had an amazing power to cloud her mind, but she couldn't afford to let it happen again. She'd managed to keep her own raging reactions under control, but it was a close call each time. Next time she might not make it.

The lawyer beside her didn't seem right either. She knew his suit was worth a small fortune, but the shoes didn't match. They were too shiny, and the black and white patent clashed with the muted colors of the suit. His hair was badly cut—more for flash than for style, and the diamond ring on his pinky simply didn't look Princeton to her. But times had changed, and there was no question that her family had been elitist snobs. Maybe large diamond pinky rings were more in vogue than she remembered.

"Not far now," the unlikely lawyer said, guiding her around a corner and down a poorly lit alley where the debris underfoot was even thicker. He smelled of expensive cologne, but it was a brand Jane particularly disliked. Sandy was following behind them, not close enough, and for a moment she regretted struggling with him. She'd rather have his hand under her elbow. His fingers wouldn't be squeezing and stroking in a nasty, encroaching sort of way.

The alley was a dead end. There was a brick wall in front of them, windowless, doorless buildings on either side, with garbage heaped around a decrepit looking dumpster. The lawyer released her, heading straight for the rusty dumpster, as Sandy came up behind her.

"Second thoughts?" he inquired gently, the soft voice at odds with the punk appearance.

Jane watched with deep misgivings as the side to the dumpster swung open, spilling forth light and noise into the alley way. She considered lying, but it would be a waste of breath. Already Sandy knew her far too well. "And third and fourth and fifth thoughts," she said. "Do I really have to walk into a dumpster?"

The sleazy-looking lawyer was beckoning them toward the narrow stairs inside the camouflage garbage container, and as Jane moved closer she noticed that every attempt at authenticity had been made. The metal bin stank of rotting garbage.

"Too late to turn back now," Sandy said, his hand replacing his lawyer's on her befeathered elbow. And she'd been right—it was strong, comforting, the human warmth enabling her to duck her teased head and step into the narrow flight of stairs.

She went down slowly, following the Armani suit, Sandy directly behind her. As the smell of garbage faded, another scent replaced it, one of expensive, musky perfumes and colognes, whiskey and humanity. Not the rank sweat of the subway, this was expensive, freshly washed sweat. When she reached the bottom of the steps she stopped, absorbing the feel of Sandy's body as he bumped into her.

It looked like an odd combination of Chinese brothel, upscale nightclub and Soho loft. The place was packed, though nowhere could Jane see anyone she'd particularly like to socialize with. Feathers, chains, leather and hardware abounded. Jane was instantly grateful Sandy had taken her glasses. She had the distinct feeling she wouldn't care to see anyone here more closely, and she followed Caldicott blindly through the thick smoke and haze, her eyes downcast, as ordered.

"Hey, Jimmy," a man's voice called out, and she could feel Sandy's hand tighten reflexively on her elbow. She waited for him to respond, but Caldicott did it for him.

"Where's Jabba, Crystal?"

"He expecting you?"

"Would I be here if he wasn't?"

"Who knows?" the husky, cheerful voice responded. "Maybe you've brought some fresh talent. Who's your little feathered friend?"

"Ask Jabba," Caldicott replied cheerfully, as Jane bit back a tiny moan of sheer panic and claustrophobia.

"You ask Jabba. He's in the back. I'll tell him you're here." Jane allowed herself a brief glance at their interrogator, and then wished she hadn't. The voice had been basso profundo, the hair a Dolly Parton wig, the dress Ralph Lauren ruffles. She dropped her gaze to a thick pair of ankles and size twelve spike heels as they disappeared toward the back.

"Great guy," Caldicott said cheerfully. "Lucky we ran into him. I might have had a hell of a time finding Jabba."

"I thought this was prearranged," Sandy said, and Jane turned to look back at him in surprise. Her easy-going partner in crime sounded downright dangerous, and Caldicott reacted with uncharacteristic nervousness.

"It's as prearranged as things get with Matteo. I explained what was going on," Caldicott said uneasily. He had a prominent Adam's apple above his silk knotted tie, and it was bobbing in agitation.

"You'd better have," Sandy said softly, his voice a very definite threat. He caught Jane's fascinated gaze, and immediately smiled at her. "You look like you've seen a ghost."

She wet her lips, tasting the strawberry flavor of the purple-black lipstick. "I just suddenly realized how dangerous you could be," she said, her voice faltering.

He seemed equally as startled. "Only to low-lifes like him," he said. "Never to you."

She managed a weak smile in the noise and smoke. "You call your lawyer a low-life? What does that make you?"

His expression was instantly veiled. "An entrepreneur," he said. "And your partner in crime, in case you've forgotten."

"I haven't." She was too nearsighted to tell if everyone was watching them, but she couldn't rid herself of the feeling that countless hostile eyes were following their every move. "Sandy," she said, her voice low and beseeching, "I think I'm frightened."

If everyone was watching them that fact had no effect on Sandy. He pulled her into his arms, feathers, leather bra and all, and he was hot and strong and safe around her. She hid there, her face pressed against his shoulder, the noise and lights swirling around them, as she slowly pulled her strength back around her. He held her just as long as she needed holding, and when she felt strong enough to move away he released her instantly.

"Feel better?" he inquired in the most casual of voices.

She managed a tremulous smile. "Yes."

"Don't worry. I won't let the bad guys get you."

"They wouldn't want me, would they?" she countered seriously.

"They'd be fools not to."

"This way." Caldicott was back between them, his cologne overpowering the other, more suspect smells of the crowded rooms, and Jane had no chance to respond. The lawyer had her hand caught tightly in his, tugging her through the maze of chattering, bright-eyed people toward a door in the back, and she followed, certain that Sandy was right behind her.

The silence of the next room was thick and shocking after the cacophony before, and the filtered light only compounded Jane's myopia as the lawyer drew her to a halt. Sandy was beside her, his hand caught her other one, and slowly she lifted her eyes to the figure in front of them.

She had never seen a human being so immense in her entire life. He seemed to fill the end of the narrow room, and in the gray filtered light he seemed an amorphous blob of semihumanity, larger than three normal people put together. He was dressed in some sort of gray suit, but his abundant flesh spilled around him. His skin was pasty gray, his eyes dark little raisins in a face of suet, his mouth was small and cruel and pink. He was smiling at them with that mouth, and he waved a fat, balloonlike hand in greeting.

"Welcome, friends," he said, and his voice was another surprise. She would have expected something low and rumbling from that mountain of flesh, but instead it came out in a high-pitched wheeze, barely carrying the length of the empty room. On second glance Jane noticed the room wasn't empty at all. Stationed at strategic points along the bare walls were studiously casual men, their loose jackets concealing their weapons. Jane shuddered, and she could feel the cool dampness of the hands in hers. Both Sandy and his nefarious lawyer were just as scared of Jabba Matteo as she was.

"How nice to finally meet you, Mr. Caldicott," Matteo purred, his voice lilting his amusement. "I've been hoping for a chance to repay the favor you did me and mine so long ago, and now that time has come. And as I live and breathe, this must be Jimmy the Stoolie. Come closer, young man, and tell me how I can assist you and this surprising young lady."

Sandy's hand clenched more tightly around hers, but his elegant profile gave nothing away. The man on her left was pale and sweating profusely, and she was glad she didn't have to count on him to defend her in court. At least Sandy could keep his head when things got difficult.

"We appreciate your seeing us, Mr. Matteo," Sandy said, his voice steady and deceptively casual. "Caldicott probably explained our problem to you."

"Your lawyer did mention something. And please, call me Jabba. Such formality distresses me. Old friends such as we shouldn't stand on ceremony. Come, come, Jimmy. Bring the little lady closer."

It was Jane's turn to be startled. She lifted her head, against Sandy's previous orders, and stared defiantly into Jabba's piglike eyes, and then wished she hadn't. For all the comic-book trappings, the absurdity of place and time, the eyes of the huge man in front of her were pure evil.

"We want to know about Stephen Tremaine." Sandy angled his body to shield her an almost imperceptible amount. "You know everything in the world of arms dealing. What is Tremaine up to?"

Jabba chuckled, a high, wheezing sound. "Why limit it to arms dealing? I know everything worth knowing, or I can find it out in minutes. Stephen Tremaine is trying to sell an advanced titanium coating process to the highest bidder he can find. Libya has already backed down—the asking price is much too high. Chile is interested, but has yet to make an offer, Chad wants it but is also too poor, and Iran doesn't want to wait. At this point it looks like he's going to sell to the President of Salambia."

"But he's a madman," Jane said, horror overriding her common sense.

Jabba's evil little eyes smiled on her. "Indeed he is, dear lady. A very wealthy madman, and one of my best customers. You mustn't judge him too harshly, dear lady. You've lived too sheltered a life."

"Shut up," Sandy hissed at her, his strong hand grinding the bones in her wrist.

"But let the little woman speak, Jimmy the Stoolie." He accented the name, as if he and Sandy shared a secret joke. "I'm not used to such innocence, and it amuses me. She's the one who wants to know, isn't she? Let her ask the questions."

Jane ignored Sandy's warning hand, pulling away from him and confronting Matteo with deceptive fearlessness. Her knees trembled, her stomach churned, and she could only hope she could ask her questions and escape without throwing up on the red Oriental carpet beneath her feet.

"Does Tremaine have the entire formula?" she demanded. "Or is he still missing a crucial part of it?"

"Dear me," Jabba said, fanning his pale basketball-size head with a copy of *Fortune* Magazine. "I hadn't realized what was causing the delay. How delicious. He went to all that trouble to silence your brother and now he's unable to profit from it. Maybe that has something to do with his interest in a certain property in Bay Head. I do love irony, don't you, Ms Dexter?''

The room was utterly, completely still. She no longer felt Sandy's restraining hand, was completely unaware of Caldicott's terrified stance. She moved forward, so close she could feel the heat and danger emanating from the mountain of flesh in front of her. "Did Stephen Tremaine have anything to do with my brother's death?" Her voice was raw with emotion, and she was no longer frightened.

Jabba's grin revealed two rows of tiny gold teeth. "Dear child, I don't know. I can assure you he didn't hire any professionals before yesterday. I would have heard if he did. But I couldn't say whether he opted for an amateur hit. The man is desperate, and your brother's death was very convenient."

Jane just stared at him numbly, listening to the words she didn't want to hear. "What do you mean before yesterday?"

Jabba chuckled. "Word has it he's retained the services of a notable knife artist named Lenny the Rip. I didn't bother to check, and sometimes any information can be...premature. If he has, I expect you'll find out sooner or later." He'd finished with her, turning his attention back to Sandy. "Was there anything else you wished to know?"

Sandy glanced over at her, then shook his head. "That about covers it."

Jabba nodded, his row of chins quivering. "Then my debt of honor is repaid. I will have to make sure my son doesn't incur another such debt."

Sandy said nothing, simply inclining his head graciously. The lawyer was still sweating in the cool room.

"And I think," said Jabba, "that you might make me a small gesture to ensure your good will and discretion."

She could feel the tension in the room. It was a palpable thing, and once again she had the eerie sense that all eyes were on her, from Jabba's evil dark ones to the deadly cold emotionless ones of the men lining the wall.

Again Sandy nodded, this time with less grace. "I'd be more than happy to oblige."

Jabba giggled. "I thought you might. Why don't you leave me Ms Dexter for the night? I can promise her an interesting time, and we'll return her in one piece."

The lawyer beside her swore, casting a desperate glance over at Sandy's immobile face. The army lining the room had straightened, clearly expecting some action, and Sandy's face was carved in stone. Jane could see his gray eyes flicker as his brain struggled for some way out of their current mess, and she resisted the impulse to start screaming in utter panic. Instead she waited, forcing herself to be calm.

Sandy shrugged. "I'd love to oblige you, Jabba. Shall I come back and fetch her or will you send her home?"

Jane's moan of outrage was drowned out by Jabba's laugh. "I'll send her home when we've finished with her. It's been a long time since we've seen such an innocent. Her costume only makes her naïveté more apparent."

"I'm rather fond of it myself," Sandy said, lifting one of the feathers and letting it flutter down. "I do trust you don't actually wish to touch her?"

"Trust away, dear boy," Jabba said with a smirk.

"Because I should warn you that much as I adore the young lady, she's not terribly...healthy." The pregnant pause said it all. "It's nothing fatal, but the results could be quite uncomfortable, if you know what I mean."

Jabba recoiled faintly, his smile fading. "I don't believe you," he wheezed.

Sandy only smiled. "I may be lying," he agreed. "But how will you know?"

Jabba stared at them, long and hard, and Jane held her breath, waiting for the ax to fall, waiting for the slit-eyed army to draw weapons and put an end to their impertinent existence.

And then he began to laugh, the sound coming from deep within the rolls of fat surrounding his body, bubbling out, shaking his huge frame until Jane thought he might choke to death in front of her eyes. Tears poured down his rosy cheeks and caught in the folds of his chins, his gold teeth glinted in the lamplight.

"Philadelphia lawyer," Jabba chuckled breathlessly. "It's just as well. My honor is compromised enough as it is. In this case I'll keep it intact."

"I thought you might see it that way," Sandy said smoothly.

"But I suggest you leave the back way. It wouldn't do my reputation any good to have it known I let you walk away without paying any duty. And I don't think you'd care for that sort of attention either, not in your line of work."

"A con man can't be too careful," Sandy said.

Jabba chuckled, dabbing at his tear-streaked face. "If you're a con man what do you call your ailing young lady?"

Sandy looked over at her, and there was a fiercely possessive gleam in his blue eyes. "My partner in crime," he said. "What else?"

JANE RAN BLINDLY, stumbling through the dark streets after Sandy, too terrified to even think. The pounding of her heart and the rasping of her labored breathing drowned out any possible sound of pursuit, but she could imagine a horde of those grim-faced men chasing after them through New York's mean streets.

She had no idea how far they'd come when Sandy pulled to a stop, dropping her abused wrist and leaning against a building to catch his breath. She could feel the cool evening air dry the sweat on her face, she could smell the exhaust and the fear that had surrounded them back in that dark, hot room, and she shivered.

"Was it worth it?" Caldicott whined. He'd ripped the Armani suit during their mad dash, and Sandy was eyeing the tear with nothing short of outrage.

"No," said Jane.

"Yes," said Sandy at the same time. "We know we're in trouble and we know Tremaine is dangerous."

"We already knew that," Jane pointed out, stripping off her black lace half gloves.

"But now we know who he's negotiating with. And we know he's still a ways from finding the rest of the formula. We have some time."

"We don't know how much," Jane said.

"At least we have a night's sleep."

"And we know where we're going tomorrow."

Sandy looked at her with deep apprehension. "All right, I'll bite. Where are we going tomorrow?"

"Bay Head. My brother inherited a house on the ocean. Tremaine must think the formula is there."

"And what do you think?"

"I think it's a good possibility. Richard used to go there and refused to invite any of the family. It would be the perfect place for a lab, and it's less than an hour from Princeton."

"All right," Sandy said wearily. "Tomorrow we go to Bay Head. Tonight we go back to the apartment."

"I was thinking I might join you after all," Caldicott began, half bravado, half edginess. "Jabba's spooked me good and proper..."

"Too bad, old man," Sandy said firmly. "But you're going to be busy with the police."

"I didn't do anything!" the lawyer declared instantly, sounding for all the world like either a criminal himself or a very naughty little boy.

"I didn't say you did," Sandy said, reaching out a long arm and hailing a taxi. The yellow cab pulled up beside them, and Sandy opened the door. "But you're going to be busy filing a stolen car report."

"Not the MG?"

"The MG," Sandy verified with only a wince of sorrow. "All in a good cause, though. Thanks for the use of the apartment, old boy. See you in court." And he slid in beside Jane, slamming the door in Caldicott's pinched little face.

The real Jimmy the Stoolie watched them disappear into the night, a mournful expression on his face. He stood there for a long time, not moving, until a skinny, ratlike figure scuttled up to him out of the darkening shadows.

"Here's the key, Jimmy," he rasped, dropping it in his outstretched hand. "But boy, that MG needs a tune."

Chapter Twelve

For all Alexander Caldicott's sleaziness, there was no denying he lived well. The taxi dropped them uptown, on East 66th Street, and the uniformed doorman was as elegant as he was discreet, ushering Sandy in with a "Good to see you again, sir" that was the epitome of understated tact.

"You spend a lot of time here?" Jane whispered as they were passed on to an equally circumspect elevator operator.

"More than Caldicott does," Sandy replied innocently. "Half the people who work here think I *am* Alexander Caldicott."

"I'm sure they had a little help in that assumption."

Sandy merely smiled. Sure enough, the elevator operator murmured, "Welcome home, Mr. Caldicott," as they exited the small gilt and walnut cage on the sixth floor. Even in her advanced state of shock and exhaustion Jane didn't miss the passing of paper money.

The apartment had the dry, musty smell of uninhabited places, and Jane stumbled into the elegant foyer with only a tenth of her usual curiosity. She wanted to ask him where Caldicott had been the past few days, but she didn't bother. Instead, she asked the question that was uppermost in her mind.

"Where's the shower?"

"Straight down the hallway. You want some clean clothes? I'm afraid your suitcase was in the MG, but I think I can come up with something."

"Anything," Jane said with a shudder.

"I'll leave something outside the door," he promised. "Though I'll miss the leather bra."

"You try and wear it," she offered, heading toward the bathroom. She stopped halfway down, turning to look at him with the last ounce of curiosity in her weary body. He was standing in the entrance, staring after her, his spiky hair rumpled.

"What is it?" he questioned softly.

"Matteo was bluffing, wasn't he? He didn't really want me?"

Sandy shook his head. "Don't count on it. You were in deep trouble at that moment."

"What if he hadn't given in? Would you have left me?"

The dim light cast eerie shadows on his face, and she remembered the steel in his voice when he'd threatened his lawyer, the danger radiating from him when he'd confronted Jabba. "What do you think?" he asked, not giving an inch.

Jane thought about it. "I think Jabba was lucky he decided to let me go," she said finally, turning back toward the shower.

The sun was rising over the canyons of New York when Jane finally emerged from the shower, her towel-dried hair dripping onto her shoulders, an oversize black sweat suit presumably belonging to Caldicott enveloping her body. At least it didn't smell of that awful cologne. The apartment was huge, with a living room, formal dining room and three bedrooms, each one the size of a studio apartment. She found Sandy in the kitchen, laying out thick sandwiches and imported dark beer.

There must have been two showers in the rambling old place. Sandy's hair was still spiky, though this time it was wet from the shower, and he was wearing faded jeans and nothing more. The jeans were zipped but not snapped, and Jane noticed that somehow in between his bouts of criminality he must have found time to work out. He'd already made it clear he'd never soil his hands with physical labor, so his smoothly muscled chest and shoulders had to come from something slightly more elitist.

"Do you want anything to eat?" he inquired, padding across the tile floor on bare feet.

"I think I just want a bed," she said in a small voice. She backed up as he advanced. She was in no condition to fight off any errant advances, in no condition to fight her own desires. He kept moving closer, and his body was even more beautiful as he drew near, and she wanted to burst into tears.

She did. He stopped within a foot of her, not moving closer, and even without her glasses she could see the skepticism in his face. "Is this part of your act?" he asked. "Or are you really crying this time?"

"You can tell when I'm really upset," she said between choking sobs, "my nose gets red and I get the hiccups." She punctuated that watery statement with a noisy "hic," and her sobs increased.

"Proof enough," he said, crossing the distance between them and pulling her into his arms. She was beyond thinking, beyond caring, and she went willingly, grateful to be enveloped against a strong, warm chest, a soundly beating heart, a male body that had protected her. So many emotions had swept over her during the past few hours that she could no longer summon the energy to fight. The rage and terror, the outrage and determination had vanished with their escape. All that was left was a shimmering desire washing through her, and all her rational, logical doubts vanished. What she wanted tonight was comfort and oblivion, and her partner in crime could provide just that.

She slid her arms around his waist, his skin firm and hot to her touch. She tilted her head up, just slightly, waiting for his mouth to claim hers, for the demand that this time she'd respond to.

His hands threaded through her wet hair, holding her still. She waited for his mouth, but he moved no closer. The tautness of his body told her he wanted her, but still he did nothing about it. Slowly, reluctantly she opened her eyes a crack.

"No," he said gently.

Her eyes flew open the rest of the way. "No, what?"

A small, self-deprecating grin lit his sexy mouth. The mouth she wanted on hers. "No, thank you."

She tried to pull away from him then, but he wasn't about to let her go. "I think I've just about lost my sense of humor, Sandy," she said in a raw voice. "Let me go."

"I don't want to."

"Make up your damned mind!" she said desperately, struggling. It was a waste of energy.

He took her shoulders and shook her, a hard, brief shake. "Listen to me, Jane. I could have you tonight, and you're not so naive that you don't know that's exactly what I want, what I've been working for since the moment you walked in my door and asked me to commit arson for you. And I'm going to have you, sooner or later, and I hope for the sake of my sanity that it's going to be sooner. But not tonight. Not when you're tired and frightened and vulnerable, not when you've been through so much that you'd go to bed with anything that moved just to blot out the last few days. When we make love I want you to know what you're doing, I want you to want me enough to trust me, to look at me, to know that it's me you're making love to and not some faceless soporific. Do you understand?"

He still hadn't released her. His long fingers were biting into her slender shoulders, and the tension running through him put her own anxiety to shame. His mind might have bought what he just said, his body was putting up a hell of a fight.

Still, she'd had enough time to come to her senses. "What makes you so sure it's going to happen? How do you know you aren't blowing your one and only chance?"

"Lady," he said wearily, "I don't sleep around. When I go to bed with someone I do it because she matters, not just to scratch an itch. And I expect my partner to feel the same way. If it's not going to be that way, it's not going to happen."

She stepped back, and this time he let her go. "The last thing I expected from you is a lecture on morals," she said, but there was a faint resurgence of humor in her voice.

"We all have to have some standards," he said, running a weary hand through his wet hair.

He was still impossibly beautiful. And she still wanted that lean, tough body pressed against hers through the long hours of the early morning. But she'd come to her senses, and next time she wouldn't be so vulnerable.

"So where do I sleep?"

"Take your pick. The back bedroom is the quietest, the front one's got the most comfortable bed."

"You've tried them all?"

"I spend a lot of time here."

"How come Caldicott has such a huge apartment that he never uses?" she asked with her last ounce of curiosity.

"It's a condo he inherited from his parents. I guess it's cheaper than a lot of studios."

"So he can afford to run a flop house for con men?" Jane asked.

"If he wants to."

"Why would he want to?"

"Why don't you ask him next time you see him?"

"Am I going to see him again?"

"Jane," he said wearily, "it is five-fifteen in the morning, and we've been through a hell of a night. Stop cross-examining me."

"Just trying to keep you in practice in case we get caught. You sure you won't change your mind?" She was teasing now, in control and marvelously self-assured. He wanted her, he wanted her as much as she wanted him, and yet she was deliciously safe.

"Go to bed, Jane," he growled. "I can always change my mind."

It was tempting, but she'd gotten her second wind. "I'll take the quiet back bedroom. See you in about six hours."

"Eight."

"Six. We have to get to the Jersey shore before dark."

"Six," he groaned. "I should have left you with Jabba."

There were sheets on the narrow bed in the back bedroom. The room was plain and austere—she could see the darker patches on the wallpaper where pictures had once hung. Children's books were piled in haphazard rows in the lateral bookcases, an old orange-and-black Princeton pennant still decorated one wall, and the musty smell was heavy in the air. It took all her strength to pry open the window to let in the cool morning air, and then she dragged her weary body to the little bed and tumbled in. When she woke up she'd think about Richard, about Stephen Tremaine and his nasty double dealings. When she woke up she'd think about Sandy and what in the world she was going to do about her overwhelming attraction to him. For now all she needed was sleep.

SANDY LEANED against the wall and breathed a sigh of relief. It had been a close call. Granted, she'd been in the shower almost half an hour, but the apartment in which he'd been raised was littered with family memorabilia, including silver-framed photographs in almost every room. He'd raced from one end of the apartment to the other, shoving pictures in drawers, under beds, between mattresses. If he'd had any sense at all he would have taken her up on her half offer, carried her to bed and made sure her brain was no longer working well enough to notice anything.

But he couldn't do that to her. He couldn't take advantage of her fear and exhaustion, he couldn't take advantage of the wanting he knew burned beneath her strong defenses, not when those defenses were down. And he couldn't make love to her when he was busy living a lie.

When it came right down to it she might very well be right—it might have been his only chance. But maybe, just maybe, when the manure hit the fan, she'd remember and give him credit for his self-control and forbearance. Or maybe she'd be too mad to think.

He needed a decent night's sleep. He needed to sit Jane down and tell her the truth, no excuses, no more lies, just the facts, ma'am. And while he was at it, he ought to call in the theft of his beloved car. For some reason the recalcitrant MGB had lost its importance in his life. While he regretted its loss, he knew it wasn't a sensible car for a married man.

What the hell was he thinking of? He must be getting punchy. Too little sleep, too much excitement. What he needed was eight hours of solid sleep in his own bed. Jane was only going to allow him six, and that would have to do. Maybe once he told her the truth she'd leave him to sleep forever.

He was sorely tempted to tiptoe down the hallway and check on her. He wanted to watch her sleep, her defenses gone, her face absurdly young and vulnerable. He wanted to take the chance that she might still be awake, that he could forget his peripatetic principles and join her in his narrow boy's bed.

He'd already taken one shower. Maybe another cold one would put a halt to the temptation. Why, he asked himself, did he have to be so damned noble?

SHE SLEPT FITFULLY in the strange bed, and her dreams were bizarre, confused ones, laden with doomed sexuality, pervaded with longing and despair. No one was as he seemed. Jabba kept metamorphosing into his Star Wars counterpart, Sandy and the sleazy Caldicott kept changing persona. Stephen Tremaine wandered in and out of her life, and sometimes he was her father, sometimes himself, always disapproving.

She herself was the most confused, alternating between martyr and avenger, virgin and whore, victim and criminal, until she woke up covered with a cold sweat, blind and terrified.

There was no clock in the room, and Sandy had confiscated her watch along with her glasses. She had no idea what time it was, no idea where Sandy was. All she knew was that she had to find him, had to find the peace and comfort only he could give her. It didn't matter that he'd turned down her tentative offer once—he'd regretted his nobility the moment he gave in to it, and it would take nothing, a glance, a smile, to have him banish his finer instincts.

She didn't care whether it was right or wrong. She didn't care whether she was making the worst mistake of her life. She needed someone, she needed Sandy, and his past no longer mattered. He couldn't have committed any more foolish mistakes than she had in marrying Frank and then relinquishing him so easily.

He'd taken the middle bedroom, but the queen-size bed was empty, the sheets pulled apart, the pillows tossed here and there. She could hear the sound of the shower in the background, and leaning over, she squinted at the digital clock. Nine-thirty—she'd slept a grand total of four hours.

She wondered if Sandy was taking a cold shower. If he was it would be a complete waste. She considered stripping off the black sweat suit and climbing naked into his bed, but she didn't quite have the nerve. Instead, she kept her clothes on, climbed into the bed and pulled the navy-blue sheets around her, awaiting his return.

He was a long time in the shower. She sat there, her nerves getting the better of her, waiting for him. She reached for a magazine from the pile stacked beside the bed. *Princeton Alumni Weekly*, she noticed. What scintillating reading material. She was about to toss it down when she noticed the photograph on the cover. There stood Sandy, surrounded by three very Princetonian looking gentlemen, and her curiosity was aroused. Why would Sandy be posing for the Princeton Alumni Weekly with a bunch of yuppies?

The caption was mistaken, of course, but then, captions often got screwed up. The men on the cover were identified as Gregory MacDougal, '73, Elroy "Max" Sullivan, '72, Alexander "Sandy" Caldicott, '75, and Jonathan Cohen, '77. All partners in the law firm of MacDougal and Sullivan.

She stared at the caption for a long moment, then turned back to the picture. Sandy was wearing the Armani suit she'd seen destroyed the night before.

It wasn't a conscious realization, a mental leap, but more like a sudden clearing in her previously befogged brain. The knowledge was surrounding her like a cold, nasty blanket of truth, and for countless moments she sat in his bed and shook.

He'd left his wallet on the dresser. The picture on his driver's license wasn't flattering, but it was definitely Sandy. The top drawer was jumbled with old photographs of Sandy and a family that looked exactly like him. Pictures of Sandy at Princeton, pictures of Sandy skiing. All the evidence of an elitist life spent far from the bowels of New York and a life of arson and petty crime.

She started hunting for a blunt instrument. Her rage was so total, so overwhelming, that violence came immediately to mind. Never mind her pacifist ideas: right now her fury was so strong that she was ready to kill.

But Alexander "Sandy" Caldicott was still locked safely in the shower. Fond thoughts of *Psycho* danced through her brain, but she dismissed them as calm slowly, painstakingly returned. He'd made a complete and utter fool of her. Like it or not, she was too civilized to kill him. She'd have to settle for revenge.

She stood there in the doorway to his bedroom, a cold, evil calm settling over her, as she listened to the shower end. She waited, prepared, as he stepped into the room, knotting a towel around his waist.

He didn't see her at first. When he did he jumped, startled, and then flashed that beautiful, ingratiating grin. "I couldn't sleep," he said, coming toward her. "Must be the strange bed."

"Must be," she said gently, ignoring his beautiful body that was still glistening from the shower.

"Are you all right?" He bent down, looking into her distant face, his wonderful gray eyes worried.

"Fine," she said. "I'm just anxious to get to Bay Head."

He smiled at her, his head ducked down, and she knew he was going to kiss her again. She considered letting him, but at the last moment she chickened out, backing away from him before his mouth could brush hers. If he actually touched her she might forget her noble resolve and strangle him with her bare hands.

"Can we get coffee on the road?" she murmured.

He looked at her for a long, puzzled moment. "Sure," he said finally. "It'll take me a few moments to get dressed. Think you can wait that long?"

"Oh, I'm very patient when I know what I want," Jane said evenly, visions of Sandy's head on a platter dancing in front of her eyes. "Take your time."

And Sandy, an uneasy light in his eyes, was ready to go in three minutes flat.

Chapter Thirteen

Sandy didn't know how he was going to explain his sudden acquisition of a late-model Audi from the basement garage, but for once Jane wasn't asking any questions. She still had that pinched, peculiar expression on her face, she wouldn't meet his eyes, and the tension vibrating through her slender body was so intense he found his own fists clenching in sympathetic response.

It was an Indian summer Sunday in New York, beautiful, and the city was practically empty. He drove through the park on the way to the tunnel, hungry for a taste of cool green after the heat and squalor of the night before. He'd been hoping to talk Jane into a leisurely brunch at one of his favorite restaurants, but one look at her averted profile and he had abandoned the idea. It was just as well—he was known by name at most places, and he'd already been pushing his luck by taking her home to his apartment.

He was used to thinking on his feet in court, and his experience had served him well when he'd come face-to-face with Hans the elevator operator who'd known him since adolescence. But Jane was a smart lady—it had been sheer luck that she hadn't tumbled onto all the amazing coincidences so far.

It was more than luck. He knew from observing human nature in and out of the courtroom that people saw what they expected to see. Once Jane got it into her head that he was Jimmy the Stoolie it would take a great deal to convince her of anything different. If he were reasonably circumspect he'd be safe.

"Penny for your thoughts," he said as he headed the Audi into the Lincoln Tunnel.

Jane turned slowly to look at him, her eyes unreadable behind the wire-rimmed glasses. "You wouldn't want to know them," she said.

"That bad, eh? I'm glad I'm not Stephen Tremaine. I wouldn't care to have your fury directed at me."

Her smile was cool. "Oh, I'm very rational and civilized. I'm not one to let my emotions overwhelm me."

"And if we find that Stephen Tremaine actually did have your brother killed, what then? Won't your emotions get the better of you? Won't you want your revenge?"

"First things, first," she said, continuing before he could ask her to explain that enigmatic statement. "I haven't been to the Jersey shore in years."

"I don't think it's changed much. It was already built up as much as it could be, and the real estate is worth so much that when things start disintegrating new money comes in and buys the old places up. How come your brother owns a place in Bay Head and you don't? A research scientist, even one at the top of Tremaine's payroll, wouldn't make enough to buy one."

"Especially not one like Richard's," she said, her voice losing some of its tight, strained quality. "It was left to him by an eccentric bachelor uncle. One who hated women. He hadn't been in the place in decades, but he'd had it kept up, and when he died he left it to the one relative who least wanted it. Typical of Uncle Oscar."

"What did Richard do with it?"

"Not much. I gather he'd come down weekends occasionally, when Princeton got too crowded. In fact he came down here the weekend before he died. I hadn't thought it made any difference, but if it really wasn't an accident..." She shuddered, her hands pleating and repleating the khaki shirt Sandy had found in a back closet for her. "I was going to come down here sooner or later, but I knew he'd never cared much for the place so I couldn't believe he would have had his private laboratory here. Maybe I was wrong."

"What are you going to do with the place?"

"I beg your pardon?"

"You inherited it, didn't you? Are you going to sell it?"

"Why?" Jane inquired sweetly. "Were you interested in buying it?"

"I don't make that kind of money with my penny ante schemes."

"Maybe Alexander Caldicott would buy it for you. He seems to be bankrolling everything as it is."

She was looking out into the early-afternoon traffic, so he couldn't see her expression, but her tone of voice had been downright caustic. She couldn't have found out... No, it was impossible. Jane wasn't the kind to take that information quietly. If she found out he'd been lying to her she'd be more likely to rant and rave. Wouldn't she?

"Don't you like Alexander?" he probed gently.

She turned then, her brown eyes limpid and innocent, and he breathed a sigh of relief. Jane wasn't that practiced a dissembler. "Of course I do," she said. "He keeps you out of jail, doesn't he?"

"Does that matter to you? Whether I'm in jail or not?"

"I wouldn't get very far in my life of crime without an experienced crook like you, now would I?"

Something was definitely wrong. Maybe it was as simple as a delayed reaction to last night, or distress about her brother, or concern about the time it was taking to get to the bottom of it. One look at her delicious, thoroughly stubborn lower lip and he knew he wouldn't find out anything more until she was good and ready to tell him.

"I guess not," he said.

Without another word she flicked on the radio, tuned it to Bruce Springsteen, and turned up the volume loud enough to preclude conversation, as they headed toward the New Jersey Turnpike.

THE MAN BESIDE HER was right, the Jersey shore hadn't changed much in the last fifteen or so years. In this transitional off-season, the streets, while not deserted, were more reasonably populated, and there were no signs of urban decay as there were in the inland cities.

Suddenly Jane was transported back to her teenage years, when a bunch of kids would pile into someone's old Beetle and drive to the shore for a day of sunburns and junk food and very little sea water. It had been a wonderful time, spent hidden behind prescription sunglasses, stuffed into a bikini she blushed to remember, playing WNEW-FM too loud and irritating everyone else on the beach. She had very few memories of such innocence—those times had been few and far between during her ordained quest for academic excellence. It wasn't until she flatly announced to her parents that she was refusing Stanford, Harvard, and Princeton in favor of a small liberal arts college in the Midwest that she once more experienced that heady feeling of youthful joy and power.

The old house on the ocean hadn't changed much. Unlike its neighbors, it hadn't been freshened with a new coat of paint, the shingles were streaked and weathered, and weeds were poking out of the cracked walkways. She'd been there once since Richard inherited it, and with him had made the tour of rusty pipes, outdated wiring, cheap furniture and rattan rugs. The house had smelled of boiled cabbage and dead fish, and four years later it smelled the same. There was no apparent sign that Richard had been back in the past few years.

The first thing Jane did was open all the windows. The second was to check that the power and phone were working. The former was, the latter wasn't, but that wouldn't matter for one night. Not unless she murdered the man with her and then wanted to turn herself in.

She couldn't think of him in terms of anything but a pronoun or a four-letter word. It didn't matter that she'd been calling him Sandy, clearly an often-used nickname for Alexander. It didn't matter that she knew him as Caldicott—she still thought of that little weasel as his lawyer, not as his client.

"We're spending the night here?" the creep inquired as he came back down the stairs.

Jane turned off the rusty tap water and turned to face him. "You can go back to your lawyer's apartment if you want," she said sweetly. "I'm staying here."

"I'll stay. Though what you think we'll find is beyond me. It doesn't look as if anyone's been here in years."

"Richard wasn't the type to settle in. He probably just brought a suitcase and ate out. That doesn't mean he wouldn't leave some sort of sign. He left directly for Vermont from here. Chances are we'll find a reason."

"I don't see any sign of a laboratory. Not unless it's hidden behind fake walls or something." He shoved the sleeves of his rugby shirt up to his elbows and peered into the empty refrigerator.

"The wiring hasn't been upgraded. He couldn't have had a lab here. His work requires some sophisticated instruments and a decent power source."

He shut the refrigerator door and leaned against it, staring out the grimy kitchen window at the ramshackle garage. "So we've come to a dead end."

"Not necessarily. That's what comes from being on the other side of the law, Jimmy," she said with just a touch of malice. "You don't have to put your energies into discovering things, you have to put them into keeping from being discovered. It's different when you're the one who's looking. There's trash in the wastepaper baskets, there are papers and envelopes less than two months old in his desk. He left his McDonald's wrappers here—we'll be able to look at it and see whether he was alone or whether there is enough trash for two."

"You do have a devious mind," he said admiringly.

"I'm probably better suited to a life of crime than you are, Jimmy."

"Call me Sandy," he said with a trace of irritation.

"Sandy's too bland and innocuous a name," she replied sweetly. "I prefer to think of you as Jimmy the Stoolie. After last night's encounter I have no doubt at all that beneath that wishy-washy exterior lurks the soul of a completely sleazy liar, but it's easy to forget and think you're a decent, upstanding citizen."

He just stared at her, at a complete loss for words, and she watched him with limpid delight. He couldn't very well insist that he wasn't a rotten liar—after all, he'd gone to a great deal of trouble to convince her that was exactly what he was. He couldn't very well insist what she termed his wishy-washy exterior was the real thing, that bland and innocuous Sandy was his real name. All he could do was glare at her from across the large, old-fashioned kitchen.

"It's always nice to know what my partner in crime thinks of me," he said finally, pushing away from the refrigerator and moving toward her.

Jane eyed him warily. No matter how furious, how outraged and murderous she felt, she couldn't rid herself of the irrational, utterly degrading attraction she still felt for him. "Why don't you go out and find us something to eat," she said, forestalling his steady approach, "and I'll make a start on the trash?"

"That sounds like an offer I can't refuse." He stopped his headlong advance. "Wouldn't you rather go out for dinner?"

"I'd rather get started. The longer we take the greater the chance that Uncle Stephen will find the missing part of the formula first. We've wasted too much time as it is."

He didn't reply to the indirect criticism. "Do you want to make a list?"

"See if you can find a place with take-out fried clams. We'll also need some instant coffee and maybe something for breakfast."

"No instant coffee. We get ground coffee or we go without. I think I'll see if I can find a bottle of Scotch, too. Something tells me it's going to be a cold night."

"It's Indian summer," she pointed out.

"I wasn't talking about the temperature. Anything else?"

Enough rope for you to hang yourself, she thought sweetly. "Anything that strikes your fancy, Jimmy."

"Let's leave it at wishy-washy old Sandy, okay?" he said, his voice just short of a bark. "I'm used to it by now." The door slammed behind him, the Audi screeched out of the driveway, and Jane stood at the kitchen door, trying to fight the burning feeling of anger and tears that had lodged in her chest since early that morning.

"Damn you, Alexander Caldicott," she whispered, trying the name on for size. It suited him, all right. How could she have been so blind and stupid?

She hadn't bothered to mention to him that the house already contained a bottle of Scotch. Her brother's one human weakness in his entire austere life had been a fondness for the best Scotch he could buy, and he could buy the best. There was bound to be a bottle of Cutty Sark or Pinch somewhere around in the dusty old cupboards. And that was exactly what she needed, right then and there.

She found it under the sink, next to the rusty can of Drano. The ice cubes in the freezer were dry and shrunken, the rusty water unappealing, so she poured herself a goodly portion, neat, and stepped out onto the screened-in back porch.

Most of the screens were ripped and shredded, but thankfully the mosquito season was well past. The house sat smack on the beach, and while its stretch of white sand leading down to the churning gray water was ostensibly private property, no one had abided by that edict. Jane noticed the charred remnants of a campfire, several cans and bottles, but nothing that couldn't be cleaned up in a few minutes.

She sank down gingerly on an aging lounge chair, propped her feet up, and took a deep sip of the warm Scotch. Despite the unseasonable warmth of the day a fresh breeze had picked up, and the strong salt scent of high tide teased her senses. The sun was setting, the purples and reds of a brilliant sunset reflecting over the ocean. It never failed to work out that she was on the wrong coast at the wrong time. The only time she'd spent on the Pacific she'd been involved in a seminar that included rising at dawn and being locked away in meetings during sunset. Here she was on the East Coast, finally able to watch nature, and the sun was setting out of sight. And she had no intention whatsoever of being up early enough to see the sun rise.

She had more than enough time to drink her whiskey, watch the tide ebb, and think about the future. She'd have to find Richard's lab on her own, without any help from her so-called partner in crime. Though she was beginning to lose interest in the chase. Richard made his life a monument to high principles, but that didn't mean she had to waste months and months trying to follow in his footsteps. She'd always felt like such a cop-out compared to Richard's high-flown standards, but maybe she'd been too harsh on herself. Maybe it wasn't such a crime to be able to see the other person's point of view, no matter how distasteful it might appear.

She toyed with the notion, as she toyed with the glass of rapidly disappearing whiskey, considering various occasions when she might have been too understanding. While she was an old-fashioned liberal, she understood the fears that drove conservatives. While she enjoyed an occasional whiskey or a glass of wine, she realized the dangers certain people ran in indulging even marginally in such social drugs.

And what about Frank? He'd made a mistake, divorcing his first wife and then marrying Jane on the rebound. He hadn't excused it, or tried to blame anyone else, he'd been terribly sorry about it. Had she been wrong to forgive him? To understand?

Jane drained her whiskey, setting it down on the smeared glass-topped table with a snap. Yes, she'd been wrong. Because she hadn't really forgiven him. She'd kept her hurt and anger and sheer outrage locked inside, tamped down beneath her well-nurtured civility, and it had done nothing but eat away at her.

Damn Frank, damn Richard and damn Alexander Caldicott. Damn all men everywhere. Revenge, sweet revenge was the answer. When she got back to Baraboo she'd see if she could find one of those companies that delivered a cream pie in the face of specified victims. It was the least she could do for the happy couple.

But more important was Sandy Caldicott. She needed him to make as big a fool out of himself as she had of herself. She still hadn't quite figured out how to do it, but she wouldn't sleep until she had. And once she'd gotten rid of him, she could concentrate on finishing her business in Princeton.

Richard didn't deserve her vengeance, but Stephen Tremaine did. Enough of this messing around—tomorrow morning she'd head back to Princeton, alone, buy whatever seemed ultimately inflammable, and torch Technocracies Ltd. If she couldn't stop Tremaine from selling the formula she could certainly make a mess out of his business.

She should get moving and go find some clean sheets, make up a bed. While she wasn't sure she wanted to stay here alone in this big, empty house, she definitely didn't want Sandy around for longer than it took to wreak a considerable amount of havoc.

Embarrassment would do it, she thought, wanting to head for another glass of whiskey but not daring to. She hadn't eaten anything all day and that first glass had hit her like a mallet. She needed to keep her wits about her if she was going to outfox her accomplice.

She was too tired to think of how she was going to do it. She'd simply have to play it by ear. Draw him out into a long, incriminating conversation, and then let him have it. Maybe simply bash him on the head and have done with it. She hadn't been thinking ahead—she'd end up being stranded here without a car. Still, it would be worth it, just to see the look on his face when she calmly, evenly, told him to go to hell.

In the meantime, she'd better get to work. There was a decent amount of old paper trash in the kitchen—she could go back there, dump it on the floor, and begin sifting through it for any sign of where Richard hid the formula. And she could help herself to just a tiny bit more of the whiskey.

IT TOOK SANDY too long to find the only open grocery store, and he had to give up on the Scotch. He'd forgotten it was Sunday, and there were still certain things you couldn't buy on a Sunday. He was getting to the point where he'd kill for a glass of Scotch.

The sun had almost set by the time he pulled the Audi back into the cracked driveway, but as far as he could see no lights had been turned on in the house. He tried to quell the sense of uneasiness that had been plaguing him all day. He'd never had any psychic ability, but all day long he'd been dogged by the feeling that something was very wrong.

He forced himself to move slowly, fetching the groceries from the back seat and walking deliberately toward the kitchen door. He saw her the moment she walked in. She was seated in the middle of the floor, surrounded by garbage. There was a smudge on her cheek, he hated to think of what, her wire-rimmed glasses had slid down her nose, and she was clutching a McDonald's bag in her hand. He could still smell the memory of the onions.

She looked up at him, and for the first time that day her expression wasn't wary, defensive, on edge. In the dim light of the kitchen he could see her cheeks wet with tears, and her mouth trembled with a vain effort at control.

"Stephen really killed him," she said in a broken voice, and without hesitation he crossed the room and sank down beside her, ready to draw her into his arms.

Chapter Fourteen

His arms felt so good around her, his body warm and strong, and for one weak, desperate moment Jane absorbed the comfort, the sheer loving presence that radiated from him. And then she remembered.

She shoved with all her might, sending him backward among the McDonald's wrappers and then scrambled to her feet. Normally she wouldn't have been strong enough to do it, but she took him off his guard. He lay sprawled there, staring up at her, a bemused expression on his too-handsome face.

"I take it you finally figured it out," he said.

If he hadn't said the word "finally" she might have kept her temper under control. That word was like a red flag to a bull, reminding her just what a deluded fool she'd been. All the frustrations of the past few years washed over her in a haze, and she reached for the first thing she could find. It was a tin pitcher that had once held iced tea, and she hurled it at his head.

He dodged, rolling over in the garbage, but she'd already followed it with the bag of groceries and the bottle of Scotch. He struggled to his feet, half laughing, half terrified, as he held his arms up to ward off the barrage.

"Calm down, Jane," he said, backing out of the kitchen. "If you'd just think about it you'd realize it was funny."

"Hilarious," she snarled, flinging a ceramic lamp at his head. "Just a complete riot." Her glasses were slipping down her nose, her hair had come loose, and she felt like an avenging angel.

"Come on, Jane, it wasn't my fault," he said, ducking the lamp and dodging behind a chair. "You were the one who decided I was a criminal."

"You *are* a criminal. You're a cold-hearted, lying, manipulative bastard." She hurled an antique copper fire extinguisher, a copy of *Shakespeare's Complete Plays*, three glass ashtrays and a box of matches. One of the ashtrays connected quite smartly with his forehead, eliciting a yelp of pain, and the matches bounced off his nose.

"Jane, I have been helping, even if I didn't admit who I am," he said. "If you'd just...put that down...listen, you'd realize...ow!" She'd gotten him with a brass hurricane lamp, and he went down into a heap, hidden behind the chair.

She was reaching for the fire poker when the silence penetrated her rage. The house was still. From outside the open windows she could hear the muffled thunder of the surf, the sound of intermittent traffic. But inside, behind the chair, all was silent.

Her sense of horror and remorse was as sudden as it was overwhelming. "Sandy?" she said, her voice weak as she dropped the poker on the ancient, sand-embedded carpet. "Say something," she pleaded. "Curse, moan, anything."

There was no sound, not even the rustle of clothing as he lay out of sight. Her last ounce of mistrust vanished, and she shoved the chair out of her way and sank down beside his prostrate body. His forehead was bleeding, his face was pale, and his taunting, teasing gray eyes were closed. Perhaps forever.

"Damn you," she said desperately, picking up one lifeless hand. "Don't you dare be dead." He didn't move, his eyelids didn't flicker, and as she reached up to touch his face he made no response. His skin felt icy beneath her hot, shaking hands, and she thought back to all the things she'd ever read about head injuries. She should pull back his eyelids and check to see if his pupils were unevenly dilated, she should take his pulse, listen to his heartbeat.

The last seemed the easiest thing to do. She pressed her head against his chest, her hair fanning out around her, and was rewarded with a slightly accelerated thumping. Not too fast to worry about, and it proved he was still alive. She sat back up, missing the hand that was just reaching to touch her, and pulled his inert body into her arms, cradling his bleeding head in her lap.

"Damn it, Sandy, wake up," she moaned. "I didn't mean to kill you. I just wanted to hurt you a little. Please, Sandy, don't die. You can't die! I can't live without you." As stupid as the words sounded, she realized with sudden shock that they were true. She didn't want to live without Alexander the Stoolie Caldicott.

Her dying lover's eyes shot open, his eyes clear and curious. "Why not?" he inquired calmly.

She considered dropping his head back on the hardwood floor, but she had vented her violent rage enough for one night. "I take it you're not dying," she managed with admirable nonchalance.

"Just mortally wounded. Why can't you live without me?"

"Don't you think you're pushing your luck? The iron poker is still in reach." She tried to pull away, but he'd somehow managed to get an arm around her while lying in her lap, and short of actually dumping him back on the floor she had to stay put.

"You're not going to beat me to a bloody pulp, Jane," he said softly. "You can't live without me, remember?"

She stared down at him for a long moment. The room was sinking deeper and deeper into shadows, with only the light from the kitchen illuminating the darkness. A wind had picked up, sweeping through the open windows, bringing the dampness and scent of the ocean around them. "I've already drawn blood," she said, her voice husky as she reached out and touched his forehead with gentle fingertips, bringing them back wet and sticky.

He winced, whether from pain or the sight of blood she couldn't be sure. "Well, then," he said, his voice not much more than a low, sexy growl, "kiss it and make it better."

She thought about it for a moment, then, leaning forward, she kissed his mouth instead, her own lips pressing softly, questioningly against his hard ones. He still felt cool against her fevered skin, and then his mouth opened, his arm slid up around her neck, pulling her down to him, and he was as hot as she was. Suddenly the darkness was all that mattered, the darkness and his body next to hers, his mouth hungry, claiming, this time taking only yes for an answer.

Moments later she was on the floor herself, the scratchy rush matting beneath her back, Sandy Caldicott above her, his body lean and hard and pressing her into the floor. He was no longer a comic-book felon or her partner in crime, he wasn't even a burnt-out yuppie lawyer. He was darkness, powerful, sexual, wiping out the terrors of the night and the anguish of loss and betrayal, he was life and heat and desire, and he was everything she ever needed.

His hands were wondrously, infuriatingly deft, sliding up her leg, beneath the khaki skirt, along the finely muscled line of her leg. Her own hands were far less practiced, pulling at the rugby shirt, ripping the buttons, needing his cooperation to strip it over his head. And then his chest was warm and bare against her, the chest she'd spent far too many moments eyeing with surreptitious longing. He was smooth-skinned, with only a smattering of golden hair in the middle of his chest, and the tactile sensation of his golden flesh beneath her fingertips was unbearably arousing. She whimpered with longing, back in her throat, and he swallowed the sound, his mouth hot and devouring on hers.

While she'd been fumbling with his shirt he'd managed to strip her of her skirt and sweater with such expertise that she'd scarcely been aware of it. When he lifted his head to look down at her with such fierce, heady desire she suddenly realized she was stretched out on a scratchy rug in nothing but her thin scrap of bikini underpants and lacy little bra. All her exposed flesh was tingling with desire, with heat and hunger that she hadn't known she could feel. All the while her heart and soul were longing for him, and her brain was screaming no.

Her mouth was connected to her brain. "I don't want this," she said clearly. "I don't want to feel this way."

For a long moment he didn't move. "If I had any sense of honor or decency I'd back off," he said finally. "But we've already proven that when it comes to you my honor and decency get shot to hell. Too bad if you don't want to feel this way—you do. You want me as much as I want you. And I'm not about to give you time and space to come up with a dozen lame excuses that will keep us both in the state of advanced frustration we've been suffering through for the last few days." He dropped his mouth back onto hers with a brief, savage kiss that left her dazed and breathless. He pulled away, and that look of fierce possession was back on his face.

With one graceful movement he stood up, pulling her with him. She swayed for a moment, hoping to keep out of his arms, but she couldn't fight both him and her own deep-rooted desires. When he swung her up into his arms she went willingly, closing her eyes in dizziness as he headed for the stairs.

"Don't do this," she muttered when he kicked open the bedroom door at the top of the stairs. The house had only twin beds, but it didn't seem to daunt him. He dropped her on the bed, then reached for his belt.

"Give me one good reason, Jane," he said, kicking off his shoes. "Just one."

She didn't bother trying to climb off the bed—he'd stop her and she didn't really want to go. "If you leave me alone I might learn to trust you, respect you."

He unzipped his pants and stripped them off. "Sorry, Jane. Tonight I don't want trust and I don't want respect. I want love."

She tried one last time. "Isn't that a euphemism?"

"Maybe for you, lady. Not for me." He climbed onto the bed beside her, pulling her into his arms.

It was close enough to a declaration on that windswept Indian summer evening. He'd left the door open, and the only light in the cavernous second floor of the old cottage was the fitful shadows bouncing off the water. There was no one to watch, no one to listen, no one to judge. For now, for tonight, she would do what she knew she shouldn't. She would do exactly what she wanted.

His hands slid down her body, beneath the thin bands of her panties, pulling them off and tossing them away from the bed. Her bra came off with equal simplicity, and then she was naked beside him, her long legs sliding, twining with his rougher ones.

She felt as if she'd been running, running, and she didn't know if it was from something or to someone, maybe a little bit of both. She wanted the darkness to close around her, to wipe out the shadows and half-light, she wanted anonymity, to be alone in bed with a man she couldn't even call by name. Alone with a man she shouldn't want, but did.

She kept her eyes tightly closed, savoring the possession of his mouth on hers, savoring the feel of his deft, arousing hands on her body, simply wanting to lie back and be pleasured by someone else who had taken control. It was no longer her responsibility.

He pulled his mouth away from hers, and she waited for its fiery possessiveness to travel down to her aching breasts, waited for the seduction to continue.

It was a long wait. Slowly, reluctantly she opened her eyes and looked up into Sandy's wary gray ones.

"I thought I told you," he said, his voice husky with strain, "that I don't provide sexual Valium and instant forgetfulness. I'm not a dream lover, Jane, here to fulfill your fantasies while you lie back with your eyes closed. This is a game for two players, lady. Ante up."

His fully aroused body was half on top of hers, holding her captive as she tried to pull away. This time he was expecting it, and clearly he had no intention of letting her go.

"Listen, buddy, I don't even want to be here," she said fiercely.

"Liar."

"I don't want you."

"Liar."

She tried to hit him, but he caught her wrist, forcing it down on the mattress and holding it there. "You're the liar," she said in a furious undertone. It didn't help that she was intimately aware of every square inch of flesh pressed against her, it didn't help that her desire, rather than abating in the face of her justifiable outrage, was only growing to unmanageable proportions.

"Maybe," he said. "Who's being honest now?"

The room was very still. She could hear the rumble of the surf, the keening of the wind through the old windows, the pounding of her lover's heart still pressed against her own, the steady, labored breathing of two people beyond the limits of stress. She looked up at him, keeping her own expression carefully blank as she tried to read his soul in the depths of those wicked, lying eyes.

She got the answer she wanted. "Let go of my wrists," she said.

He stared down at her cynically. "So you can hit me again?"

"Let go of my wrists."

He did so after only another moment of hesitation. Once released, she slid her arms around his neck, pulling him down to her, her mouth eager beneath his.

He rolled onto his back, taking her with him, and she was on fire, her hands desperate for the feel of his flesh beneath her, her mouth bold with deep, hurried kisses. He put his mouth on her breasts, and she arched her back like a cat in the intensity of her reaction, he slid his hand between her thighs and she shattered at his first gentle touch.

"Easy," he whispered. "Easy now." But she couldn't, wouldn't slow down. She was shaking all over, covered with a fine film of sweat, shivering and helpless as her needs raged out of control, unable to even say the words to beg him.

She didn't need to. He didn't bother to roll over. Instead he lifted her trembling body astride his, settling her carefully against him so that the heat of him rested at the center of her pulsing desire.

With a moan of fear and anticipation she sank down, guided by his hands on her hips, until he filled her. She let out a muffled cry at the unexpected feel of him, and the hands on her hips held her still, giving her time to accustom herself to his invasion. She bowed her head for a moment, absorbing the impact, and then she opened her eyes to meet his fierce gaze.

"I still don't trust you," she whispered, not giving an inch.

He grinned then, and his fingers dug into her hips as he slowly withdrew. "It doesn't matter." And he arched up, deep within her.

She reached out and caught his shoulders for balance, her hair a tangled curtain around her face. She rocked slightly, reveling in the sense of power it brought her, the way it made her insides clench and vibrate. She tried it again, this time more forcefully, and Sandy reacted, driving into her.

Reaching up, he put his hand behind her neck and brought her mouth down to meet his. His other hand moved between their bodies, touching her, and suddenly everything dissolved, her body, the night, the ocean air, until she was nothing but a shimmering mass of sensation.

From a long distance she felt him tense beneath her, heard the hoarse cry against her mouth, but she was past all conscious thought. She slumped against him in a welter of sweat and tears, unbearably exhausted.

Sometime later she felt his hand brush the hair from her tear-streaked face. She waited in an odd state of nerveless, lethargic tension, for him to say, "I told you so."

He said nothing at all. His hands were impossibly gentle as they moved her to his side, his lips were warm and lingering as they brushed her mouth, her eyelids, her tear-drenched cheeks. His warm, strong body wrapped around hers, tucking her into his shoulder, protecting her. And when she heard the even cadence of his breathing, sure that he had fallen asleep, she finally gave up, nestling against him, and slept, too.

WHEN JANE WOKE UP hours later, she was chilled. Sandy had managed to find a blanket to pull around them on the stripped bed, but the open window blew in a stiff, northerly breeze off the ocean, and Jane knew Indian summer had gone.

It was getting light. There was no clock in sight, and it probably wouldn't have done her much good if there'd been one. Sometime in the debacle of last night she'd been divested of her glasses, and the world was the tiniest bit fuzzy about the edges.

She only wished it could stay that way, but she knew better. Sandy was deeply asleep, protesting only faintly when she carefully slipped out of his arms. His forehead showed a fairly sizable lump beneath his tousled hair and the matted blood, and she stifled her overwhelming guilt. Their relationship had been fraught with danger from the very beginning, it was no wonder that things had escalated to full-scale disaster.

She scooped up her clothes from the floor and crept downstairs, past the debris-littered living room, on into the trashed kitchen. She surveyed the results of her fury with mixed emotions. On the one hand, she was horrified at the destruction she had wrought. On the other, she was gratified that she had finally allowed herself to vent her emotions instead of being so self-controlled.

She picked up the ripped bag of groceries, dumping the melted container of Ben and Jerry's ice cream in the sink, sniffing the heavy cream to make sure it hadn't turned during its sojourn on the chilly floor, finding the French Roast coffee Sandy had bought. Her glasses were sitting on the counter—she had no idea how they got there, but she placed them on her nose with a sigh of relief as the world came into focus. Maybe everything would become clearer.

The porch was chilly when she stepped outside, a cup of strong brewed coffee in one hand, a handful of papers in the other. She opened the sagging screen door and went out onto the beach, digging her bare feet into the sand. The wind was whipping the waves into foaming whitecaps, the day was gray and stormy in the early-dawn light, and it matched her mood. Sinking down on the step, she took a warming sip of coffee, opened the first scrap of paper, and started to reread how Stephen Tremaine attempted, and eventually succeeded, in murdering her brother.

And that was where Sandy found her, two hours later.

Chapter Fifteen

Sandy had pulled on his jeans and a cotton sweater against the early-morning chill, and he'd washed the blood from his forehead, but he still looked half-asleep. Jane could see the coffee steaming from his mug, and she wished she could ask him for a refill. But right then and there she was determined never to ask him for anything again.

Her expression must have made her feelings clear. He skirted the doorway, his face wary, and sank down cross-legged in the sand. The day had warmed up slightly, but the gray mist proved stubborn against the encroaching sun, and the chill in the air had more to do with winter than a balmy autumn.

She waited, tense, for him to say something about last night. Chances were he had a killer of a headache, chances were he wasn't going to let things pass without making some sort of comment.

He took a sip of coffee, and the lines in his brow relaxed a bit beneath the tousled blond hair. "You said something about Stephen Tremaine killing Richard," he said, peering out at the horizon. "What did you mean?"

She was both relieved and miffed. While she wanted last night over and forgotten, a momentary aberration in an otherwise well-regulated life, she wanted it to be her decision, not his. Nevertheless, she couldn't afford to be choosy.

"I went through all the trash. There was a letter from Richard to his lawyer. He must have changed his mind and decided to call him instead of sending it, but he never got the chance."

"What did the letter say?"

"That he didn't trust Tremaine. That there'd already been an accident at Technocracies that was just a bit too coincidental, and that he wouldn't put it past Tremaine to try it again."

"Did he know what Tremaine wanted?"

"Apparently. My brother had a fairly cynical view of the mankind he professed to love so much. If Tremaine was trying to sell the titanium coating process to an unfriendly government, Richard would have found out. And he would have done anything, absolutely anything, to stop him. Richard could be a royal nuisance when he made up his mind about something. Tremaine wouldn't have had any way to stop him, short of murder."

Without a word Sandy leaned over and poured half of his still-steaming cup of coffee into her empty mug. She usually drank it back, while he laced his with cream and sugar, but still she was reluctantly grateful, gulping it down with a muttered "Thanks."

"Show me the letter," he said, finishing off his coffee.

She held up a crumpled, grease-stained piece of paper. "It's taken me a while to decipher it. He said he'd call Bennett, his lawyer, from the house in Vermont. That he was going to be up there to do a little work, and to figure out how to put a spoke in Tremaine's wheels. Which answers our question. The lab must be somewhere on our grandmother's property in Newfield."

"Seems logical," Sandy said.

"But he never made it there. And when I talked to Bennett about Richard's will he said he hadn't heard from him in months. He must have died before he made the phone call."

"Exactly how did Richard die?"

She glanced at him, then looked determinedly out at the rushing waves. For all the danger of her feelings for him, for all the perfidy he'd shown, she still felt pulled with an intensity she could barely fight. "His brakes failed. His car plunged over a cliff in upstate New York and ended up five miles downstream."

"Were the brakes tampered with?"

"I wouldn't take any bets that they weren't. No one bothered to check. At the time it just seemed like a tragic accident. Richard wasn't capable of simple car maintenance. He hadn't registered or inspected his car in more than three years. It was entirely possible that he could have run out of break fluid and never noticed that his brakes were losing power."

"What was the official cause of death?"

"I beg your pardon?" She turned her gaze from the ocean, blinking slightly. He had a red mark under his stubby jaw, a mark that could only have come from her voracious mouth. She stared down at the sand, at two pairs of bare feet.

"On the autopsy," he said patiently. "Was his neck broken? Any chance he was dead before he went over the cliff? We'd have a better chance of pinning something on Tremaine if we could wipe out all possibility of an accident."

"I thought you knew," she said, still staring at their toes.

"Knew what?"

"Richard's body was never found. It had washed away before the car was found."

"Damn," Sandy muttered. "We'll never get an indictment."

She stirred restlessly. "I'm not interested in an indictment—Tremaine would just get off anyway. I hate to tell you, but my plans haven't changed. The fact that you're really a lawyer has nothing to do with this. If I wanted to work with lawyers I would have talked with Bennett. At least I know I can trust him.''

"If your darling Bennett had done his homework he would have known he could have gotten a restraining order to keep Tremaine from selling off the process," Sandy snapped.

"My darling Bennett is one of the finest lawyers in Princeton. He was my parents' lawyer before he worked for Richard, and he's a happily married sixty-seven-year-old grandfather.''

His shoulders relaxed slightly. "That explains it, then. He was too old.''

"He's better than a young shyster like you.''

She was hoping to infuriate him, but instead he merely smiled. "All right, so we don't go about this legally. What are we going to do about it?''

"*We* aren't going to do anything," she said loftily. "I had need of a felon, not a broken-down lawyer.''

"I thought everything worked pretty well last night," he said softly.

Jane could feel the color flood her face. "Forget about last night.''

"Even if I wanted to, I couldn't.''

"It was a mistake, an aberration. It won't happen again," she said in a fierce little voice, glaring at him.

Unmoved by her animosity, he stretched out in the sand and eyed her with nothing more than casual curiosity. "Of course it will, Jane," he said gently. "And you know it as well as I do. Maybe not right away—we've got some things to sort out first. But sooner or later we're going to have a relationship.''

"Sooner or later I'm going to torch my brother's laboratory and head straight back to Baraboo, Wisconsin.''

"We'll see about that."

"We'll see about nothing. I don't want your help, I don't need..."

"Too bad," he interrupted. "You're getting it. I'm too deep in this already, and I'm certainly not going to walk away without knowing the outcome. Besides, if you insist on your illegal schemes, you're going to need a qualified defense attorney by your side."

"You don't really strike me as a model of rectitude. It was your idea to break into Technocracies, wasn't it?"

"It was."

A sudden thought struck her. "What would have happened to you if we got caught?" she asked in a less strident voice.

He shrugged. "It's always possible I could have been disbarred. I imagine I would have gotten off with a reprimand."

"Uncle Stephen would have prosecuted."

"Yes, well that might have made things more difficult," he agreed.

She said nothing for a long moment. "You risked your career because of me?"

"Don't get all sentimental on me," he said with real horror. "I risked my career for the same reason I went along with your mistaken assumption that I was Jimmy the Stoolie. I was bored, miserably, fatally bored. If I'd been caught and it had gone all the way to being disbarred I would have relished the challenge."

"Of course," she said flatly. "It was silly of me to think you might have had any noble motives in mind."

"Jane..."

She rose in one fluid motion. "If you want to go straight back to the city I can find my own way to Princeton."

"I want to go back to Princeton with you, and then I want to drive to Vermont and see if we can find your brother's lab."

"And if I refuse?"

"I can always go to Tremaine and tell him where the lab is."

"You wouldn't."

"I would. If you don't let me go with you you're going to run into a whole mess of trouble. The only way I know to stop you is to tell Tremaine. So take your pick. Him or me."

She stood with her hand on the rusty door handle. "It's a hard choice."

"Not that hard, Jane. Give in gracefully. I'm coming to Vermont with you, whether you like it or not."

"I don't like it," she said. And they both knew she lied.

THE RIDE DOWN to Princeton, while devoid of the simmering, unnamed hostility of the day before, was riddled with sexual tension. He would have thought the previous night's tumultuous encounter would have taken the edge off his desire for her. It only seemed to make it worse.

Jane, however, appeared entirely unmoved by the whole thing. She kept her distance, treating him like one of those beneficial garden insects, the sort of pests you tolerate because they happen to eat slugs, or something. She accepted the fact that he was going to keep tagging along, but the few hours they spent in the darkness upstairs in the old cottage might well have never happened. And she could have carried it off, if she didn't happen to blush occasionally, for no apparent reason. And if she didn't happen to steal small, surreptitious glances in his direction when she thought he wasn't looking.

He knew, for all her year or so of married life, that she wasn't as sexually experienced as he was. He'd known it from her hesitancy, her initial passiveness, her unfeigned surprise at the depth of her own reaction. That surprise had touched him more deeply than he cared to admit. Jane got to him on all sorts of levels, conscious and unconscious, and for all his casual talk about something as trendy as a relationship, he knew he wanted more than that. For the first time he wanted to spend his life discovering all there was to know about someone. He wanted to wake up with her, fight with her, father her children and grow old with her. With a sudden, alarming intensity he knew that he wanted to marry her, and the shock of it kept him silent for most of the drive back to Princeton.

It was going to be rough going for a while. She didn't trust him, and with good reason. She hated lawyers, also with good reason. She was so tied up in knots about her brother and Stephen Tremaine's villainy that she didn't have much to spare for her unwanted suitor. What he needed to do was help her find some sort of resolution to that whole affair, preferably with Tremaine in jail and Jane still relatively law-abiding. Then he could work on regaining her trust and breaking down her prejudices.

In the meantime, the best thing he could do once they got back to the sleazy splendor of the Princeton motel was take a long, cold shower, maybe run a couple of miles, then go for another icy shower. Then maybe he'd be too tired to think about the way Jane shivered when she wrapped her beautiful legs around him.

He shifted uncomfortably in the leather seat of the Audi, and Jane looked at him, fortunately at his face and not at his pants. "Did someone really steal your MGB?" she asked. "I assume it *was* your MGB and not Jimmy's?"

"It was mine, and yes, it was really stolen. I called my secretary and had her file a report on it. Not that I expect to ever see it again," he added mournfully.

"Don't be so sure. Any self-respecting thief would abandon it as soon as it started acting up. Tell the police to look within a couple of blocks of where we parked it."

"Very funny. That car was a classic."

"That car was a disaster." She rolled down her window, letting in some of the crisp autumn air and the recycled exhaust fumes. "You have a secretary?"

"Two, actually." He sounded apologetic, but he couldn't help it.

"Well, Mr. Hot-Shot lawyer, if you're a partner in a major law firm and you're so busy you need two secretaries, what were you doing staying in a dive like the Princeton Pike motel, and how come you can just disappear off the face of the earth and start running around with me? Or do you make a habit of doing things like this?" He could tell by the way her adorable nose wrinkled and the glasses slid down it that she didn't like that notion one tiny bit. A good sign, he thought.

"No, I don't make a habit of doing things like this," he said patiently. "Until I called yesterday they thought I was on vacation in the Canary Islands. I was all set to go once Jimmy's trial was over—I had tickets and my bags were packed."

"How could you be certain the trial would end that day? I thought trials tend to drag on and on. What if you hadn't gotten an acquittal?"

"That was unlikely."

"Okay, Mr. Perfect, why were you at such a sleazy place?"

"For the same reason I went along with your outrageous proposition instead of spending last week sunning myself and having meaningless sex," he snapped. "I told you, I was bored. Burned out, fed up and bored. The trial with Jimmy was just the last straw in a list of cop-outs and compromises and I got sick of it. I was tired of getting slimy little criminals and rotten huge corporations out of the trouble they so richly deserved. I thought for once I could put my energies into something that mattered, helping the underdog.''

"Me being the underdog?" she questioned, but there was a blessed trace of humor in her voice.

"And there was one more overriding reason," he added, knowing he was pushing his luck.

"Dare I ask?"

He wanted to tell her he'd fallen in love with her the first time he saw her. In retrospect it seemed as if he had, but he knew what her reaction would be if he said any such thing. "I took one look at you," he said instead, "and developed a case of advanced lust."

Her expression didn't change. "Well," she said briskly, "you must be well on the road to recovery after last night."

At that point he laughed out loud. "Lady, were we in the same bed? After last night I think it's terminal."

"I'll send flowers."

"No physical therapy?"

"You're on thin ice, Caldicott."

"Yes, ma'am." He subsided, satisfied at having completed his objective. Once more her cheeks were stained red, and she had trouble keeping her gaze from straying toward his face, his hands, and points south. He managed to swallow his grin, but suddenly he felt a great deal more hopeful. "Lovely weather, isn't it?"

Jane looked out at the gray sky. "Just peachy."

THE PRINCETON PIKE Sleep-a-While Motel looked, if possible, even sleazier. The cold gray weather didn't help, and the turquoise paint job that surely dated back to the fifties seemed to be peeling at an even faster rate. While the place had never been fully occupied, it now appeared that they were the only guests registered. Jane, already depressed, sank into a deeper gloom.

"I'm going to take a nap," she said outside her door, backing away from him to try to minimize some of the difference in their heights. She didn't like him towering over her—it made her nervous and far too aware of him.

"Jane, you fell asleep at six-thirty last night, and you must have slept at least until six this morning. Why do you need a nap? Did I tire you out that much?"

"This will only work," she said in a fierce, angry little voice, "if you stop reminding me about last night. I'm not going to sit around having you throw that mistake in my face. It's over and done with. The next time you bring it up will be the last." She didn't know what she could threaten him with, but at that moment she felt capable of restaging her moments of fury from the night before. However, there wasn't anything handy to throw at him, and the sight of his cut forehead still had the power to make her flinch.

He must have thought better about goading her. "Yes, ma'am," he said meekly enough, but she could see the laughter lurking in the back of his gray eyes. She decided she could ignore it for now.

"Maybe I'll go for a drive instead."

"You just went for a two-hour drive."

"That was with you. I find I'm feeling a little claustrophobic." She turned her back on him, heading for her parked car, but his hand reached and caught her arm, the first time he'd touched her since she left the bed.

She yanked her arm free, glaring at him, but he was singularly unmoved. "Listen, sweetie, we're talking about murder here. If Tremaine has any brains at all he'll know you're getting too close to the truth. So I'm not going to let you out of my sight. If you want to go for a drive, I'll drive you."

"I'll drive. You can tag along if you want."

Traffic was still heavy when Jane tore out onto Route One. She stomped on the accelerator, and the rental Escort did its valiant best, inching its way up toward fifty. She sped along the highway, turning off past the Mercer Mall, and the Escort inched up toward sixty. She cast a tentative glance at her reluctant passenger, but he appeared unmoved by her maneuvers. He did have his seat belt on, and his hands were clutching the sides of the seat, but he was keeping his expression calm and serene.

"I bet you're a good poker player," Jane said, pushing the car to sixty-five. The road narrowed, turning by the Delaware Canal, but she'd driven those roads for years and had no doubt that with a light touch of the brakes she could control the curve.

Sandy didn't have the same assurance. "That's a fairly sharp turn up ahead," he said faintly.

"I know." She grinned.

"You might want to slow down a bit."

"I might." She sped a little faster. The road was completely deserted—most cars either took the highways or the more direct shortcuts through the back areas outside of Princeton.

"Damn it, slow down!" Sandy finally snapped.

She was being unforgivably childish, and suddenly she was ashamed of herself. "Yes, sir," she acquiesced, stepping on the brake.

Her foot sank to the floor as the car hurtled forward on the deserted back road.

Chapter Sixteen

"This isn't funny, Jane!" Sandy shouted as they skidded around a gentle curve in the road.

"The brakes are gone!" She tried to shove the automatic transmission into a lower gear and the Escort responded with a shriek of pain and a hideous grinding noise. The road had only a gentle downhill slope, but they were fast approaching a sharp right-hand turn at a speed too high for her to cope with it. She could yank the wheel and hope they'd make it, but the alternative to the narrowing road was a thick forest on either side. Or she could go straight through the flimsy wooden barrier at the end of the road and end up in the Delaware Canal.

Neither choice was appealing, but water was a lot more forgiving than oak trees. "Get ready to jump," she muttered, steering with one hand and reaching for the door with her other.

A moment later they were soaring through the air, through the splintered fence. Jane was out of the car before it hit, landing smack in the middle of the cold brown water.

The car almost made it to the other side. It crashed into the bank, then slowly sank, tail first, into the cold, murky water.

She treaded water for a moment, dazed, scarcely noticing the icy temperature of the old canal. "Sandy?" she called, but the sound came out as only a hoarse croak. She watched in horror as the Escort sank down beneath the surface, only the headlights showing for one brief moment before it settled on its side. She could feel the pull of the suction, and she had to use all her limited strength to keep from being sucked under with it.

"Sandy!" she screamed again, the sound echoing in the sudden stillness that was broken only by the gurgling water. "Sandy!"

The water erupted beside her, and there he was, blessedly intact and mad as blazes. "Thank God you're alive," she sobbed, flinging her arms around his neck. They both sank beneath the cold brown water, only to rise again, sputtering.

With more force than tenderness he detached her clinging arms and pushed her toward shore. "Let's get out of here before we freeze to death." His voice was terse through chattering teeth, and she went obediently enough, scrambling onto the bank from the steep sides with the last ounce of her energy. She fell in the grass, and Sandy collapsed beside her. For a moment there was only the sound of their hoarse, labored breathing, mixing with the wind through the trees overhead. And then the rain began to fall: thick, fat drops of icy precipitation. Jane sat up and sneezed.

Sandy didn't move. He was soaked to the skin, covered with a brown sludge, and Jane knew she didn't look much better. The wind had picked up along with the rain, and if they didn't get warm and dry soon they were both going to die of pneumonia. "Are you just going to lie there?" she demanded with some asperity. "I know it was my fault, I know I was driving too fast. You don't have to ignore me. I admit it. If I hadn't been so furious, if I hadn't come down this back road..."

"You would have been keeping up with traffic on Route One and the first red light you came to you would have smashed into another car, probably killing all of us. That doesn't mean you weren't driving like a bat out of hell, and if you ever do that again I'll wring your neck. But it wasn't your fault." He sat up, shaking the water out of his hair like a large wet dog.

"Whose fault was it?"

He looked at her through the miserable gray drizzle. "Do you have to ask?"

She shut her eyes in horror. "Oh, no," she whispered. "Uncle Stephen."

"You told me he could be ruthless. He probably murdered your brother. It looks as if you're next in line." He rose, reaching a hand down and pulling her up beside him. "Let's get out of this godforsaken rain."

"How?"

"By standing on the road and looking forlorn. Someone's bound to take pity on us sooner or later."

It was a great deal later, fifty-three minutes by Sandy's still functioning Rolex, when a sod truck pulled to a stop. The rain had been steady the entire time, getting colder by the minute, and Jane thought that if another moment passed without getting under cover she'd dive back into the canal.

She sat huddled in the corner of the truck, barely conscious of Sandy's directions, of the effortless stream of pleasant conversation, as if it were afternoon tea and her partner in crime weren't as cold and wet and miserable as she was. When the truck stopped at a rambling split-level on Cherry Hill Road she dutifully climbed out of the cab, following Sandy's drenched figure. It was only when they were standing under the shelter of the front entryway, waiting for someone to answer the doorbell, that she roused herself enough to ask where they were.

"My ex-wife's house," Sandy said cheerfully. "It was the closest place I could think of."

Jane stared at him with complete loathing, wishing he'd stayed in the canal. She was about to tell him so when the heavy walnut door opened and a spectacularly beautiful, enormously pregnant woman appeared.

"Sandy!" she cried, her face glowing with delight as she flung the door open and enveloped her ex-husband in an embrace that showed a complete disregard for his wet muddy clothes and her designer maternity jumpsuit. "What in the world are you doing here, and looking like that?" She pulled him inside, chattering a mile a minute. "And what have you done to that poor woman?" She flung a gorgeous smile at Jane, who tried to resist its charm and found she couldn't. "You never did know how to treat a date."

"This is Jane Dexter." He disentangled himself gracefully as he made the introductions. "My sister-in-law, Margery Caldicott."

Relief swamped Jane. "I thought you were his ex-wife," she blurted, then could have cursed her thoughtless tongue.

Things could only get worse. "I am," Margery said cheerfully.

"Oh," said Jane.

"I think," Sandy said, wrapping a protective arm around Jane's drenched, shivering shoulders, "that my partner in crime needs a very hot shower, a glass of Scotch, and clean dry clothes. We came to you because we knew you were the softest touch in Princeton."

"Not to mention that Peyton would kill you if you came back to town and didn't see us. Partner in crime, eh? Sounds fascinating. We have three showers, lots of clothes, and enough Scotch to float an ocean liner, particularly now when I can't drink. Once you're feeling better you can tell me exactly how you got into whatever mess you're in."

"Later," Sandy promised, leading a benumbed Jane down the hallway with unerring instincts. "Just let me take care of my lady first."

She opened her mouth to protest, then shut it again. Right then and there she didn't have the energy to fight it. For just a short while she wanted to be taken care of, she wanted to be his lady. Later, when she was clean and dry and nicely tipsy, she'd be independent again. For now she wanted to cling.

She took her time in the huge, sybaritic shower. When she got out, there were clean clothes waiting for her, clearly pre-pregnancy clothes of Margery's. The sweatpants bagged around her ankles, the sleeves drooped over her fingers until she pushed them up, but it was warm and soft and dry and wonderfully comfortable.

She found them by their voices, and when she walked into the living room she had to work hard to stifle the sudden, irrational sweep of jealousy that threatened to reduce her to tears. Sandy and his sister-in-law cum ex-wife were sitting on the white leather sofa, looking closer than any divorced couple had the right to look. While they both rose and greeted her with seeming delight, she couldn't help feeling like an intruder in their scene of domestic bliss. She wondered how Sandy's brother would feel.

"So you've run afoul of Stephen Tremaine," Margery said, rising with cumbersome grace and pouring Jane a drink. "I can think of people I'd rather meet on a dark night in an alleyway."

Jane took a huge, warming gulp of her drink, allowing herself a furtive glance at Sandy's bland face. "I told Margery that Tremaine is trying to get hold of one of your late brother's inventions." His voice matched his face.

"Yes, I was sorry to hear about the accident." Margery's gorgeous face rumpled in real sympathy, and Jane gave up trying to hate her. It wasn't her fault she was six feet tall, spectacularly beautiful and pregnant by the man she loved. Not to mention that she had the ability to say no to Sandy, an ability Jane didn't seem to share.

"I told Margery I couldn't really go into detail." Sandy rose, crossed the room and put his hands on Jane's shoulders, pushing her gently into an overstuffed chair. "Drink your whiskey while I see about notifying the police."

She wanted to protest, but the soft leather felt too comfortable, the room too cozy, the drink too warming. "Better call the rental place, too," she said, settling back and pulling her legs underneath her.

Margery sank into the chair beside her, her face thoughtful. She waited until Sandy was out of earshot, waited until they could hear the muffled sound of his voice on the telephone, before she spoke. "He's in love with you."

Jane spilled her whiskey on her borrowed sweat suit. "I beg your pardon?"

"I said Sandy's in love with you," Margery said, sipping her Perrier and lime.

"He told you that?" The possibility was so overwhelming that she didn't even bother to mop up the icy drink that was slowly chilling her thigh.

"Of course not. I'm not even sure he realizes it himself yet, though I suspect he does. Sandy was never slow on the uptake, and he has more than his share of intuition."

Jane began mopping up her thigh. "I'm going to smell like a distillery," she said.

"You don't believe me?"

Jane met Margery's huge blue eyes, disarmed, but fighting it. "In a word, no."

"I know him better than any human being on this earth. Better than his parents, who are too distant and polite to ever ask him a personal question, better than his own brother, who's only open with me, better maybe than he knows himself. He never loved me, even though he felt he should. But he surely loves you."

Jane ignored the latter as only a theory, impossible to prove. "If he didn't love you, why did he marry you?" she asked bluntly, draining her depleted glass of whiskey. If Margery could be outspoken, so could she.

"We were supposed to be the perfect couple," she said with a sigh, looking out the wall of windows into the rainy evening. "We met when he was at Exeter, I was at Concord. We dated through college, we got engaged when he graduated, we got married when he passed his law boards. We love each other very much, but we're not in love with each other and never were, and neither of us noticed that wasn't enough until Peyton moved back from South America. And then I realized that the things I loved in Sandy were the things that made me fall in love with Peyton. Sandy noticed before I did, Peyton was all set to move back to Buenos Aires and I was ready to enter a convent."

"And what happened?"

"Sandy flew to Haiti and got a twenty-four hour divorce, without telling either of us where he was going, without saying a word. And Peyton and I were married six months later, five years ago."

"Happy ever after," Jane murmured. "But what about Sandy?"

"He's looking forward to the birth of his nephew." She patted her swollen tummy.

"And he's had no regrets?"

"No regrets," Margery said. "I won't tell you it didn't hurt. No one likes to admit failure, no one likes it when someone chooses another person over you, even if you didn't want them in the first place. I had moments of feeling miserable because he didn't fight for me. I wanted Peyton, not Sandy, but I wanted him to put up more of a fuss. Ridiculous, isn't it?"

"A little."

Margery's smile was rueful. "I never pretended to have much more than common sense and a certain intuition. And my intuition tells me Sandy's in love with you."

Jane thought longingly of another glass of whiskey, but resisted the temptation to beg. "I think this time you're wrong," she said firmly.

"And, of course, you're in love with him."

Jane stared at her, open-mouthed in shock, just about to wreck whatever amity had sprung up between them, when Sandy strolled back in. "I've called us a taxi. The police will meet us at the motel and get our statements. Margery, thank you for giving us a port in the storm."

"Of course." She rose and waddled over to her former husband. "But what's this about a motel? Why aren't you staying with us?"

"We prefer our independence, but thanks for the offer." He raised a questioning eyebrow at Jane, who rose dutifully enough, still struggling with outrage at Margery's last announcement before Sandy came in the room.

"Where are you staying? Maybe we could have dinner together or something."

"Jane and I are leaving for Vermont tomorrow," Sandy said. "But thanks for the offer. Take care of Junior for me." He patted her belly with an affectionate air, and Jane wanted desperately to slap his hand away.

"Which motel, Sandy?" Margery demanded, undeterred.

"Princeton Pike Sleep-a-While Motel," Jane said, as Sandy shook his head.

"That dive? But why?"

"It has character," Sandy said softly.

"It has anonymity," Jane added.

"Curiouser and curiouser," Margery murmured. "You're sure I can't talk you into staying?"

"Positive," Sandy said.

"And I can't worm any more information out of either of you?"

"Absolutely not," Jane said.

Margery sighed. "Peyton will be sorry he missed you."

"We'll catch up after the baby is born." Sandy was ushering Jane toward the door. In the background she could hear the taxi honking its horn, her bare feet were wet and cold as Sandy thrust her out into the rain.

"Your clothes..." she said to Margery.

"I'll get them next time I see you," Margery said cheerfully. "I'll be closer to fitting back into them by then."

"Bye, Margery," Sandy said, giving her a casual kiss on the cheek.

"Don't dunk Jane in any more canals," she ordered. "Your nephew is going to want cousins."

Jane didn't say a word as they drove through the pouring rain back out toward Route One, and Sandy seemed similarly inclined. They used the Alexander Road route rather than pass the old canal, and Jane could only be grateful. They hadn't even come close to drowning, but for the next few months, even years, she planned to keep her distance from cold dark bodies of water.

She padded barefoot in the rain to her motel-room door while Sandy paid the taxi driver with some soggy paper money. She'd almost managed to shut the door in his face when he reached her, and he had no compunctions whatsoever about forcing it open and thrusting her inside.

"I didn't invite you in here," she said, stalking into the bathroom and grabbing one of the threadbare white towels they replaced every three days to dry her damp, chilly feet. She sat on the bed, knowing she was asking for trouble, not giving a damn.

"I just wanted to get our stories straight." He was uncowed by her hostility. He strolled over to the connecting door and unlocked it. "How much are we going to tell the police? Everything?"

She eyed the door warily, deciding to wait until he left to relock it. "What do you think? You're the lawyer here."

"Yes, but I'm here as your coconspirator, not as your counsel," he pointed out. "I think we should tell them the truth. That your brother died in a similar accident two months ago, that you haven't any idea who could have tampered with your car if indeed it was tampered with. I don't think we need to burden them with our theories and suspicions. They're pretty smart fellows—they can add two and two and come up with four."

"Why shouldn't we tell them our suspicions?"

"For one thing, we could let ourselves in for a charge of libel. For another, there's no way we could head for Vermont tomorrow if they suspect we're involved in attempted murder. Let them work that out for themselves while we're gone. If we have to wait, Tremaine could get the jump on us, and by the time we find the lab the entire place could be cleared out."

"That makes sense." She was very cautious in her agreement.

"Then we'll deal with just the facts, ma'am," he said, heading for the door. "I'll see if I can keep them away from you entirely. They might be satisfied with my statement."

"That would be nice." She yawned, squirming on the bed, and noticed with momentary surprise that she was sore in the oddest places. And then she remembered her activities of the night before, and blushed. "I'm going to take a hot bath and go to bed," she said with studied calm. "That dunk in the canal took a lot out of me."

"Among other things," he murmured, opening the door into the neon-lit night. She could see beyond his shoulder that the rain had finally abated, but the wind had picked up, and there was a northerly tinge to it. He paused, gazing at her, and for the first time she noticed how weary he looked. There were lines between his clear gray eyes, bracketing his sexy mouth, across his broad forehead, and she suddenly realized that his last thirty-six hours hadn't been a piece of cake, either.

Sympathy, however, would get her into nothing but trouble. She scooted up the bed, ending at the pillows. "Good night," she said in a cool, dismissive voice.

Clearly he was in no mood to fight it, and she told herself she was relieved. "One last question," he said. "What did Margery say to you just before I came in?"

If she could feel herself blush before, this time her cheeks grew positively inflamed. She said the first thing that came into her mind. "She asked me if you were still good in bed." The moment the words were out she clapped her hands over her mouth in utter horror.

But Sandy only laughed. "I don't believe a word of it, darling," he said, some of the shadow leaving his eyes. "But if she asked you, what would you have said?"

She could think of a dozen instant responses, all of which were guaranteed to have him close the door and jump on the bed with her. But she had enough self-control, or self-destructiveness, to keep those thoughts to herself. "I'll tell you when we stop Stephen Tremaine."

He shook his head in weary amusement. "I'm too tired to get it out of you tonight, Jane. Tomorrow." The words were both a threat and a promise.

"It'll be a cold day in hell."

Sandy looked out into the windy night. "It might be, at that. Good night, Jane."

She didn't say another word as he slowly closed the door behind him. She waited until she heard him unlocking his own door before she jumped up and double-locked the outside door. Then she went to the connecting door, relocking it and moving the rickety armchair under the handle for extra protection. Not that she thought she had anything to worry about—Sandy wasn't the sort to use force. Not when he had such formidable powers of persuasion.

She heard the voices of the policemen next door while she lay soaking in her hot bath. Apparently Sandy gave them more than enough information—there were no peremptory knocks on her motel room door. She stayed in the tub until the water grew tepid, then pulled on an oversize T-shirt and was heading for the dubious comfort of the motel's best mattress when she heard the connecting door rattle.

She smiled smugly at the chair blocking the doorknob. "Go away," she said. "I'm going to bed."

Sandy's reply was short and graphic, and the door rattled with the force of his shaking it. She decided to ignore him, climbing into bed and turning off the light, prepared to enjoy the sound of his futile struggles.

A second later there was a huge, crashing noise, the chair went flying across the room, the door frame splintered, and the room was flooded with light outlining a very angry man.

"Don't," he said with deceptive calm, "lock the door again."

Jane raised her head off the pillow, matching his even tone. "I don't think that's possible anymore."

"We'll leave at six tomorrow morning. Is that all right with you?" He didn't make any effort to come into the room, and somehow she knew he wouldn't.

"Just dandy," she said. "Am I allowed to close the door?"

"Certainly," he replied with great courtesy. "I'll even do it for you." And without another word he pulled the splintered door closed, shutting out the light.

Jane lay on the sagging mattress, listening to the sounds of her accomplice as he moved about his bedroom. He was whistling softly, apparently well pleased with his brief act of violence.

At least, Jane thought, she wouldn't have Margery's problem. Alexander Caldicott wasn't going to give up without one hell of a fight. And with that thought, Jane fell asleep. Smiling.

Chapter Seventeen

Jane Dexter had to be the most infuriating, pigheaded, cold-hearted, sexless woman in the entire world, Sandy told himself. And then he quickly amended his judgment. Sexless, she wasn't; she'd simply prefer to be. No woman had ever melted in his arms the way she had, had ever turned as hot and demanding, as overwhelmed and overwhelming as she had during that too-short night in the old house in Bay Head.

He wanted her again. He'd wanted her last night when he'd given in to a childish fit of pique and smashed open the connecting door. One word, one sign of softening on her part and they could have spent the night a lot more profitably than he had, alternating between tossing and turning and taking cold showers. But she hadn't exhibited any signs of relenting, and he'd felt like a damned fool smashing through the door like that, and so he'd spent the night in misery. His only consolation was the certain knowledge that she'd had just as wakeful a night. The paper-thin walls carried every creak of the mattress, every weary sigh. He lay there in his bed, staring at the clock, wondering how much longer he could reasonably wait before he could get up. Wondering how much longer it would be till Jane came back to his bed.

He groaned, punching his pillow and rolling over. He was going to have a hell of a time driving four hundred miles on approximately fifteen minutes of sleep. Maybe he could catch just a few more minutes. Maybe he could blot Jane out of his mind long enough so he could get a short nap. He pulled the pillow over his head, nestling his face into the scratchy sheets. If he could just blot out the evocative sound of her mattress creaking, he might have a chance.

THE FIRST COOL GRAY LIGHT of dawn was filtering through the lime-green curtains of the motel room when Jane awoke. She squinted at her watch, moaned, and shut her eyes again. It was 4:45 a.m. Too early to get up, even if they were planning to leave by six. She wouldn't need to pack—everything was still jumbled in her suitcase anyway. All she had to do was stumble through her morning ablutions and climb into that sinfully comfortable Audi. There was nothing to keep her awake.

Except the certainty that Stephen Tremaine, the bluff, avuncular figure from a distant past, had murdered her brother. She still couldn't comprehend, couldn't accept the fact that her brother died from someone else's act of violence. Had he known when the car went over the embankment? Was he afraid of dying?

She shivered, sitting up in bed. Horrible, nightmare thoughts. Richard had never been afraid of anything in his life, not draft boards or the national guard or rural, reactionary sheriffs or dying for a cause. She'd seen him lie down in front of a bulldozer that was trying to raze a building Richard considered a historic monument. She'd known him to walk in front of snarling police dogs, to starve himself down below a hundred pounds, to risk death in numerous ways, and he'd never been frightened. When it came right down to it, he was too self-absorbed to consider himself mortal. When death came he probably reacted with no more than surprise and mild outrage.

She found herself smiling in the darkened bedroom, and a small part of the clutching around her heart eased a bit. For the first time some of her brother's noble, infuriating characteristics seemed to have some side benefits. At least they might have made death easier.

She only wished she were blessed with a similar self-absorption. It was always possible that the brakes on the Escort had failed normally. And it was remotely possible the moon was made of green cheese and the astronauts who landed there didn't happen to notice.

She supposed she ought to be more frightened. If she were alone she would be. But the knowledge that Sandy was beside her, that another living, breathing soul was stuck in the mess along with her, gave her enough courage to face even another case of tampered brakes. If she'd had any plans to sever her relationship with her duplicitous partner, those plans had vanished after their dip in the canal. She needed all the help she could get, and no matter how mad she was, she preferred to have that help from Sandy.

Besides, it was clear Uncle Stephen hadn't the nerve for a direct attack. He could tamper with someone's automobile with impunity, and given his background that was understandable. Stephen Tremaine was a self-made man, and he just happened to have paid his way through undergraduate school by working at a local auto repair shop.

In the past thirty years he'd been involved in too many things for Jane to even contemplate, if she had to guess where the next attack might come from. As far as she knew, after college none of his work had been particularly hands-on. Maybe his murderous expertise was limited to cars. They'd better go over the Audi with a fine-tooth comb.

These thoughts weren't conducive to going back to sleep, she thought, climbing out of bed and pulling back the hideous nylon curtain. The gray-blue light of early dawn bounced off the glaring streetlights, and there was frost on the Audi. Trucks rumbled past on Route One, but the rest of New Jersey was asleep.

She could stay in the room and brood, or she could get her last chance for a little exercise before being cooped up in a car for eight or nine hours, depending on how fast Sandy drove. While she thought jogging was a sign of insanity, she missed her early-morning walks that used to start her day in Baraboo. The parking lot of the motel lacked a certain jungle charm, but it was better than nothing. A little fresh air, even laden with chemicals and exhaust fumes, was better than nothing.

She pulled on Margery's designer sweat suit, which had to be the most comfortable thing she'd worn in years, slipped on her Nikes, tied her long hair back with a scarf, and stepped outside into the early-morning chill. She closed the door behind her, taking a deep breath and watching the ice crystals on the air as she exhaled. Stuffing the keys in her pocket, she stepped out past the silver Audi, onto the pitted tarmac.

Her only warning was the sound of gravel beneath a noiseless tread. An arm snaked around her neck, a hand clamped over her mouth, shutting her scream off before it got past her throat, and something sharp jabbed into her ribs, something that could only be a knife.

She had a faint, panicked hope that it was Sandy trying to scare her. But the solid body behind her was too tall, even for Sandy, the arm across her throat was too thick and burly, the voice rasping in her ear too hoarse and obscene.

"Shut up," he hissed in her ear. "You try to scream, lady, and you'll be dealing with a heart transplant the hard way. Understand?"

She nodded, trying to swallow her terror along with her scream, hoping the pressure of the knife against her ribs would lessen. It didn't.

The man began dragging her back toward the motel, back into the shadows. She wanted to beg him not to hurt her, but his hand was still tight over her mouth, and it took all her concentration to breathe through her nose, to keep calm, to keep from kicking and screaming and crying in sheer, childish terror.

Was he going to rape her? Kill her? Simply rob her? She'd come out without her wallet, with nothing but the keys to her room. Even if she were able to get away from him, she wouldn't be able to unlatch the ancient lock on her door before he caught her again. Maybe she could reason with the man.

She felt the sharp point of the knife leave her rib cage, and she breathed a sigh of relief, only to experience the even greater horror of having the cold, sharp steel pressed up against the fragile underside of her jaw, just above the man's arm.

"That's right, honey. You know I mean business, don't you? Jabba told you about Lenny the Rip, didn't he? But you don't learn too quickly, do you? First your brother's car, then yours, and you still go around asking questions, talking to the police. My employer doesn't like that. He wants you to butt out of his business. You'd like to do that, wouldn't you?" He gave her a rough little shake, and the tip of the knife grazed her skin. "Just nod if you agree."

She didn't have much choice. She nodded, very carefully, so as not to impale herself on the tip of the knife. "So you tell your lawyer friend that you aren't interested in your brother anymore. That he should go on back to New York, and keep out of places in the East Village where he doesn't belong. And you go back to Nebraska or wherever it was you came from, and in a few months a nice fat check will arrive. Now isn't that better than driving a car with crummy brakes? Just nod.''

She nodded, but the knife still bit into the tender skin. "I'm glad we had this little discussion. I'd be more than happy to go into detail, but I think you get my drift. Don't you, honey?''

Once more she nodded, and she felt her body propelled along the walkway, back toward her room. "Reach in your pocket for the keys, lady," he said in that same, hoarsely affable voice. "And unlock your door.''

Her hands were shaking so hard she could barely find the keys. Finding the lock without being able to look for it was even harder, but he was still holding her in that vicelike grip, and when she tried to move her head downward the knife jabbed deeper.

"Come on, lady, you can do it without looking, I know you can. A smart girl like you," he sneered gently.

Getting the key in the lock was only half the battle. The lock was old and rusty and usually required careful handling and just the right amount of jiggling. She wasn't going to stand and jiggle while her backside was pressed up against someone named Lenny the Rip.

Finally the lock gave, and the door opened in front of her. She didn't move, terrified to precipitate something she couldn't fight. Would he follow her in, out of sight of possible witnesses, and make his point more violently and more effectively?

"We're agreed on this, aren't we, lady?" he muttered in her ear. "You're going back to Kansas, right?" He moved his hand a fraction of an inch away from her mouth, ready to slap it down again if she made the wrong sound, and the knife still rested against her throat.

"Right," she said, her voice a thin croak of sound.

"Good," he said cheerfully. And then she felt herself propelled forward, sprawling full-length on the seedy carpet, as the door slammed shut behind them.

She lay without moving, shivering in reaction as she listened to the sound of a car gun its engine and tear away. She heard the slamming of doors, the pounding of footsteps, and then her room was flooded with light from the connecting door, and she was no longer alone.

Sandy was on the floor beside her, pulling her into his arms, his hands gentle, reassuring, as they pushed the hair away from her face. It wasn't until she felt his arms around her that she started crying, great, gasping sobs of reaction and relief.

He held her tightly, murmuring to her, meaningless words of comfort as he stroked her face. She could see streaks of darkness on his hand, and knew with a sort of benumbed horror that it was her blood on his hand. Instead of calming down, she could feel the tension building inside her, bubbling forth into what might very well turn into hysterics, when she heard Sandy's prosaic voice in her ear.

"Thank God he left when he did. I was afraid I might have had to rescue you."

Jane's tears halted abruptly. She stiffened in his arms, pulling back the few inches he'd let her, and stared up into his bland face. "You knew he was attacking me?"

"I could hear every sound you made during the night, every toss and turn. As a matter of fact, I didn't sleep too well, either. When I heard you get up and go outside I decided to join you. I was just getting my clothes on when I heard Lenny grab you."

She just stared at him, her hysterics forgotten. "And you didn't want to step outside without your pants on, is that it?"

"It is cold," he agreed. "But even more important is the fact that Lenny has had a great deal of experience with that nasty knife of his, and I had no weapon at all. Not to mention the fact that he's about half a foot taller than I am and a hundred pounds heavier.''

Jane could feel outrage and loathing bubbling up inside her. "But he could have raped me," she said furiously. "He could have murdered me.''

"Unlikely. Jimmy told me that Lenny's gay. And he charges too much for murders—I don't think Tremaine would be willing to pay that much just for an inconvenience like you.''

His arms were still around her. She whirled out of them, scrambling across the floor out of reach as the words tumbled forth, epithets she hadn't used since she was fourteen and on the tough girls' softball team. "You rotten, degenerate, low-living coward," she snarled. "You self-centered, dishonorable, lily-livered, chicken-hearted pig. You . . .''

"Chicken-hearted pig?" Sandy echoed, unmoved by her fury. "Aren't you getting your metaphors mixed? And I'm not the slightest bit degenerate, as you should know by now. I'm very healthy in my wants and desires. And I may be a coward, but I'm not stupid. It didn't make any sense to make a heroic stand and risk getting myself knifed if there was no need to.''

She could feel the warm, sticky dampness of blood on her neck. "So instead you let me get knifed," she said, her voice very quiet.

"Don't be melodramatic, Jane," Sandy said wearily. "He didn't knife you. Lenny's too smart for that.''

"What's that on your hand, then? Ketchup?''

He froze. He stood up with one swift movement, and turned on the dim bedside light.

If Jane had been surreptitiously proud of her cursing a few moments earlier, it was nothing compared to Sandy. She didn't even have time to duck before he swooped down on her, scooping her up in his arms and heading for the door.

"Put me down, dammit," she demanded, squirming fruitlessly. She hadn't realized Sandy was quite so strong. "Where do you think you're going?"

"I'm taking you to the hospital."

"It's not that bad. He only scratched me." Sandy was fumbling with the lock, and she decided it was time for more forceful action. She didn't want to go to an emergency room and have to answer a lot of unfortunate questions, she wanted to get out of New Jersey.

She rammed her elbow into Sandy's unprotected stomach. He dropped her with a thud, doubling over in pain as he tried to catch his breath. She tried not to feel guilty as she dashed across the shadowy room for the bathroom. "I don't want to go to the hospital," she said as she switched on the fluorescent light and stared at her pale, bloody reflection. "It's not nearly as bad as it looks, and I always hated Princeton Hospital ever since I had my tonsils out." She began daubing at her bloody neck with a wet washcloth, wincing slightly as she cleaned it. There were two long, shallow scratches, and the bleeding had slowed down to a mere trickle.

Sandy pulled himself to his feet, staggered across the room and collapsed on her unmade bed. "You could have said something," he groaned, still clutching his belly like a man in mortal pain. She hadn't elbowed him that hard, she thought, grimacing at his reflection in the mirror.

"I believe I did," she said. "Consider it my thanks for so gallantly coming to my rescue." The bleeding had stopped, and now that the first stages of reaction had passed she was no longer hysterical, she was blazingly mad.

"Sorry," Sandy said, sliding up and propping himself on her pillows. "Next time I'll be more than happy to be virgin sacrifice for your bloodthirsty visitors."

"It's a little late for the virgin part, isn't it?" She came and leaned in the bathroom doorway.

"You should know the answer to that as well as I do." Suddenly he dropped his indolent air. "If I'd known he was hurting you I would have stopped him."

She thought about it for a moment, then shrugged. The gesture was a mistake, causing her to wince in pain, but she did her best to cover her flinching. As usual, nothing escaped Sandy. "If you'd done anything he might very well have killed me," she said. "It's probably just as well you waited. What it lacks in romance it makes up for in common sense. I'd rather be mad and have a tiny scratch on my neck than be lying in Intensive Care right now."

"I guess I can't be your knight in shining armor."

"I wasn't looking for one."

He sat up, looking suddenly cheerful. "True enough. You were looking for a cowardly sleaze. Maybe you didn't do so badly after all."

She looked at him for a long, thoughtful moment. His long, lean body was stretched out on her bed, his hands were still stained with her blood, his face, despite the jaunty grin, showed that he'd been far from untouched by Lenny's attack. Even she wasn't too self-absorbed to see the guilt and worry shadowing his eyes. It was dangerous, but she couldn't resist it.

"Maybe I didn't," she said softly. And quickly closed herself in the bathroom before he could react. "It's getting close to six," she called out, reaching for the bloody washcloth and rinsing it in the sink. "Are you almost ready to leave?"

There was a long silence. "Give me ten minutes," he said finally. And she could hear the connecting door shut quietly.

She stared at her reflection in the mirror. Her brown hair was a witchy mass around her pale face, her eyes were huge and shadowed, her mouth pale and tremulous. Maybe once she put on makeup, wound her hair back in a bun and found her glasses she'd look more normal. But she knew she wouldn't be able to wipe away the truth.

Margery Caldicott was right. Jane was in love with her partner in crime. And all her own common sense, all the common sense in the world couldn't talk her out of it.

THEY WERE ON THE ROAD in fifteen minutes, stopping at McDonald's for a fast-food breakfast and three cups of coffee each before heading up the turnpike. The weather stayed cool and crisp, and Sandy kept the heater on low and the tape player on medium. "You sure you don't want to tell the police?" he asked for the final time as they were heading over the George Washington Bridge.

"Positive," she said sleepily, curled up against the leather-lined door. "They'd only hold us up. We don't know where Stephen is right now, but I bet if he isn't heading for Vermont already, he'll be there soon enough. You pointed it out yourself, we don't have any proof, just suspicions."

"We might be heading into more danger," he felt compelled to point out. Guilt was still riding him hard—every time he saw the long, shallow scratches on Jane's neck his hands would clench around the steering wheel.

"I know," she murmured.

"Aren't you worried?"

"Nope." She gave him a sleepy smile. "You'll keep the bad guys at bay. You've got enough guilt to keep you on your toes for the next ten years."

"It shows that bad, eh?"

"Sure does. And you deserve every rotten pang of it."

"Jane," he said sweetly, "that's what I love about you. Your generous, forgiving nature."

"Drive on, Sandy," she said, closing her eyes again. "And remember, next time you're attacked by Elinor Peabody don't look to me to save you."

"Promises, promises," he muttered. But Jane was already sound asleep.

Chapter Eighteen

The weather, already a bit brisk in New Jersey, turned sharply colder by the time they reached Connecticut. A cold hard drizzle was falling by the Vermont border, and the road grew slick and icy as the sun began to sink.

All the glorious color of Vermont in autumn was long past. The trees were bare, the ground brown and hard, the sky and the mountains bleak and gray. The Audi shook a bit as the wind buffeted it along the deserted highways, and Jane shivered as she thought about her grandmother's old house on the lake.

"I hope you brought some warm clothes," she said, breaking one of the long silences that were surprisingly comfortable.

He turned to look at her. "That sounds ominous. Doesn't your grandmother's heating system work very well?"

"My grandmother's cottage doesn't have a heating system."

"Oh, God."

"Was that a curse or a prayer?"

"A little bit of both. I hope there are motels in Newfield, Vermont."

"Nary a one. Don't worry, though. Nana's cottage has a huge fieldstone fireplace. If we just put our sleeping bags on the floor in front of it we should do all right."

"Sleeping bags?" Sandy's voice was rich with horror. "You're asking me to sleep in a sleeping bag? Inside?"

"Nana's cottage won't feel much like inside this time of year," Jane assured him.

"Small comfort."

"In more ways than one."

"I don't suppose I get to share my sleeping bag?" Sandy asked in a hopeful tone.

"Well," she said doubtfully, "sometimes squirrels get in and make their nests in the house. You could always ask one of them."

"Thanks, I think I'll pass. I presume you can provide the sleeping bags?" He sounded resigned but gloomy.

She thought about the big brass bed up under the eaves, piled high with quilts and handwoven coverlets, and sighed. She had to gather her self-preservation about her, not give in to her baser instincts. "I can provide the sleeping bags."

The snow started some fifteen miles south of Newfield, in the slightly larger town of Hardwick. Jane wasn't surprised. If the weather was going to be bad, it was going to be worse heading out of Hardwick toward Newfield. The steep hill out of the bustling little village was already slick with sleet, and by the time they reached the first dip in the road the sleet had turned into hard white pellets, halfway between snow and ice.

"I'm not crazy about the driving conditions," Sandy said between his teeth. "For heaven's sake, it's still October."

"They often get a first snow by October tenth. I will admit this seems a little intense for this time of year." She peered out through the whirling whiteness. "I suppose we should have checked the weather report before we took off. I'd forgotten how bad things could be."

The Audi's sideways skid immediately gave a perfect demonstration of just how bad things could be. Sandy proved himself more than capable, however, turning into the skid and bringing the car back under control with seemingly no effort at all. The snow was getting thicker, spattering the windshield between each swipe of the wipers, and Sandy slowed their headlong pace.

"Lovely weather," Sandy muttered.

"You're handling it perfectly," she said with only the slightest bit of resentment in her voice.

"I was on the ski team in college. If you like to ski, you get used to driving through new snow. However, I usually had snow tires."

Jane gave him a look of pure, unadulterated horror as they crested another icy hill and began sliding down the other side. Fortunately all Sandy's attention was on the slippery road and not on his companion's sudden lack of confidence. "No snow tires?" she managed in a sickly gasp. The snow was sticking to the roads now, a thin layer of white on top of the icy scum.

"No snow tires," he verified. "Look at it this way, Jane. You wanted adventure."

"I didn't want adventure, I wanted justice. You're the one who was terminally bored."

"Well," said Sandy, as the car began traveling sideways toward the bank on the side of the road, "I'm not bored now." He touched the accelerator, nudged the wheel, and averted disaster once more.

Jane leaned back against the seat and shut her eyes. If she had to die she didn't want to watch. She'd been brave enough for the past seventy-two hours, facing gangsters and near drownings and knife attacks. A snowy drive was suddenly her limit. "Neither am I," she said faintly. "I only wish I were."

NEWFIELD HADN'T CHANGED MUCH in the years since Jane had been there. The snow slackened a bit as they drove into the village, and the light flurries only enhanced its perfect

New England charm. From the white-spired church to the charming general store, from the barn-red mill that had been converted into a gift shop to the rows of perfect white clapboard houses, the place reeked of photo opportunities. The village was shutting down for the night when they drove through at just after five, and they had barely enough time to grab something for dinner before they headed up the road to the old Dexter cottage.

It had been snowing longer in Newfield, probably since early afternoon, and no one had bothered to plow the long, winding drive up to the house. Sandy tried twice, gunning the motor and taking a running start, but even he had to admit defeat. This time he wasn't able to regain control, and the Audi ended up in a shallow ditch, the headlights pointing crazily at the old cottage.

"We're here," Jane said faintly. Sandy only snarled, as the two of them scrambled out of the lopsided Audi and headed up the embankment toward the house.

Even in the fading light Jane could see it, still unchanged after almost seventy-five years. It was the perfect prewar summer cottage, with weathered shingles, porches surrounding three sides, gables and dormers and multipaned windows looking blankly out into the snowy evening. Sandy stood there, ankle-deep in the snow, staring up at the old place, and his expression wasn't encouraging.

"No heat, eh?" he said gloomily.

"The sooner we get a fire going the sooner we'll be warm." She sounded disgustingly hearty, even to her own ears, as she trudged up the broad front steps. She stopped for a moment, looking down. For an instant it had looked as if someone had walked up those steps before the snow had gotten so deep. She thought she could see the faint trace of a man's boots beneath the fresh layer of snow. She peered down, but she couldn't be certain. It was probably just Ephraim, checking the empty summer cottages as he'd been hired to do. If anyone had come up to the old house, they were certainly long gone.

It was about thirty degrees in the autumn night air. It was about twenty in the house, the high ceilings and curtainless windows keeping the air icy. Sandy dumped his suitcase on the floor and headed straight for the fireplace as Jane went around turning on lights. At least someone had left a fresh supply of wood and kindling. She listened to Sandy curse, a low, steady stream of profanity beneath his breath, as she wandered through the old place, turning on lights and looking back over her past.

She hadn't been there in three years, not since Sally had brought her kids back East for a stilted summer reunion. Things had been too hectic then, chasing around after Sally's hellions, dealing with Richard's absentmindedness, all the while trying to use her time away from Baraboo to make up her mind whether she should marry Frank or not. No wonder she'd made the wrong decision.

Richard's idea of a family reunion was to sit in the old Morris chair, smoking his pipe and telling everyone to be quiet. Sally's idea was to dump the kids on Jane and go off to visit with her childhood friends. And Jane's idea was to do all the cooking, all the cleaning, all the child-care, and then simply walk out halfway through the allotted vacation time.

She hadn't seen Richard since, though she'd spoken to him on the phone. Suddenly she missed him, missed him terribly. She could almost picture him sitting in that chair, scowling at everyone over his thick glasses. She could practically smell the rich, pungent smell of his pipe tobacco lingering in the chilly air.

By the time she finished her tour of the house and returned to the cavernous living room, laden with sleeping bags and pillows, Sandy had managed to start a decent fire. The heat penetrated a few feet into the icy vastness of the room, and her accomplice looked well pleased with himself.

He looked up at her, and the flickering firelight danced across his face. "Why don't we use the electric space heater? It's going to take a long time for this fireplace to warm the room."

"We don't have any electric heaters. The wiring's too old to take it. We were going to upgrade it but we never got around to it. The three of us inherited the place equally, and no one's got enough of a stake in it to make any sort of push."

Sandy rose, stretching his limber body. "Then what's that in the corner?"

Jane stared. "An electric heater," she said, suddenly uneasy.

"Looks like there are some new outlets, too. Want to risk it?" Sandy had already crossed the room and picked up the portable baseboard heater.

Jane shivered, but whether it was from the cold or something else she wasn't sure. "All right," she said, concentrating on unpacking the groceries.

"What's wrong?"

She shook her head. "I'm not sure. That heater shouldn't be here, for one thing. For another, I thought there were footprints on the front steps. The refrigerator is on, when the last person here would have been sure to turn it off. And I have the oddest feeling that someone's been here."

"Tremaine?"

She shrugged. "I guess so. Who else would come up here without saying anything? Except that I can't imagine Uncle Stephen hiding out in any place as cold and uncomfortable as this. He'd be staying in a first-class motel in Stowe, not lurking in a deserted summer cottage."

"Do me a favor, Jane," Sandy said suddenly, his voice tight with tension. "This man is apparently a conscienceless murderer, a man who not only killed your brother but has done his best to kill or terrorize you. For God's sake stop calling him Uncle Stephen!''

"Excuse me," Jane said stiffly, pressing a hand against her throbbing neck.

"And stop doing that!" Sandy snapped.

"Doing what?"

"Rubbing your neck. I feel guilty enough—you don't have to remind me."

"I hate to tell you this, Alexander 'the Sleaze' Caldicott, but I'm not doing it to make you feel guilty. All my actions are not motivated by how you're going to react. My neck happens to sting!"

Sandy's mouth compressed in a thin, angry line that still managed to be sexy. "Are we going to spend our entire time arguing?"

"Probably."

He glared at her for another long moment. And then a slow, reluctant smile started, first in his gray eyes, then traveling to his mouth, relaxing that tight, tense line. "Well, I guess I'd rather fight with you than be peaceful with anyone else."

"Anyone else?" She was momentarily disarmed, a danger she recognized and decided to ignore.

"Anyone else. What's for dinner?"

"Steak and baked potatoes and salad. Except that I don't want to go out to the kitchen and make it. It's too cold."

"We can cook the steak over the fire if you have a grill. And we can roast the potatoes in the ashes. I'm afraid one of us will have to freeze to make the salad." His smile was just a bit too ingenuous.

Jane sighed. "You know no woman in her right mind likes to cook over a fire. We had too much of it five million years ago. I'll make the salad."

"I don't suppose this house comes with a liquor supply?"

Jane smiled sweetly. "Treat me nice and maybe I'll break it out. I like my steak practically raw."

"Savage," he muttered. "I like my Scotch practically straight."

"Yes, sir."

By the time she came back into the living room with a hastily tossed-together salad, two glasses and a half-empty bottle of Johnny Walker Red she was shivering, chilled to the bone. The living room was redolent of broiling steak and wood smoke, and the heat had finally penetrated even the chilliest corners of the room.

Sandy had spread the sleeping bags out on the floor, one on top of the other, and Jane contented herself with a skeptical glance before seating herself cross-legged on them. It certainly wasn't the softest surface she ever hoped to sleep on, and once she made Sandy take his sleeping bag and move a decent distance away it was going to be even harder. She allowed herself a moment of delicious indecision, and then hardened her heart. She couldn't afford to get any closer to him than she already had, not until she decided she could trust him, not until she had some sign, other than his ex-wife's fantasy, that he was involved with her for any other reason than to alleviate boredom.

She had to make one more icy dash into the kitchen for plates and silverware, but the steak was well worth it. Sandy had managed to simply sear it on one end and cook it to his own tastes on the other, a talent Jane properly appreciated. The potatoes were a little uneven, but absolutely delicious with Vermont butter, and the Scotch, without ice and only a trace of water, did a great deal toward advancing the truce.

"Where are we going to look for the lab?" Sandy said once they were finished and the dirty dishes stuffed unhygienically and aesthetically under the sofa until tomorrow. "I presume it's not in the house?"

"I checked when we got here. Not that I thought he'd bother. This place is impossible to heat when it gets much colder. The lab could be any one of a number of places. There's a boathouse down by the lake, a garage, a couple of hay barns, even an old icehouse out back by the pond. We'll just have to check them out one by one." She reached up to touch her stinging neck, then caught his eyes watching her hand and instead pushed her hair away from her face.

He said nothing. He was stretched out on the sleeping bags, his second glass of Scotch in his hand, and his eyes were hooded, watchful. He was wearing faded jeans which clung to his long legs, and he'd dispensed with his sweater an hour ago. His navy blue corduroy shirt looked worn and soft to touch, and she had to remind herself that she shouldn't touch, didn't dare to touch.

"There's some long winter underwear upstairs in one of the drawers," she said, knowing she was babbling slightly. "Even in the summer Vermont can get cold enough to need them. We can put them on tomorrow before we go out looking." She'd taken off her own sweater and unbuttoned her cotton knit shirt, pulling it away from her sore neck.

"All right." His voice was deep, slumberous, almost erotically soothing.

Fight it, Jane, she ordered herself. *Fight it.* "I tend to think he would have chosen one of the hay barns," she said, reaching for her neck again. It was stinging, and a cold wet washcloth would have felt wonderful, but she didn't want to call attention to it. She no longer wanted Sandy to feel guilty. She didn't know what she wanted.

She dropped her hand on the sleeping bag between them, staring down at it. There was no mark where her wedding ring had rested, no sign of that tumultuous, painful period in her life. No sign either that she'd used that hand to fling things at the man lying so close to her. His forehead still bore the mark of the few times she'd connected, and then it was her turn to feel guilty. She'd almost gotten him killed in the canal—if it weren't for her he'd be safely away in the Canary Islands or wherever he'd been planning to go.

And if Lenny the Rip found out she ignored his warning, ignored the warning lightly etched on her neck, he might very well follow them and make his point a little clearer. And if Sandy got in the way this time...

She shivered. "Maybe you should go back to New York," she said abruptly. "I can rent a car, take over from here."

She could feel the sudden tension in his body. "I thought you forgave me for not coming to your rescue."

"It's not that." Her voice sounded desperate. "I don't want to be responsible for your getting hurt. Getting killed." She tugged at her shirt, pulling it up around her stinging neck.

He reached out and stopped her hand, pulling it away. "No one's going to kill me," he said. "No one's going to kill you, either. And if anyone lays a hand on you again I'm going to be the one who does the killing."

She lay perfectly motionless, staring into his eyes, and she knew he was absolutely serious. And she knew he would do just that.

"In the meantime," he continued, his voice low and beguiling, "we need to see about your battle scars. You've been tugging at your collar all day." His hand, deft and strong and warm, reached into her shirt.

"I'm fine." She tried to push him away, but he was too fast for her, capturing her combative hand in his while he pushed her back on the sleeping bags.

"We can turn this into a wrestling match," he said, leaning over her, a glint of laughter in his eyes, "and you know I'd prefer that. Or you can humor me. I should have insisted you go to the hospital this morning, but I'm sure we could still find one..."

"Thirty miles away," she said. "All right, you can check it out. I hate to admit it, but it stings like crazy."

She tried to look anywhere but into his face as he leaned over her, pushing her shirt back over her shoulders to expose the long scratches on her throat. She heard his swift intake of breath, and she tried to sit up. He simply pushed her back down.

"What is it?" she demanded. "Why did you make that sound? Does it look infected?"

"Don't be such a sissy. I wasn't reacting to your neck," he said calmly, and belatedly Jane realized that the bra she was wearing, now fully exposed to his interested gaze, consisted of not much more than two triangles of white lace.

She tried to pull her shirt back around her, but he pushed her hands out of the way. "Stop leering," she said grumpily, giving up the fight.

"I'm not leering. I'm just being properly appreciative. Your neck does look painful. What did you put on it?"

"Earlier? Just water."

"I think it needs some disinfectant." He sat up and reached for the bottle of Scotch. "This is the best I can do at the moment. Relax, Jane. This will hurt you more than it does me." He poured a generous amount on the dish towel Jane had found to serve as a napkin and pressed it gently to the side of her neck.

She let out a loud, piercing scream, more of surprise than actual pain. The sting of the whiskey wasn't much worse than the scratches themselves had been, and she'd barely noticed when they'd been inflicted.

"It's not that bad," Sandy muttered, pouring a little more Scotch onto the dish towel as he held it against her skin. The cold whiskey trickled down her neck, sliding over her shoulder and down between her breasts. "Now who's being a coward?"

She took a deep intake of breath as the burning liquid slid over her flesh, and from her supine position she looked up at him, into his hooded eyes. "I am," she said, her voice husky, and they both knew she wasn't talking about the pain.

For a long moment he didn't move. The flickering fire-light danced across his face, and the hiss and pop of the burning pine was the only sound in the huge room. Then he leaned forward, his voice low and husky, his breath warm and sweet on her skin. "It would be a sin to waste good Scotch, don't you think?" he whispered, moving the saturated cloth away. And he kissed her neck, his lips feather soft, and his tongue snaked out to taste the trickle of whiskey along the slender white column of her neck.

Chapter Nineteen

Jane lifted her hands to his shoulders, to push him away. Instead her fingers dug into the faded corduroy, feeling the bone and muscle and sinew beneath, and she was lost. Lost as she'd been since the night in Bay Head, lost as she'd been since she first got up enough nerve to knock on a stranger's door and ask him to commit arson with her.

His tongue slid across her jaw, down her chest, to the vee between her breasts, tickling her, sipping at the spilled whiskey. Her shirt was spread around her, and suddenly the front clasp of her bra was free. Some small part of sanity, of self-preservation, reared its ugly head, and she said in her most prosaic voice, "Are you really going to do this?"

If the result came out sounding rather breathless, it was only to be expected, since his tongue had abandoned the quest for spilled Scotch and was now concentrating on the tightly budded nipple beneath his mouth.

He raised his head for a moment, his eyes gleaming darkly in the firelight. "Yes," he said. "Unless you have any objections?"

She had a thousand, but right now she couldn't bring a single one to mind. She was lying on her back in her grandparents' living room, about to be seduced in the same room where she'd once played jacks. The sleeping bags beneath her had seen many a teenage slumber party—she should feel hopelessly decadent.

What she felt was hopelessly in love. "No objection, counselor," she said. And then he kissed her.

Her arms slid around his neck, pulling him down to her, and her mouth opened beneath his, sweetly, generously, kissing him back with all the passionate enthusiasm she had in her. His mouth slanted across hers, nibbling, teasing, and she could taste the whiskey, the saltiness of her skin, on his tongue. She kissed him back, reveling in her sudden freedom, reveling in the dizzying wonder of it, so caught up with the mingling of their mouths that she was scarcely aware of his deft hands on her zipper, unfastening her jeans and sliding them down over her hips. He broke the kiss for a moment, long enough to toss the jeans into a corner, and then just as quickly divested her of her shirt and bra, with the same deft grace.

His eyes were dark with desire, and there was an expression of almost smug possession on his face as he sat back to unbutton his shirt. It was an expression she knew she should hate, and yet somehow she found it deeply flattering. The shirt joined her clothes in a pile, followed by his jeans, and his flesh was gilded by the firelight, a golden bronze color glowing with heat and desire. He sank down beside her, taking her willing hands in his and pressing them against his smoothly muscled chest, and the tips of her fingers caressed him, absorbing the feel of him.

"You aren't going to change your mind?" he asked, his voice a husky rasp. "I don't think I could stand it if you changed your mind."

"You could always change it back for me," she said, her hands drifting along his torso, the smooth, sleek hide of him.

"I don't want to do that. I want you to want me." He wasn't touching her now, instead he was letting her touch him, letting her fingertips dance over his gilded flesh, explore the smooth muscles, the trace of hair, the ribs, drifting downward with inexorable purpose.

She touched him, the hard, wanting part of him, and listened with sensuous gratification to his sharp intake of breath. "I want you," she said, using the same delicate, arousing touch on that most sensitive part of him. "I never said I didn't. I just thought I shouldn't."

"Why?" he groaned.

She shook her head. "I can't remember. Maybe it will come to me."

"Don't," he whispered. "Don't remember. Just feel." He reached for her, his hands strong and certain, cupping her full breasts, holding them, arousing them as he brought his mouth back.

She released him, reluctantly, sinking back on the sleeping bag and arching her back with a moan of pleasure. She didn't know when she'd had such a barrage of delight assaulting her senses. The heat from the fire, the smell of wood smoke and whiskey, the flickering firelight and the softness of the old flannel sleeping bag beneath her, all combined to make her feel almost drunk with sensation. She opened her eyes to look over Sandy's golden head, and outside the frosty window she could see snow swirling down. She closed her eyes again, feeling safe and warm in Sandy's arms.

Except that safety and comfort were fast disappearing beneath his practiced mouth. Her breasts felt swollen, burning against his mouth as he suckled them, giving each lingering, devouring attention. His hand slid between her thighs, touching the heated center of her, and she whimpered slightly in the back of her throat, a sound of longing and instinctive wariness. She reached out a hand to stop him, to slow him down, to hurry him up, but he ignored it, sliding his mouth down her body, glancing off her flat stomach, down to the juncture of her thighs.

"Sandy!" she gasped, trying to jackknife up in sudden panic, but he simply pushed her back down on the padded floor, his hands cradling her hips.

"Objection noted and overruled," he murmured, and his mouth found her.

She shivered in helpless delight, reaching down to push at his shoulders. Instead her nails dug in as she writhed beneath his practiced mouth, afraid to let go. Her body felt coated with a sheet of burning ice, her heart was pounding so hard and fast she thought it would explode from her chest, and all she knew was his mouth on her, his tongue, and a delight she wanted to fight and then suddenly no longer could, as wave after wave of sensation smashed over her.

Vaguely she could hear her voice, sobbing in helpless reaction. She could see him move up and cover her, sliding into her with a deep, sure, hard thrust that sent her spiraling out of control. The ice had melted, they were both covered with a film of sweat, and through the dizzying firelight she thought she could see their bodies, locked together in an undulating dance of love.

He reached down and held her hips, striving with unquestionable intent, and his mouth covered hers, his tongue in her mouth, a dual invasion. She was crying, she knew she was, she could feel her face wet with tears, but all she could feel was the man within her body, carrying her places she hadn't even dreamed existed.

Suddenly his body tensed, and he lifted his head, his eyes glittering down into hers with a fierce intensity. She could feel the life, the love pumping into her, and then everything shattered around her, dissolving into a maelstrom of sensation and dark, dangerous release.

It went on forever, wave after wave of delight wringing a convulsive reaction from her exhausted body. Her mind had long ago stopped working, and for a moment she could feel herself slipping into some sort of alternative reality, a place of infinite rest. The last bit of tension left her body, and she sank back, floating for a bit, entirely at peace.

The pop and crackle of the fire brought her awake. Her eyes shot open, and she knew why she felt so warm and so lethargic. Sandy's one hundred and eighty-some pounds were still stretched across her like a deadweight.

He must have felt her stir, for suddenly his muscles tightened, and he lifted his head from its place on her shoulder and looked down at her.

She waited for him to say something, but he just looked at her, an odd, indecipherable expression on his face. She could feel the dried tears on her face, and her body still thrummed with latent tremors. She might as well end these games, she thought briefly. There was no way he couldn't know.

"Did I just die and go to heaven?" she whispered in a hoarse voice. "Or did I just faint?"

She managed to get a small, wary smile from him. "I'm not sure," he said. "I was on cloud nine myself. Weren't you with me?"

"Oh, is that where we were? I wasn't sure," she murmured lazily. He was still looking very serious, whereas she felt positively buoyant. She resisted the urge to tickle him, but just barely. Instead she brought her hands up over his back, stroking his still-damp skin.

His shiver of reaction brought a small, secret smile to her face. "Be careful," he warned, not moving. "The next time might just kill us."

She kept stroking, moving her sensitive fingertips down his sides. "It might be worth it."

His hands reached up and cupped her face, holding her still. "We have plenty of time."

"Do we?"

"We have the rest of our lives."

"Do we?" She held her breath, waiting. She wasn't sure for what. Not something as formal as a proposal. She wanted a promise, a commitment.

But Sandy only moved to lie beside her, and while the loss of his body heat and weight should have been a relief, she felt cold and lonely and bereft.

"Yes," he said, drawing her into the shelter of his arms.

For a moment she wanted to fight, but she was too weary, to sated to hold out for what she still needed. "Yes," would have to be good enough. For now.

WHEN SHE AWOKE she was very, very cold. Sometime during the night Sandy had managed to wrap one of the sleeping bags around them, and he must have stoked the fire at least once, but now, as an eerie gray-white dawn crept through the windows the coals were an orange-red memory and Jane could see her breath.

She was also naked beneath the sleeping bag, and even Sandy's strong, warm body wasn't enough to keep the chill at bay. She slid out from under the covers, but her accomplice, her lover, she reminded herself, didn't stir. Scrambling across the room, it took her too long to find all her clothes. She settled for his sweater since he'd ended up using hers as an extra pillow, and she stuck her bare feet in his shoes as she headed for the great outdoors and the use of nature's plumbing since the cottage water had been turned off for the winter.

The moment she stepped out onto the broad front porch she realized why the light was strange. It was just after dawn, and the entire world, or at least Newfield, Vermont, was covered with almost a foot of freshly fallen snow.

She stopped, daunted. "For crying out loud," she said, her voice loud in the hushed stillness, "it's only October!"

Not even the birds were awake. In the distance she could see wood smoke rising from some of the village houses and from the farms lying on the outer edges of the hills. They needed a little wood smoke of their own, she thought, biting her lip and trudging out into the snow for the convenient patch of woods. Not to mention some water for washing—maybe if she could wash away the remnants of last night she might be able to rid herself of her sudden vulnerability.

Sandy was blessed with the gift of heavy sleep. He barely stirred when she came back in and stoked the fire into a roaring inferno that threatened the safety of the old fieldstone chimney. He only turned over and began snoring as she came back in with two buckets of lake water and began heating them. It wasn't until she'd managed to wash, change into fresh clothes, and was just beginning to think about breakfast when his hand snagged her ankle as she tiptoed by, and he pulled her down on top of him.

"Don't give me that look, partner," Sandy muttered, flipping her on her back and looming over her.

"What look?"

"That wary, I-don't-know-what-I'm-going-to-do-with-you-but-I-know-it-won't-be-much kind of look," he said.

She thought about it for a moment. "All right," she said, reaching up and pulling his face down to hers. "I won't." And she kissed him, full on the mouth, a slow, lingering good-morning kiss that had him flipping up the edge of the sleeping bag and trying to pull her back in.

She escaped, rolling out of his reach before he had time to react. "You slept too late. And unless you want to spend another night in this icebox you'd better get dressed. It's going to take some time to find Richard's lab, and a fair amount of time to burn it."

"I wouldn't mind spending another night here," he said quietly, sitting up and scratching his shaggy head. "If we could spend it the same way."

"I don't know if I'd survive another night like the last one," she said, busying herself with the fire, afraid to look at him.

She didn't hear him move, didn't know he was behind her until she felt herself caught and turned, wrapped in his arms. "But what a way to go," he whispered against her mouth.

It was sorely tempting. He wasn't wearing any clothes, of course, and even without her glasses she could see how much he wanted her. There was nothing she wanted more than to sink back onto the pile of sleeping bags with him and wait for the snow to melt, but she couldn't. She had to pay her debt to her brother, and for now her own considerable desires would have to wait.

Of course, she'd already plastered herself against his body and kissed him back with mindless enthusiasm. And she wasn't saying a word as he was lowering her back onto the floor. Maybe family debts could wait a few hours, she thought. Maybe everything unimportant could wait a few hours. Maybe all that really mattered was Sandy.

SHE MANAGED TO FIND a half-frozen bottle of Deer Park water in the kitchen, so they were able to have coffee. Sandy had to make an extra trip to the lake for more wash water, and it took him far too long to find the dishes they'd stashed under the sofa. The sleeping bag was a mess, and Jane considered tossing it out, then changed her mind. When it was over, when she came back here alone, maybe she'd wrap herself up in it and remember. She didn't have much faith in happily ever after.

The snow was melting to a freezing slush when they were finally ready to start their quest. In the light of day the Audi proved to be only slightly mired, and it took a push from Jane and clever driving from Sandy to get it back on the narrow driveway.

"Where to now?" Sandy asked, climbing out of the car and wincing as his soaked running shoes settled into the snow.

"We look for the lab. We can start with the boathouse. I didn't see anything interesting when I went down to get water but I didn't look all that carefully. Then we'll head for the hay barns. Once the store opens we can get you a decent pair of boots and some kerosene."

"Jane, we're not going to burn the laboratory unless we have to."

"We have to," she said flatly, heading toward the lake. Her own boots were only ankle high, and the snow had already soaked them, but she was determined to ignore physical discomfort. She had already paid far too much attention to physical pleasure in the past twelve hours.

"Jane, arson is a crime." He headed after her through the snow, cursing under his breath.

"So I'll get a fire permit."

"No one's going to give you a fire permit on such short notice. Not to burn an existing structure," he argued.

"Then I guess I'll just have to break the law."

"Jane, as your lawyer I have to tell you—"

She stopped, whirling around in the snow, and he almost barreled into her. "You're not my lawyer, Sandy," she said with great reasonableness. "You're my partner in crime. If you don't want to aid and abet this particular endeavor, go back to the cottage."

He looked at her for a moment, and then he sighed. The cool crisp air brightened his eyes and brought color to his cheeks, and for one rash moment she was tempted to tackle him and roll in the snow with him.

A slow smile lit his face. "I can read your mind."

"Don't. I have work to do."

Sandy sighed, resigned. "We have work to do. Lead on, Macduff. I'll just have to do a hell of a job defending you."

The boathouse held nothing but boats, fishing tackle, aging outboard motors and bird droppings. For years it had been a favorite nesting spot for swallows, and as far as Jane could see the population during the summer had only increased.

The hay barns held nothing but hay. The family leased them to a local farmer in return for keeping them reasonably intact, and they were full of neat bales, ready for winter feeding.

The garage held nothing but broken, rusty tools that no one would ever possibly use. Richard's brilliance hadn't extended to earthly matters, and it was unlikely anyone had worked in the building since the early sixties.

Which left the icehouse. It was a small wood structure out by the ice pond, near the edge of the property adjoining the old Wilson place, and it hadn't been used for anything other than kids' games and teenage necking since electricity had come to Newfield in 1922 and people had discovered the wonders of refrigeration.

As long as Jane could remember the entryway had been a splintered pine door on one rusty iron hinge. They weren't within twenty feet of the place before she noticed the heavy steel door, the steel locks. "Eureka," she said softly, trudging through the woods at a faster pace.

Now that she bothered to look, she could see the new power box on the side of the building. Richard had had electricity and running water brought to the small, seemingly ramshackle structure, and the new roof was made of rustic-looking cedar shakes. Nice and inflammable, Jane thought.

Sandy stood there surveying the building. "Don't bother asking me to pick the locks," he said. "That time at Technocracies was merely a fluke."

"That's what I thought." She made a halfhearted attempt at forcing the door, then stepped back. "We'll head back to the store and get some kerosene."

"No."

"Yes," she said firmly. "Have you bothered looking down? Someone's been here recently. Someone with large feet and expensive boots, the kind you get at upscale New Jersey malls, not the Newfield General Store. I can think of only one other person left alive who has any stake in this place, and that's Stephen Tremaine. If we don't burn it now he's going to win, and I'm damned if I'm going to let him. I'll do it with you or without you, but I'm going to do it."

He just stared at the building for a long, contemplative moment. "I guess you do it with me," he said finally. "I just hope we can find me some better shoes at your general store."

She moved fast, flinging her arms around his neck and smiling up at him. "Thank you," she said, her voice soft in the morning air.

"Anytime," he said, the wary expression almost leaving his eyes. "That's what you hired me for."

YOU'RE CRAZY TO DO THIS, Sandy told himself as he circled the old building, splashing kerosene against the foundations. Arson was a felony, and it would take all his powers of persuasion to get her off. Hell, he was aiding and abetting—maybe he wouldn't even be able to defend her, he'd be standing trial alongside her.

It wasn't as if she didn't own the place—she was Richard Dexter's sole heir. And it wasn't as if she was going to make an insurance claim. The blaze would provide no danger to other structures—the slowly melting snow would keep the fire from spreading, and the nearest structure was an old white farmhouse barely visible through the woods. A young widow lived there with her twin sons, Jane said. Doubtless they kept her too busy to even look out her windows, much less notice a suspicious fire.

Jane was staring at the wooden roof of the icehouse, biting her lower lip as she pondered how best to use her five gallons of liquid. He wished he could be the one to bite her lower lip, and not spend his time worrying about her criminal tendencies. He ended up pouring the last of his kerosene around the window frame, stepped back, and waited for Jane.

The icehouse was set into a hillside. Jane had climbed up the bank and bathed the entire rooftop with kerosene. It was already soaked with melted snow, and Sandy had grave doubts about the inflammability of the whole thing. If he was lucky it would simply refuse to ignite, and Jane would have to consider more reasonable alternatives.

She jumped back, rubbing her hands against her jean-covered thighs, and stared at the structure. It was midafternoon by then, already well past full sunlight, and the area stank of kerosene.

"Got a match?" she inquired cheerfully.

Sandy reached in his pocket, handed her the box of kitchen matches, and stepped back. Directly into a solid figure.

He whirled around, only to look into a pair of chilly brown eyes. The man in front of him looked like a cross between a Vermont hermit and an aging hippie, with a bald pate, long stringy brown hair hanging to his shoulders, a full beard, and wire-rimmed glasses with a Band-Aid securing one corner. He was wearing well-aged denims, and the expression on his face was extremely disgruntled.

"What the hell do you think you're doing?" he demanded.

Sandy turned to Jane. She was staring at the apparition, open-mouthed, the lit match burning her fingers.

Sandy turned back to the newcomer. "Richard Dexter, I presume?"

Chapter Twenty

Sandy stood there, waiting for Jane to fling herself in her brother's arms in joy and relief, but she did no such thing and merely stood, staring, in shock.

And then she turned to Sandy. "You knew!" Her voice was richly accusing.

He shook his head. "Of course, I didn't. I won't say I didn't consider the possibility though."

"And you didn't say a word."

"I didn't want to get your hopes up," he said in what he felt was his most reasonable voice. Jane, however, wasn't in the mood to be reasonable.

Fortunately Richard distracted her. "What in hell are you doing with the kerosene, Jane?" he demanded in righteous indignation. "Do you realize the years of work you were about to burn?"

"What the hell would it matter to you—you're dead!" she shot back.

Richard Dexter appeared only slightly abashed. "I'm sorry if you were upset at the thought of my death. We were never particularly close...."

"Never particularly close?" Jane echoed, her voice a furious shriek in the chilly air. "I thought you'd been murdered."

"So did Stephen Tremaine," said Richard with satisfaction.

Jane's fury died abruptly. "Did he try to kill you, Richard?"

"Oh, probably not," Richard said with an airy wave of his hand. "Stephen's not quite that cold-blooded. I think he only intended to incapacitate me a little. He knew I never drove fast—I think he figured I'd get a little banged up and not pay any attention to his Salambian schemes. Little did he know I'd already spiked his guns."

"He knows now," Sandy said. "Do you have the missing part of the formula?"

Richard stared at him out of disgruntled brown eyes that were eerily akin to Jane's at her most distrustful. "Who is he?" he asked his sister. "And what was he doing setting fire to my laboratory?"

Jane turned to look at him and Sandy had the uncomfortable feeling she was considering him from a fresh viewpoint. "Oh, him," she said dismissingly, "he's my lawyer."

"Some lawyer," Richard snorted as Sandy swallowed a choked laugh. "Does he make a practice of committing arson?"

"Only with the woman I love," Sandy said smoothly, noting with pleasure Jane's look of complete shock. He left it at that, deliberately. If she didn't know he was in love with her, if she hadn't caught on to that very apparent fact, he'd have to explain it in more intimate detail later. Next time they got a few moments alone, with or without a sleeping bag beneath them.

"Put the matches away, Jane," Richard said sternly, and Jane meekly complied. "Come back to the house with me and we can talk about our mutual godfather. Any chance you can leave *him* behind?"

"*Him* is Sandy Caldicott," Jane said, her meekness gone. "And he goes where I go."

"Can you trust him?" Richard demanded, and Sandy found himself holding his breath, waiting for the all-important answer.

"More than I trust you, my dear departed brother," she snapped back, and if it wasn't quite the declaration Sandy had in mind, it would do for now.

Richard headed off toward the woods, his narrow shoulders slightly hunched, his long stringy hair floating in the wind. "Where are you going?" Jane demanded. "The house is back the other way."

"Not that house," Richard said loftily. "I haven't been to the old cottage in weeks. It's too cold to stay there in October." He didn't bother to slow his deliberate pace through the snow.

"Oh, I don't know," Sandy murmured. "We managed to heat it up last night."

Jane tried to glare at him, and failed miserably. "What did you mean by that?" she asked in a low voice, making no effort to follow her brother's lanky figure.

"Well, what with the fireplace and the selected use of body heat . . ."

"I'm not talking about that," she said stubbornly. "Why did you tell Richard I'm the woman you love?"

She wasn't about to move until he said something. On impulse he reached down, scooped up a handful of fresh snow and advanced on her.

She looked at him warily, standing her ground when he reached her. "Not down my neck," she warned.

"I wouldn't think of it." Very gently he placed some of the icy whiteness against her mouth. And then he followed it with his own, dissolving the crystals between them, and her mouth was cold and delicious and hot and melting as her arms wrapped around him.

"You're as bad as your sister," Richard's disapproving voice floated back to them. "Come along now. I haven't got all day."

Reluctantly Sandy released her. "Exactly where are we going?" he questioned, taking Jane's hand and following Richard through the woods.

"Who knows? Richard's not going to explain until he's good and ready. If we want answers we'll have to follow him. Besides, we've got a little problem."

"Which is?"

"Richard said he hasn't been back to Nana's cottage in weeks. There were fresh footprints on the steps, remember? If it wasn't Richard it has to be..."

"Don't say Uncle Stephen," he warned.

"I was going to say Tremaine." She glared at him. "I wish you wouldn't..."

"What the hell is that?" Sandy demanded, interrupting her mid-tirade. They'd come through the other side of the woods and were approaching a brightly lit farmhouse. In the twilight he could see signs of dereliction, of a badly needed paint job and a roof in need of repair. Hanging from a hook on the front porch was what appeared to be the body of a hobo. Two small hooligans were dancing around the grisly figure, whooping wildly. Richard walked past them without seeming to notice them, disappearing into the house without a backward glance.

Even Jane looked momentarily startled at the macabre apparition. "It's a Guy Fawkes," she said. "I'd forgotten it was almost Halloween. Around here they stuff old clothes with dead leaves and leave them around—on front lawns, rooftops, hanging from trees. They're creepy but basically harmless—it's an interesting ethnological phenomenon."

"That doesn't explain the two demons." They'd reached the sagging porch by then, and he was relieved to see that it was indeed a dummy hanging from a noose. The two demons, on closer inspection turned out to be two red-headed boys so exact that they could only be twins. They were approximately six years old and making enough noise for a score of children as they danced around their macabre plaything.

Jane smiled at them cheerfully enough, unmoved by their bloodthirsty demeanor, and headed toward the door, Sandy in tow. He knew his own smile was more of the sickly variety, but at least he had the immediate and happy certainty that Jane would be a great mother. Only someone who truly loved children could have reacted to those two monsters with such unaffected friendliness.

As night had fallen, the temperature had also dropped, and while they had attempted to dress for it, the warmth of the house was welcome. They followed the noise and light down the narrow hallway to a huge old kitchen. A woman stood at the sink, watching their approach with friendly interest.

Richard was already slumped down at the table, drinking coffee, completely immersed in an issue of *Organic Gardening*, and his introductions were cursory at best. "This is my sister," he announced, leaving it at that.

The woman, a hefty, dark-haired lady in her late thirties with a smile as warm as the wood cook stove, held out a rough, work-worn hand and cast a cheerfully disparaging look at Richard's preoccupied figure. "Not much for the social graces, is he?" she said with an unexpected Southern accent. "But I guess you know that better than I do. I'm Hazel Dexter, and those are my two boys out there, Derek and Erik. You must be Jane."

Jane managed a weak smile. "Dexter?"

"We were married last month," Richard roused himself long enough to answer. "Figured I'd let you know once I decided what to do about Tremaine."

Jane glared at her brother, dropped Hazel's polite hand and pulled her into her arms to give her a hug. "Welcome to the family," she said. "I'm not sure if you got the better part of the deal."

"Oh, Richard and I get along just fine. And the boys mind him, which is more than I can say for me. They just ride roughshod over me."

"Really?" Jane said faintly. "I never pictured Richard as much of a disciplinarian."

"Self-defense," Richard said cryptically, not raising his eyes.

"Are you Jane's husband?"

Richard raised his head to that. "Yes, what happened to your husband, Jane? Doesn't he mind you running around with an arsonist?"

"I've been divorced for more than a year, Richard," she said patiently. "I told you at the time."

"I can't remember every little detail of my sisters' lives," he said loftily, putting down his magazine. "Come and sit down and tell me what Stephen Tremaine's been doing since my unfortunate demise."

Jane seated herself in one of the pressed-oak chairs and took a mug of coffee from Hazel's hands. "Apart from trying to find the missing part of the formula?"

"He'll never do that," Richard said smugly. "I've got it up here."

"For your information, Dexter, we think Tremaine's up here, too," Sandy said. His instincts had been right, he didn't like Richard Dexter one tiny bit, and the more he saw of him with his sister the more he wanted to smash his teeth in. He was doubly grateful for his own cup of coffee. Not only did it warm his chilled hands but it kept him from knocking Richard off his chair.

For once Richard showed some consternation. "You idiot," he said to Jane. "You must have led him up here. If it weren't for you..."

Sandy set the coffee down and advanced on the soon-to-be-unfortunate Richard Dexter. "Your sister has been busting her buns trying to keep Stephen Tremaine from soiling your stained legacy," he said in a light voice. "I'd suggest you show a little gratitude for all she's done for your sake."

"I don't see that she's done that much," Richard said in a snooty voice, then backed down hastily as he recognized the menace in Sandy's eyes. "Not that I don't appreciate it, Jane," he added. "But I could have taken care of it myself."

"I don't think you could take care of a housefly by yourself, much less a scorpion like Stephen Tremaine," Sandy snapped.

"Where did you get this young man, Jane? Are you certain he's a lawyer? He seems more like a thug to me."

"Richard," Hazel said reproving, stirring a large pot of some divine-smelling concoction on the back of the cook stove. "Watch your manners."

And to both Sandy's and Jane's amazement, Richard nodded sheepishly. "Yes, dear."

"What are we going to do about Stephen? Someone was lurking around the cottage before we got there. He's had his own cadre of hired thugs that make Sandy seem like a lamb in comparison. I wouldn't put anything past him."

"Neither would I," Richard said. "I guess I've been sentimental. That's what country living and a sensible life-style will do for you. Makes you forget what a dog-eat-dog world it is out there. If I were you, Jane, I'd leave Michigan and move up here to Vermont, where the air is clean and men are men."

"Wisconsin," Jane corrected absently. "And I'm not about to live anyplace where it snows in October. And I'm not looking for a man."

"I do think you should trade in your current model," Richard said, ignoring Sandy's presence. "And you get used to a little snow."

"No thanks."

"At least keep out of New York. It's a cesspool of danger, toxic wastes and perversion."

"I live in New York," Sandy announced in a dangerous voice.

"I rest my case." Richard gave Jane his most angelic smile, and Sandy wondered whether she was gullible enough to be won over by it.

"I appreciate your concern," was all she said, looking at neither of the two quarreling men in her life. "What are you working on in your laboratory? Is it something Uncle Tremaine will want to get his hands on? You're still under contract to him, aren't you?"

"I'm dead. The contract is null and void."

"It doesn't work that way," Sandy volunteered.

Richard ignored him. "Anyway, I've changed my area of interest. I don't think Stephen Tremaine will have the slightest use for my latest research, even though it has the potential to change the free world as we know it."

Jane stared at him, her eyes round behind the wire-rimmed glasses. "What is it?" she breathed, suitably impressed.

"Carrots," Richard said triumphantly.

"Carrots?" His sister's reaction wasn't quite what he would have hoped, but Richard charged on.

"A new strain of organic carrots," he announced, beaming. "Resistant to carrot weevils, crown rot, scab..."

"Yuck," Jane said. "I'm never going to eat carrots again."

"You certainly are. Tonight, as a matter of fact. Hazel's making carrot chowder, aren't you, my dear? Along with carrot bread, carrot salad and carrot cake for dessert. And it will all taste wonderful. Besides, the new strain of carrots is a miraculous source of protein, calcium, and vitamin A. Not to mention they're a natural laxative."

Hazel was still placidly stirring her pot on the stove, the delicious odor now taking on a definitely carroty scent. "Did your kids start out with that color hair," Sandy drawled, "or is Richard's research responsible?"

"Their father was a redhead," Hazel said. "And the boys hate carrots."

"They'll learn," Richard said firmly. "Anyway, they can't grow carrots in Salambia, even my carrots, and I don't think the profit will be enough to excite old Stephen. He's just going to have to sit and watch Technocracies go under. Serve him right, running a death factory under our very noses."

"He won't give up without a fight," Sandy pointed out.

Richard nodded, clearly reluctant to agree with him on anything. "I've known him long enough to realize he can be completely ruthless. I've been much too remiss. I should have destroyed the formula weeks ago." He rose, dropping the magazine on the scrubbed wooden table. "I'll do it now."

"Dinner's almost ready," Hazel said in a slow, tranquil voice. "You two are staying." It was a statement, not a question, and Jane nodded.

"It won't take long, dear," Richard said meekly. "Just back at the lab."

She nodded. "Don't take the boys. We'll never get them out of there before Thanksgiving, and that's a fact."

"We'll come with you," Sandy announced.

Richard stared at him, deeply affronted. "Don't you trust me? It doesn't matter whether I destroyed it or not, I still have the formula in my brain."

"Great," Sandy muttered. "That means Tremaine will have to kill you."

"Nice of you to be so concerned," Richard said, glaring.

"I'm not concerned. If it were up to me Stephen Tremaine could sell *you* as a secret weapon to Salambia. I'm merely looking after Jane."

"Jane's never needed looking after before." Dexter bristled.

"Everyone needs looking after now and then," he snapped back. "If you could see farther than the tip of your nose..."

"Let's go back to the lab and watch Richard burn the formula," Jane interrupted hastily. "Unless you need some help, Hazel?"

"Everything's just fine. I just have to feed the boys their hot dogs and potato chips. You two go ahead and keep Richard from falling into a snowbank or getting involved in some project. He has a habit of forgetting what he was doing in the first place."

"I can believe that," Sandy muttered.

"And I'll get some fresh sheets for your bed. You'll be spending the night. It's going to get down into the single numbers tonight, and that old summer cottage is too cold."

"Sheets for their beds," Richard corrected. "Separate rooms. I won't have my sister cohabiting under my roof."

"It's under my roof," Hazel said, "and you and I cohabited before we were married."

"That's different."

"No," said Hazel firmly, "it's not. Go burn your formula. When you come back supper will be on the table."

"Yes, dear."

The night had grown colder when the three of them stepped back out on the porch. The twin demons of the night had disappeared, and from deep within the house Sandy could hear the echo of a violent television show. A light snow had begun to fall again, and Jane shivered.

"Lovely climate," he said, taking her arm and heading down the sagging steps.

She looked up at him. He could read everything in her eyes, her irritation, relief, and concern for her brother, her fear of the unknown. Her love for him. "Lovely," she said, huddling up against his body for warmth and maybe something else. "I think I prefer Baraboo."

"What about that cesspool of danger, toxic wastes and perversion?" he countered softly, wrapping his arms around her slender body.

She held herself very still. "What about it?"

"It's where I live."

"I know that, Jimmy."

He winced at the deliberate taunt. "I like living there. The Upper East Side is beautiful, I inherited the apartment, and I like the energy in New York."

"So do I."

"It's not a good place for children, I suppose," he continued in a musing voice. "Maybe we should move out to some sort of yuppie suburb in a few years. Buy a place with lots of land and maybe some apple trees. Would you like that?"

She didn't move, she didn't say a word. He could no longer read the expression on her face, it was one of blank incomprehension. "I'm not doing this very well," he said. "But then I haven't had a whole lot of practice. I'm asking if you could find happiness with a sneaking, lying sleaze of a lawyer?" He threw her own words back at her, gently.

"No," she said. "But I could find happiness with you."

He smiled, a wide, mouth-splitting grin of sheer joy and relief. "You'll marry me? I don't know if that gun-toting brother of yours will let us sleep together unless we're at least engaged."

"Sandy, great sex is not a good enough reason for marriage," she warned, putting her hands against his shoulders to keep him from kissing her.

"No, it's not," he agreed. "And maybe being desperately in love with you isn't enough, and maybe sharing the same ridiculous interests isn't enough, and maybe just having a good time together isn't enough. But if you put them all together they make a pretty good case."

"Yes, counselor." She wasn't pushing quite as hard. "But aren't you taking something for granted? What if I'm not in love with you?"

He laughed softly. "Jane, my precious, do you have any idea how transparent you are? Of course you're in love with me."

The hands started pushing again. "In that case," she said sweetly, "there's no need for me to say it, is there? Let's catch up with Richard."

Sandy suddenly knew he'd made a very grave error. He was so happy, so sure of her and him, that he'd been a little too hasty. "Jane..."

"Let's go." She gave him a shove, sharp enough so that he stumbled backward, landing in a pile of snow. "I'll meet you at the lab."

She was moving after her brother's ungainly figure at a swift pace, and Sandy sat in the wet snow for a moment, watching her with mingled admiration and dismay. "Does this mean you won't marry me?" he called after her.

"Not at all," she answered from a distance. "I'll marry you. But I'll make your life holy hell for a while."

He watched her go, then pulled himself out of the wet slush, brushing at the soaked seat of his jeans. "I just bet you will," he muttered. And he started after her.

JANE CAUGHT UP with her brother when he reached the edge of the woods. The huddled shape of the old icehouse was partially obscured by darkness and the lightly falling snow.

"Lover's quarrel?" Richard asked in a cheerful tone of voice.

"Don't get your hopes up. We just got engaged," Jane snapped.

"You don't look like a woman who just got engaged."

"How would you know? Maybe engagements don't agree with me." Sandy was catching up with them, his long legs eating the distance between them. Jane watched his approach with absent longing. Sooner or later the man was going to have to learn tact in his declarations of love.

They could smell the kerosene from halfway across the field, and Richard wrinkled his aristocratic nose. "I really wish I'd come across you two arsonists before you had a chance to make such a mess. It'll be weeks before I can get rid of the smell, not to mention..." His words trailed off in sudden horror, and some distinctly un-Richard-like cursing tumbled from his mouth.

Jane felt her stomach cramp in sudden dread. "What is it?"

"Someone's broken into the lab." Richard's voice was bitter as he took off in a dead run across the stubbled field. "Damn, damn, damn."

The heavy metal door was hanging open. Without hesitation Richard dashed into the darkened interior, with Jane and Sandy close at his heel.

Even in the inky darkness Jane could tell that the place had been trashed. She stumbled over piles of paper on the floor, peering through the blackness, Sandy close behind her, as Richard fumbled for the light switch.

"Do you think he found it?" she questioned anxiously.

The room was flooded with light, illuminating the three of them, illuminating Stephen Tremaine blocking the doorway, impeccably dressed in Abercrombie and Fitch country wear, a nasty-looking black gun in his hand.

"Oh, most definitely," he said in a smooth voice. "Most definitely, indeed."

Chapter Twenty-One

"I do regret doing this," Stephen continued, backing toward the door. "Normally I like to keep things a bit more civilized. But my dear Richard, you have always been the consummate pain in the rear. You even had the lack of consideration to die when I only meant for you to be injured, and then the audacity not to be dead after all. I doubt I would have gone so far down this particular road of illegality if I hadn't thought I was already guilty of murder."

"But you're not," Jane pointed out, staring at the gun as if mesmerized.

"Not yet," said Tremaine. "But there's really no turning back at this point. The Sultan of Salambia has ready cash, and I am in dire need of that cash. And the three of you are quite expendable. Even you...I'm sorry, I don't know your name," he said to Sandy.

"Alexander Caldicott," Jane supplied politely. "You wouldn't want to shoot a stranger."

"My dear Jane, you're almost as big a pain as your brother," Stephen announced with mild distaste. "As a matter of fact, I'm not going to shoot anyone. The police can trace bullets, you know. I'm afraid the three of you are going to burn to death in this old firetrap. I imagine they'll remember who bought the kerosene this morning, if anyone bothers to investigate. They might think it a bizarre ménage à trois. Or they might blame the two little monsters, who kept throwing rocks at me every time I tried spying, for the fire. I really don't care.''

"They'll blame Derek and Erik, all right," Richard announced gloomily. "They already set fire to the old Grange hall last April."

"Richard!" Jane warned.

Tremaine merely smiled. "You see how tidy everything will be? And trust an old veteran of the divorce wars, Jane. You wouldn't want to marry the man. This way you'll never have to be disillusioned." He stepped out into the darkness.

"You can't do this," Jane cried.

"Yes, my dear, I can." The door shut in their faces, and without hesitation Sandy flung himself at it. It was already tightly locked, and the smell of kerosene was thick in the air.

With great aplomb Jane began screaming and beating on the door. They could smell smoke, and the first evil tendrils of it began snaking under the doorway.

"We stand a pretty good chance," Richard announced calmly. He'd taken a seat on a stool by his workbench and was sorting through his papers at a leisurely rate. "Kerosene isn't that efficient for burning places—gasoline would have done a faster job. And it's been a very wet autumn. The wood in this place is old, but snow's been sitting on it for several days. Someone may see the smoke before it really catches." He picked up a pencil, made a little note, and then continued reading.

Jane looked at Sandy as the first wave of smoke hit her lungs. She started coughing, tears coming to her eyes, and she took the handkerchief he offered with gratitude, covering her mouth with it.

"Normally we should get down on the floor to get away from the smoke," Sandy said, his own voice similarly muffled, "but that's where the smoke is coming from, and this place isn't big enough to get away from it.'' He was coughing now, too, tears pouring down his face from the smoke.

Jane began pounding again, not bothering to cover her mouth. ''Uncle Stephen, you get the hell back here,'' she shrieked through her spasms of coughing. ''You can't leave us to die in here, damn it. Unlock the door! Unlock the damned door!''

Her furious voice faded in a paroxysm of coughing, and she sank against the door in defeat.

''Maybe I can break it down,'' Sandy muttered. ''Move out of the way.''

''For God's sake, Richard, help him!'' Jane pleaded.

Richard looked up from the abstract he was perusing. ''Let your fiancé be a hero,'' he said. ''Stephen will relent eventually. If he doesn't, there's nothing we can do about it. I had the door installed to keep everything out. Your young man won't be able to do a thing about this.'' He coughed a bit, then lifted his glasses from his streaming eyes. ''And I must say, Jane,'' he added sternly, ''I blame you for all this. If you hadn't doused the place with kerosene I doubt Stephen would ever have thought of burning us. He never was the creative sort—he worked best in a managerial capacity.''

''I'm not interested in Stephen's talents!'' Jane shrieked between fits of coughing. ''I'm interested in getting out of here.''

''Just wait,'' Richard said, replacing his glasses as Sandy kept hurling himself at the door.

''Just wait?'' Jane echoed in a furious croak. ''Wait for what? For hell to freeze over? That's where you're going to be in a few minutes, brother dear, and I can't think of anyone who deserves it more....''

''Wait a minute.'' Sandy stopped his useless assault. ''Someone's unlocking the door.''

A moment later the door opened, filling the tiny room with acrid, blinding smoke. Someone took her hand, it had to be Sandy, and together they stumbled out into the snowy night. She landed in the snow, on top of his large, warm body, and she just lay there, taking deep, wonderful lungfuls of cold night air.

It took a moment for her eyes to clear. Stephen Tremaine was standing over them, an expression of extreme self-disgust on his face. "I couldn't do it," he said, his voice rich with regret. "I'm afraid I couldn't kill you. Just don't have what it takes after all."

"I hate to interrupt this soul searching," croaked Jane, looking around her, "but Richard's still trapped inside."

"He would be," Tremaine said gloomily. Without hesitation he dashed through the sheet of flames obscuring the doorway, and moments later came back out with Richard's semiconscious body slung around his shoulder. He dumped him in the snow, rubbing his hands together in the age old gesture of one getting rid of a nasty project.

Richard lay in the snow coughing for a moment, then managed to pull himself to a sitting position. "I didn't finish the article," he said accusingly. "Now it's in cinders. You're going to have to get me another copy, Stephen."

"Richard," said Stephen Tremaine, "you always were a pain in the rear, and you always will be."

Richard only waved an airy hand at him. Tremaine turned his back to look at Jane. She still hadn't moved. Sandy felt too good, too strong and solid and comforting beneath her, for her to be noble. "I suppose you want to call the police," he said in a resigned voice. "I won't fight it. There's not much I can do—this was a last-ditch effort and it failed. It appears," he said wearily, "that I am simply too damned civilized for murder."

"It's quite a failing," Sandy agreed from beneath Jane.

Reluctantly she got to her feet, her knees still a bit wobbly in the aftermath. "Are we going to call the police?" she asked Sandy, giving him a hand to help him up and wincing in sympathy as she realized his back was soaked with melted snow.

"We might be open to other possibilities," Sandy agreed, correctly reading her tone of voice.

"Police?" Richard roused himself from his perusal of the burning lab. "I don't want the police involved. Come back to the house, Stephen. Hazel has plenty for dinner, and you deserve to spend some time with my stepchildren. I'm sure we can come up with something mutually agreeable. Something not involving Salambia."

"Your stepchildren?" Stephen echoed. "The twins? I think I might prefer jail."

"Your preferences are not the issue right now," Sandy said. "I'm feeling cold and wet and quite angry, and I would love to take out that anger on someone who richly deserves it. Get back to the house. Now."

Richard pulled himself upright, strolled over to Stephen Tremaine and took the gun that was resting loosely in the older man's hand. "Nasty business," he said, tossing the weapon toward Sandy. He missed, it landed in the snow, and Sandy left it there, stepping over it and taking Jane's arm in his. "You know, Stephen," Richard said in a musing voice, "I can think of two things responsible for your aberrant behavior. First, you must have been given war toys when you were a child to encourage this hostile streak of yours. And you eat too much red meat. It messes up the bowels and makes people quite savage. Less animal flesh, Stephen, that's the ticket. Do you like carrots?" They wandered off, Richard chattering a mile a minute in his inanely cheerful voice.

Sandy and Jane watched them go. "I don't suppose we can just go home?" she questioned hopefully.

He shook his head. "Tremaine might murder them all in their sleep." He reached down and picked up the gun, tucking it in his pocket.

"With someone like Richard, who could blame him? Is he really going to stay for dinner with us?" Her voice was still raw from the inhaled smoke, and Sandy's beautiful gray eyes were puffy and red.

"Probably the night, too, if I read Hazel's hospitable tendencies properly," Sandy said.

"Let's go to bed early."

"Sounds like an excellent idea. I love you, you know. Even with your demented brother, I still want to marry you."

She cocked her head to one side, looking up at him. "I won't bother telling you anything you already know," she murmured. "Besides, you're no prize yourself. You may not have a loony brother but you're a pathological liar..."

"Jane..."

"You're going to have to earn it," she said fiercely. "You took my declaration of love before I offered it, so you're just going to have to wait until I'm ready."

"Jane, I'm freezing. Couldn't you...?"

"No. But I can take you back and strip off your clothes and warm you up."

He smiled down at her, and there was nothing but heat between them. "I'll settle for that. For now."

IT WAS LATE when they finally got to bed. Hazel put them in an old Victorian sleigh bed up under the eaves. The mattress sagged, but the sheets were ironed, the blankets wool, and the quilts were made by hand. Jane was wearing an old flannel nightie of Hazel's, the sleeves drooped over her wrists, the hem hit the floor and the neckline floundered around her shoulders, but it was soft and warm and much more welcome than a negligee.

Sandy had to make do with long winter underwear. When Richard had first presented him with it he'd refused, but five minutes in the icy confines of the upstairs bedroom and he changed his mind.

"This isn't what I had in mind for tonight," he said, climbing into the high bed, his teeth chattering. "I don't think I'll ever get warm again."

"You should have stayed up with Richard and Stephen. When I left they were taking off their sweaters."

"There are two reasons for that," Sandy said, pulling her into his arms and wrapping his shivering body around her. "One, they're sitting by the wood stove hogging all the heat that doesn't seem to get much farther than the kitchen. Number two, they've polished off one bottle of Scotch and they're well into their second."

"They were very drunk, weren't they?" Jane said, rubbing her face against the soft thermal cotton covering his shoulder. He still smelled faintly of smoke, despite the icy shower he'd insisted on suffering, and she felt a momentary apprehension. "They're safe down there, aren't they? Uncle Stephen isn't going to murder us all in our beds?"

"Dear old Uncle Stephen has given up. He managed to agree to our terms in writing, and there's not much he can do about it without the whole mess coming out in the open. Whether he likes it or not he's going to have to sell the process to a peaceful, emerging nation of Richard's choice. He won't make much money on it, neither will your brother, but at least it'll be used for the good of mankind."

"What I particularly like," Jane admitted, sliding her hand up under the thermal shirt, "is the mess Uncle Stephen made of his future. Here he thought he was safeguarding the company by putting it in Elinor Peabody's hands, and she goes behind his back to the board of trustees and stages a palace coup. Uncle Stephen gets kicked upstairs and Elinor takes over. It serves him right—he always thought the trustees were just a formality."

"He shouldn't have underestimated Elinor," Sandy said, emitting a small groan of pleasure as her hand moved across his chest underneath the shirt. "I could have told him she was a man-eater."

"Humph," said Jane. "Why don't we lie here and *not* talk about Elinor Peabody?"

"Sounds good to me," he said, moving a thick strand of her hair away from her neck and nuzzling her ear. She shivered, and he knew for a fact she wasn't cold. "What do you want to talk about? Your godfather's future travel plans? Around the world with his long-suffering wife?"

"She'll probably push him overboard somewhere in the Orient," Jane said, letting her hand run down his flat stomach. "Maybe in Australia, where they still have great white sharks."

"I've tried to curb this bloodthirsty streak of yours," he said with a long-suffering sigh.

"I'm impossible to curb."

"Thank God."

Her hand slid beneath the elastic waistband of the thermal long johns, but before she could reach her destination his hand shot out and caught hers, stopping her.

"Wait a moment," he said with mock sternness.

"Don't worry, Sandy, I'll respect you in the morning," she assured him with an impish smile.

"It is the morning," he pointed out. "It's after two, and I'm exhausted."

"Too tired for me? That doesn't sound like a promising beginning for our life together. Maybe I'd be better off with the real Jimmy the Stoolie."

"Come here, Jane," he growled, "and stop teasing me." He released her hand, caught her shoulders and hauled her up so that her face was level with his.

"It's fun to tease." She kept her voice light, waiting.

"Not at two-something in the morning, after we've been through hell and back at the hands of that drunken old man downstairs. You owe me, lady."

"What do I owe you?"

He caught her face between his hands, his thumbs smoothing her taut cheekbones and he looked into her eyes. "Anything you want to give me," he whispered. "Whatever it is, I'll take it."

She couldn't play games anymore, she couldn't summon up any lingering vestiges of outrage or hurt pride, she couldn't feel anything more except what she had to tell him. "Okay, you win," she said. "I'm in love with you."

He shook his head. "We both win, Jane," he said softly, placing his lips on hers in a featherlight kiss. "We both win."

IT WAS AFTER MIDNIGHT two days later when they arrived back at the Park Avenue apartment. Sandy insisted on carrying her over the threshold, even though they weren't officially married yet, and Jane went willingly, losing her shoes in the hallway, dropping pieces of clothing as she headed for the master bedroom. She stopped halfway down the hall, wearing nothing but a pair of lace bikini panties and her glasses, and turned to look at Sandy.

His shirt was off, his pants were unzipped, and he was hopping on one foot while he was trying to take off his other sock. In the background the phone rang and his answering machine clicked on.

"Are your calls more important than me?" Jane demanded. "Whoever it is can wait."

"You're right," he said, reaching to turn it off, when Jimmy the Stoolie's nasal tones stopped him.

"Listen, pal, you owe me. I'm calling from the twelfth precinct. They've got me on a charge of grand theft, auto, and I need you to bail me out of here, pronto. There's an old friend of mine in here who's got no reason to feel too friendly, and a person of indeterminate sex who's fallen in love with me. Get me out of here, Caldicott, and I won't say a word to the little lady about who you really are. Come on, what's a car between friends? The MGB was a piece of crap, I'm sorry I totaled it, but you owed me for getting you in to see Jabba. Save me, pal.'' The answering machine clicked off.

Jane just looked at Sandy. ''Are you going to leave that poor man rotting in jail? After all, he brought us together.''

Sandy pulled off his other sock and stripped off his pants. ''Does that mean he gets to be best man?''

''At least we don't have to leave the church in an MGB,'' Jane said brightly. ''We wouldn't have gotten two blocks in that car.''

''Don't speak ill of the dead,'' Sandy said, stalking her down the long dark hallway, ''or I'll buy another.''

''How about an Edsel? Or maybe a nice little Chevy Vega? Mavericks had a certain *je ne sais quoi*... or we could—''

He caught up with her by the door, scooped her up in his arms and carried her into the bedroom. ''We'll use taxis,'' he said. ''Or walk.'' He dumped her on the king-size bed and followed her down.

''Or maybe,'' she said, ''we'll stay right here and not go anyplace at all.''

''Now that sounds like the best idea I've heard in a long time,'' Sandy said.

''And if I get bored I can always burn down the apartment. I still haven't had my chance to commit a crime. You were always so repressive.''

''Someone has to keep you in line. That's what a partner in crime is for.''

"I thought it was for aiding and abetting."

"There's that, too." He ran a string of kisses down her neck. "And at least I'll give you a discount on my fees if I have to defend you on a charge of arson."

"Big of you."

"Indeed."

"You're indecent, you know that?"

"I try my best."

"And you get spectacular results," she said fervently.

"What can I say?" He was all modesty.

"Say good-night, Sandy."

"Good night, Sandy."

"Indecent," breathed Jane in a pleased voice. And then all was silence, but the sound of the phone ringing and the plaintive voice of Jimmy the Stoolie wailing away on the answering machine.

PAMELA BROWNING

...is fireworks on the green at the Fourth of July and prayers said around the Thanksgiving table. It is the dream of freedom realized in thousands of small towns across this great nation.

But mostly, the Heartland is its people. People who care about and help one another. People who cherish traditional values and give to their children the greatest gift, the gift of love.

American Romance presents HEARTLAND, an emotional trilogy about people whose memories, hopes and dreams are bound up in the acres they farm.

HEARTLAND...the story of America.

Don't miss these heartfelt stories: American Romance #237 SIMPLE GIFTS (March), #241 FLY AWAY (April), and #245 HARVEST HOME (May).

HRT-1

Harlequin American Romance

COMING NEXT MONTH

#249 MATCHED SET by Karen Toller Whittenburg

There was plenty of room in Lesley's Texas home for her and her son, as well as her aunt and uncle, but she had no intention of taking in boarders. But Aunt Bentley had other ideas and, on her own, struck a deal with Adam Frazier and his young daughter. Suddenly the sprawling house seemed stifling. Could Lesley keep her distance from the handsome stranger?

#250 WE GIVE THANKS by Linda Randall Wisdom

Sara Murdock had been ostracized from the small North Carolina town of her birth ever since she had returned fifteen years ago with her infant son—and no husband. But she'd struggled to make a home in the only place she had roots. Then the new preacher arrived. The appearance of Jess Larkin meant one thing: the truth about her son's parentage was about to explode all over town.

#251 HONEYMOON HOTEL by Barbara Bretton

Pocono Mountain honeymoon hotels meant waterbeds and heart-shaped tubs to John. But to Maggie they meant adventure. Ringed by barbed wire, surrounded by security guards, her little inn had been commandeered by PAX, the secret organization that was about to plunge Maggie and John into an exciting and dangerous world where fantasy and reality become one.

#252 A COLONEL FOR JENNY by Anne Henry

Researching the history of an old mansion introduced Jenny Bishop to Colonel Stephen Carmichael. But too quickly Stephen became more than a client, and too late Jenny found out he was not a free man. She'd heard the lies, now she wanted the truth. What was the real story about his wife and daughter?

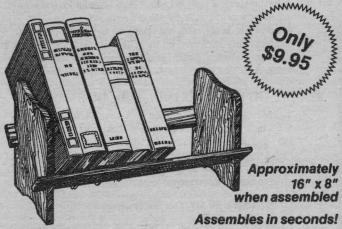

Take 4 best-selling love stories FREE
Plus get a FREE surprise gift!

Penny Jordan

Stronger than Yearning

He was the man of her dreams!

The same dark hair, the same mocking eyes; it was as if the Regency rake of the portrait, the seducer of Jenna's dream, had come to life. Jenna, believing the last of the Deverils dead, was determined to buy the great old Yorkshire Hall—to claim it for her daughter, Lucy, and put to rest some of the painful memories of Lucy's birth. She had no way of knowing that a direct descendant of the black sheep Deveril even existed—or that James Allingham and his own powerful yearnings would disrupt her plan entirely.